k

THE LAST OF THE MOHICANS

THE LAST
OF THE MOHICANS

by

J. FENIMORE COOPER

ABRIDGED

A BANCROFT

CLASSIC

BANCROFT BOOKS
LONDON

BANCROFT BOOKS
49–50 Poland Street
London W. 1

First published in the "Bancroft Classics" 1967
This impression 1973

430 00084 7

Chapter 1

Mine ear is open, and my heart prepared:—
The worst is worldly loss thou canst unfold:—
Say, is my kingdom lost?   *Shakespeare.*

IT was a feature peculiar to the colonial wars of North America that the toils and dangers of the wilderness were to be encountered before the adverse hosts could meet in murderous contact. A wide and apparently an impervious boundary of forests severed the possessions of the hostile provinces of France and England. The hardy colonist and the trained European who fought at his side, frequently expended months in struggling against the rapids of the streams or in effecting the rugged passes of the mountains, in quest of an opportunity to exhibit their courage in a more martial conflict. But, emulating the patience and self-denial of the practised native warriors, they learned to overcome every difficulty; and it would seem, that in time, there was no recess of the woods so dark, nor any secret place so lonely, that it might claim exemption from the inroads of those who had pledged their blood to satiate their vengeance, or to uphold the cold and selfish policy of the distant monarchs of Europe.

Perhaps no district, throughout the wide extent of the intermediate frontiers, can furnish a livelier picture of the cruelty and fierceness of the savage warfare of those periods, than the country which lies between the head waters of the Hudson and the adjacent lakes.

When, therefore, intelligence was received at the fort which covered the southern termination of the portage between the Hudson and the lakes, that Montcalm had been seen moving up the Champlain with an army "numerous as the leaves of the trees," its truth was admitted with more of the craven reluctance of those who court the arts of peace, than with the stern joy that a warrior should feel in finding an enemy within reach of his blow.

After the first surprise of the intelligence had a little abated, a rumour was spread through the intrenched camp, which stretched along the margin of the Hudson, forming a chain of outworks to the body of the fort itself, that a chosen detachment of fifteen hundred men was to depart with the dawn for William Henry, the post at the northern extremity of the portage. That which at first was only rumour soon became certainty, as orders passed from the quarters of the commander-in-chief to the several corps he had selected for this service to prepare for their speedy departure.

According to the orders of the preceding night, the heavy sleep of the army was broken by the rolling of the warning drums, whose rattling echoes were heard issuing, on the damp morning air, out of every vista of the woods, just as day began to draw the shaggy outlines of some tall pines of the vicinity, on the opening brightness of a soft and cloudless eastern sky. In an instant the whole camp was in motion: the meanest soldier arousing from his lair, to witness the departure of his comrades and to share in the excitement and incidents of the hour. The simple array of the chosen band was soon completed. While the regular and trained hirelings of the king marched with ready haughtiness to the right of the line, the less pretending colonists took their humbler position on its left, with a docility that long practice had rendered easy. The scouts departed; strong guards preceded and followed the lumbering vehicles that bore the baggage; and before the grey light of the morning was mellowed by the rays of the rising sun, the main body of the combatants wheeled into column, and left the encampment with a show of high military bearing that served to drown the slumbering apprehensions of many a novice who was now about to make his first essay in arms. While in view of their admiring comrades, the same proud front and ordered array was observed, until the notes of their fifes growing fainter in distance, the forest at length appeared to swallow up the living mass which had slowly entered its bosom.

The deepest sounds of the retiring and invisible column had ceased to be borne on the breeze to the listeners, and the latest straggler had already disappeared in pursuit, but there still remained the signs of another departure, before a log-cabin of unusual size and accommodations, in front of which those sentinels paced their rounds, who were known to guard the person of the English general. At this spot were gathered some half dozen horses, caparisoned in a manner which showed that two, at least, were destined to bear the persons of females, of a rank that it was not usual to meet so far in the wilds of the country. A third wore the trappings and arms of an officer of the staff; while the rest, from the plainness of the housings and the travelling mails with which they were encumbered, were evidently fitted for the reception of as many menials, who were seemingly already awaiting the convenience or pleasure of those they served. At a respectful distance from this unusual show, were gathered divers groups of curious idlers,—some admiring the blood and bone of the high-mettled military charger, and others gazing at the preparations with the dull wonder of vulgar curiosity. There was one man, however, who, by his countenance and actions, formed a marked exception to those who composed the latter class of spectators, being neither idle, nor seemingly very ignorant.

The person of this remarkable individual was to the last degree ungainly, without being in any particular manner deformed. He had all the bones and joints of other men without any of their proportions; erect, his stature surpassed that of his fellows; though, seated, he appeared reduced within the ordinary limits of our race. The same contrariety in his members seemed to exist throughout the whole man. His head was large; his shoulders narrow; his arms long and dangling, while his hands were small, if not delicate; his legs and thighs were thin, nearly to emaciation, but of extraordinary length; and his knees would have been considered tremendous, had they not been outdone by the broader foundations on which this false superstructure of blended human orders was so profanely reared.

His eyes fell on the still, upright, and rigid form of the "Indian runner," who had borne to the camp the unwelcome tidings of the preceding evening. Although in a state of perfect repose, and apparently disregarding with characteristic stoicism, the excitement and bustle around him, there was a sullen fierceness mingled with the quiet of the savage, that was likely to arrest the attention of much more experienced eyes than those which now scanned him in unconcealed amazement. The native bore both the tomahawk and knife of his tribe; and yet his appearance was not altogether that of a warrior. On the contrary, there was an air of neglect about his person, like that which might have proceeded from great and recent exertion, which he had not yet found leisure to repair.

A young man, in the livery of the crown, conducted to their steeds two females, who, it was apparent by their dresses, were prepared to encounter the fatigues of a journey in the woods. One, and she was the most juvenile in her appearance, though both were young, permitted glimpses of her dazzling complexion, fair golden hair, and bright blue eyes, to be caught, as she artlessly suffered the morning air to blow aside the green veil, which descended low from her beaver. The flush which still lingered above the pines in the western sky was not more bright nor delicate than the bloom on her cheek; nor was the opening day more cheering than the animated smile which she bestowed on the youth, as he assisted her into the saddle. The other, who appeared to share equally in the attentions of the young officer, concealed her charms from the gaze of the soldiery with a studious care, that seemed better fitted to the experience of four or five additional years. It could be seen, however, that her person, though moulded with the same exquisite proportions, of which none of the graces were lost by the travelling dress she wore, was rather fuller and more mature than that of her companion.

No sooner were these females seated, than their attendant sprang lightly into the saddle of the war-horse, when the whole three bowed to Webb, who, in courtesy, awaited their parting on the threshold of his cabin, and turning their horses' heads, they proceeded at a slow amble, followed by their train, towards the northern entrance of the encampment. As they traversed that short distance, not a voice was heard amongst them; but a slight exclamation proceeded from the younger of the females, as the Indian runner glided by her unexpectedly, and led the way along the military road in her front. Though this sudden and startling movement of the Indian produced no sound from the other, in the surprise, her veil was allowed to open its folds, and betrayed an indescribable look of pity, admiration, and horror, as her dark eye followed the easy motions of the savage. The tresses of this lady were shining and black, like the plumage of the raven. Her complexion was not brown, but it rather appeared charged with the colour of the rich blood that seemed ready to burst its bounds. And yet there was neither coarseness nor want of shadowing, in a countenance that was exquisitely regular and dignified, and surpassingly beautiful. She smiled, as if in pity at her own momentary fortgetfulness, discovering by the act a row of teeth that would have shamed, by their dazzling whiteness, the purest ivory; when, replacing the veil, she bowed her face and rode in silence, like one whose thoughts were abstracted from the scene around her.

Chapter 2

Sola, sola, wo ha, ho, sola! *Shakespeare*.

WHILE one of the lovely beings we have so cursorily presented to the reader was thus lost in thought, the other quickly recovered from the slight alarm which induced the exclamation, and, laughing at her own weakness, she inquired playfully of the youth who rode by her side—

"Are such spectres frequent in the woods, Heyward; or is this sight an especial entertainment ordered in our behalf? If the latter, gratitude must close our mouths; but if the former, both Cora and I shall have need to draw largely on that stock of hereditary courage of which we boast, even before we are made to encounter the redoubtable Montcalm."

"Yon Indian is a 'runner' of our army, and, after the fashion of his people, he may be accounted a hero," returned the young officer, to whom she addressed herself—"He has volunteered to guide us to the lake, by a path but little known, sooner than if we followed the tardy movements of the column; and, by consequence, more agreeably."

"I like him not," said the lady, shuddering, partly in assumed, yet more in real terror. "You know him, Duncan, or you would not trust yourself so freely to his keeping?"

"Say, rather, Alice, that I would not trust you," returned the young man, impressively; "I do not know him, or he would not have my confidence, and least of all, at this moment. He is said to be a Canadian too; and yet he served with our friends the Mohawks, who, as you know, are one of the six allied nations. He was brought amongst us, as I have heard, by some strange accident, in which your father was interested, and in which the savage was rigidly dealt by; but I forget the idle tale: it is enough that he is now our friend."

"Should we distrust the man, because his manners are not of our manners, and that his skin is dark?" coldly asked Cora.

Alice hesitated no longer; but giving her Narraganset a smart cut of the whip, she was the first to dash aside the slight branches of the bushes, and to follow the runner along the dark and tangled pathway. The young man regarded the last speaker in open admiration, and even permitted her fairer, though certainly not more beautiful companion, to proceed unattended, while he sedulously opened a way himself, for the passage of her who has been called Cora. It would seem that the domestics had been previously instructed; for instead of penetrating the thicket, they followed the route of the column; a measure, which Heyward stated, had been dictated by the sagacity of their guide, in order to diminish the marks of their trail, if, haply, the Canadian savages should be lurking so far in advance of their army. The youth had turned to speak to the dark-eyed Cora, when the distant sounds of horses' hoofs, clattering over the roots of the broken way in his rear, caused him to check his charger; and as his companions drew their reins at the same instant, the whole party came to a halt, in order to obtain an explanation of the unlooked-for interruption.

In a few moments, the person of the ungainly man described in the preceding chapter came into view, with as much rapidity as he could excite his meagre beast to endure, without coming to an open rupture.

The frown which had gathered around the handsome, open, and manly brow of Heyward, gradually relaxed, and his lips curled into a slight smile, as he regarded the stranger.

"Seek you any here?" demanded Heyward, when the other had arrived sufficiently nigh to abate his speed; "I trust you are no messenger of evil tidings."

"Even so," replied the stranger, making diligent use of his triangular castor, to produce a circulation in the close air of the woods, and leaving his hearers in doubt to which of the young man's questions he responded; when, however, he had cooled his face, and recovered his breath, he continued: "I hear you are riding to William Henry; as I am journeying thitherward myself, I concluded good company would seem consistent to the wishes of both parties."

"If you journey to the lake, you have mistaken your route," said Heyward, haughtily; "the highway thither is at least half-a-mile behind you."

"Even so," returned the stranger, nothing daunted by this cold reception. "I have tarried at 'Edward' a week, and I should be dumb not to have inquired the road I was to journey; and if dumb, there would be an end to my calling." After simpering in a small way, like one whose modesty prohibited a more open expression of his admiration of a witticism, that was perfectly unintelligible to his hearers, he continued with becoming gravity: "It is not prudent for one of my profession to be too familiar with those he has to instruct; for which reason, I follow not the line of the army: besides which, I conclude that a gentleman of your character has the best judgment in matters of wayfaring: I have therefore decided to join company, in order that the ride may be made agreeable, and partake of social communion."

"A most arbitrary, if not a hasty decision!" exclaimed Heyward, undecided whether to give vent to his growing anger, or to laugh aloud in the other's face. "But you speak of instruction, and of a profession; are you an adjunct to the provincial corps, as a master of the noble science of defence and offence? or, perhaps, you are one who draws lines and angles, under the pretence of expounding the mathematics?"

The stranger regarded his interrogator a moment in open wonder; and then, losing every mark of self-satisfaction in an expression of solemn humility, he answered:

"Of offence, I hope there is none to either party: of defence, I make none—by God's good mercy, having committed no palpable sin since last entreating his pardoning grace. I understand not your allusions about lines and angles; and I leave expounding for those who have been called and set apart for that holy office. I lay claim to no higher gift than a small insight into the glorious art of petition and thanksgiving, as practised in psalmody."

"The man is, most manifestly, a disciple of Apollo," cried the amused Alice, who had recovered from her momentary embarrassment, "and I take him under my own especial protection. Nay, throw aside that frown, Heyward, and, in pity to my longing ears, suffer him to journey in our train. Besides," she added, in a low and hurried voice, casting a glance at the distant Cora, who slowly followed the footsteps of their silent but sullen guide, "it may be a friend added to our strength in time of need."

The cavalcade had not long passed, before the branches of the bushes that formed the thicket were cautiously moved asunder, and a human visage, as fiercely wild as savage art and unbridled passions could make it, peered out on the retiring footsteps of the travellers. A gleam of exultation shot across the darkly painted lineaments of the inhabitant of the forest, as he traced the route of his intended victims, who rode unconsciously onward; the light and graceful forms of the females, waving among the trees in the curvatures of their path, followed at each bend by the manly figure of Heyward.

Chapter 3

Before these fields were shorn and tilled,
    Full to the brim our rivers flowed;
The melody of waters filled
    The fresh and boundless wood;
And torrents dashed, and rivulets played,
And fountains spouted in the shade.
                                        Bryant

LEAVING the unsuspecting Heyward and his confiding companions to penetrate still deeper into a forest that contained such treacherous inmates, we must use an author's privilege, and shift the scene a few miles to the westward of the place where we have last seen them.

On that day, two men might be observed lingering on the banks of a small but rapid stream, within an hour's journey of the encampment of

Webb, like those who awaited the appearance of an absent person, or the approach of some expected event. The vast canopy of woods spread itself to the margin of the river, overhanging the water and shadowing its dark glassy current with a deeper hue. The rays of the sun were beginning to grow less fierce, and the intense heat of the day was lessened, as the cooler vapours of the springs and fountains rose above their leafy beds, and rested in the atmosphere. Still that breathing silence which marks the drowsy sultriness of an American landscape in July, pervaded the secluded spot, interrupted only by the low voices of the men in question, an occasional and lazy tap of a reviving woodpecker, the discordant cry of some gaudy jay, or a swelling on the ear from the dull roar of a distant waterfall.

These feeble and broken sounds, were, however, too familiar to the foresters to draw their attention from the more interesting matter of their dialogue. While one of these loiterers showed the red skin and wild accoutrements of a native of the woods, the other exhibited, through the mask of his rude and nearly savage equipments, the brighter though sunburnt and long-faded complexion of one who might claim descent from a European parentage. The former was seated on the end of a mossy log, in a posture that permitted him to heighten the effect of his earnest language, by the calm but expressive gestures of an Indian engaged in debate. His body, which was nearly naked, presented a terrific emblem of death, drawn in intermingled colours of white and black. His closely shaved head, on which no other hair than the well known and chivalrous scalping tuft was preserved, was without ornament of any kind, with the exception of a solitary eagle's plume, that crossed his crown, and depended over the left shoulder. A tomahawk and scalping knife, of English manufacture, were in his girdle; while a short military rifle, of that sort with which the policy of the whites armed their savage allies, lay carelessly across his bare and sinewy knee. The expanded chest, full-formed limbs, and grave countenance of this warrior, would denote that he had reached the vigour of his days, though no symptoms of decay appeared to have yet weakened his manhood.

The frame of the white man, judging by such parts as were not concealed by his clothes, was like that of one who had known hardships and exertion from his earliest youth. His person, though muscular, was rather attenuated than full; but every nerve and muscle appeared strung and indurated by unremitting exposure and toil. He wore a hunting-skirt of forest-green, fringed with faded yellow, and a summer cap of skins, which had been shorn of their fur. He also bore a knife in a girdle of wampum, like that which confined the scanty garments of the Indian, but no tomahawk. His moccasins were ornamented after the gay fashion of the natives, while the only part of his under dress which appeared below the hunting-frock, was a pair of buckskin leggings, that laced at the sides, and were gartered above the knees with the sinews of a deer. A pouch and horn completed his personal accountrements, though a rifle of a great length, which the theory of the more ingenious whites had taught them was the most dangerous of all fire-arms, leaned against a neighbouring sapling. The eye of the hunter, or scout, whichever he might be, was small, quick, keen, and restless, roving while he spoke on every side of him, as if in quest of game, or distrusting the sudden approach of some lurking enemy. Notwithstanding these symptoms of habitual suspicion, his countenance was not only without guile, but at the moment at which he is introduced, was charged with an expression of sturdy honesty.

"My tribe is the grandfather of nations," said the native, "but I am an unmixed man. The blood of chiefs is in my veins, where it must stay for ever. The Dutch landed, and gave my people the firewater; they drank until the heavens and the earth seemed to meet, and they foolishly thought they had found the Great Spirit. Then they parted with their land. Foot by foot they were driven back from the shores, until I, that am a chief and a Sagamore, have never seen the sun shine but through the trees, and have never visited the graves of my fathers."

"Graves bring solemn feelings over the mind," returned the scout, a good deal touched at the calm suffering of his companion; "and often aid a man in his good intentions; though for myself, I expect to leave my own bones unburied, to bleach in the woods, or to be torn asunder by the wolves. But where are to be found your race, which came to their kin in the Delaware country, so many summers since?"

"Where are the blossoms of those summers!—Fallen, one by one: so all of my family departed, each in his turn, to the land of spirits. I am on the hill-top, and must go down into the valley; and when Uncas follows in my footsteps, there will no longer be any of the blood of the Sagamores, for my boy is the last of the Mohicans."

"Uncas is here," said another voice, in the same soft, guttural tones, near his elbow; "who wishes Uncas?"

The white man loosened his knife in its leathern sheath, and made an involuntary movement of the hand towards his rifle, at this sudden interruption; but the Indian sat composed, and without turning his head at the unexpected sounds.

At the next instant, a youthful warrior passed between them with a noiseless step, and seated himself on the bank of the rapid stream. No exclamation of surprise escaped the father, nor was any question made, or reply given, for several minutes, each appearing to await the moment when he might speak without betraying a womanish curiosity or childish impatience. The white man seemed to take counsel from their customs, and relinquishing his grasp of the rifle, he also remained silent and reserved. At length Chingachgook turned his eyes slowly towards his son, and demanded—

"Do the Maquas dare to leave the print of their moccasins in these woods?"

"I have been on their trail," replied the young Indian, "and know that

12

they number as many as the fingers of my two hands; but they lie hid like cowards."

"'Tis enough!" returned the father, glancing his eye towards the setting sun; "they shall be driven like deer from their bushes. Hawk-eye, let us eat to-night, and show the Maquas that we are men to-morrow."

"I am as ready to do the one as the other," replied the scout; "but to fight the Iroquois, 'tis necessary to find the skulkers; and to eat 'tis necessary to get the game—talk of the devil and he will come; there is a pair of the biggest antlers I have seen this season, moving the bushes below the hill! Now, Uncas," he continued in a half whisper, and laughing with a kind of inward sound, like one who had learnt to be watchful, "I will bet my charger three times full of powder, against a foot of wampum, that I take him atwixt the eyes, and nearer to the right than to the left."

"It cannot be!" said the young Indian, springing to his feet with youthful eagerness; "all but the tips of his horns are hid!"

"He's a boy," said the white man, shaking his head while he spoke, and addressing the father. "Does he think when a hunter sees a part of the creatur, he can't tell where the rest of him should be!"

Adjusting his rifle, he was about to make an exhibition of that skill on which he so much valued himself, when the warrior struck up the piece with his hand, saying,

"Hawk-eye! will you fight the Maquas?"

"These Indians know the nature of the woods, as it might be by instinct!" returned the scout, dropping his rifle, and turning away like a man who was convinced of his error. "I must leave the buck to your arrow, Uncas, or we may kill a deer for them thieves, the Iroquois, to eat."

The instant the father seconded this intimation, by an expressive gesture of the hand, Uncas threw himself on the ground, and approached the animal with wary movements. When within a few yards of the cover, he fitted an arrow to his bow with the utmost care, while the antlers moved, as if their owner snuffed an enemy in the tainted air. In another moment the twang of the bow was heard, a white streak was seen glancing into the bushes, and the wounded buck plunged from the cover, to the very feet of his hidden enemy.—Avoiding the horns of the infuriated animal, Uncas darted to his side, and passed the knife across his throat, when, bounding to the edge of the river, it fell, dyeing the water with its blood to a great distance.

"'Twas done with Indian skill," said the scout, laughing inwardly, but with vast satisfaction; "and was a pretty sight to behold! Though an arrow is a near shot, and needs a knife to finish the work."

"Hugh!" ejaculated his companion, turning quickly, like a hound who scented his game.

"By the Lord, there is a drove of them!" exclaimed the hunting scout, whose eyes began to glisten with the ardour of his usual occupation; "if they come within range of a bullet, I will drop one, though the whole

Six Nations should be lurking within sound! What do you hear, Chingach-gook? for to my ears the woods are dumb."

"There is but one deer, and he is dead," said the Indian, bending his body till his ear nearly touched the earth. "I hear the sounds of feet!"

"Perhaps the wolves have driven that buck to shelter, and are following in his trail."

"No. The horses of white men are coming," returned the other, raising himself with dignity, and resuming his seat on the log with all his former composure. "Hawk-eye, they are your brothers; speak to them."

"That will I, and in English that the king needn't be ashamed to answer," returned the hunter, speaking in the language of which he boasted; "but I see nothing, nor do I hear the sounds of man or beast; 'tis strange that an Indian should understand white sounds better than a man who, his very enemies will own, has no cross in his blood, although he may have lived with the redskins long enough to be suspected! Ha! there goes something like the cracking of a dry stick, too—now I hear the bushes move—yes, yes, there is a trampling that I mistook for the falls—and—but here they come themselves; God keep them from the Iroquois!"

Chapter 4

Well, go thy way, thou shalt not from this grove,
Till I torment thee for this injury.
Midsum.-Night's Dream.

THE words were still in the mouth of the scout, when the leader of the party, whose approaching footsteps had caught the vigilant ear of the Indian, came openly into view. A beaten path, such as those made by the periodical passage of the deer, wound through a little glen at no great distance, and struck the river at the point where the white man and his red companions had posted themselves. Along this track the travellers, who had produced a surprise so unusual in the depths of the forest, advanced slowly towards the hunter, who was in front of his associates in readiness to receive them.

"Who comes?" demanded the scout, throwing his rifle carelessly across his left arm, and keeping the fore finger of his right hand on the trigger, though he avoided all appearance of menace in the act—"Who comes hither, among the beasts and dangers of the wilderness?"

"Believers in religion, and friends to the law and to the king," returned he who rode foremost of the party. "Men who have journeyed since the rising sun, in the shades of this forest, without nourishment, and are sadly tired of their wayfaring."

"Then you must have lost your eyesight afore losing your way; for the road across the portage is cut to a good two rods, and is as grand a path, I calculate, as any that runs into London, or even before the palace of the king himself."

14

"We will not dispute concerning the excellence of the passage," returned Heyward, smiling, for as the reader has anticipated, it was he. "It is enough, for the present, that we trusted to an Indian guide to take us by a nearer, though blinder path, and that we are deceived in his knowledge. In plain words, we know not where we are."

"An Indian lost in the woods!" said the scout, shaking his head doubtingly; "when the sun is scorching the tree tops, and the watercourses are full; when the moss on every beech he sees will tell him in which quarter the north star will shine at night! The woods are full of deer paths which run to the streams and licks, places well known to every body; nor have the geese done their flight to the Canada waters altogether! 'Tis strange that an Indian should be lost atwixt Horican and the bend in the river! Is he a Mohawk?"

"Not by birth, though he is adopted in that tribe; I think his birthplace was farther north, and he is one of those you call a Huron."

"Hugh!" exclaimed the two companions of the scout, who had continued, until this part of the dialogue, seated, immoveable, and apparently indifferent to what passed, but who now sprang to their feet with an activity and interest that had evidently gotten the better of their reserve by surprise.

"A Huron!" repeated the sturdy scout, once more shaking his head in open distrust; "they are a thievish race, nor do I care by whom they are adopted; you can never make any thing of them but skulks and vagabonds. Since you trusted yourself to the care of one of that nation, I only wonder that you have not fallen in with more."

"Of that there is little danger, since William Henry is so many miles in our front. You forget that I have told you our guide is now a Mohawk, and that he serves with our forces as a friend."

"And I tell you that he who is born a Mingo will die a Mingo," returned the other, positively. "A Mohawk! No, give me a Delaware or a Mohican for honesty; and when they will fight, which they won't all do, having suffered their cunning enemies, the Maquas, to make them women—but when they will fight at all, look to a Delaware or a Mohican for a warrior!"

"It seems that may depend on who is your guide. One would think such a horse as that might get over a good deal of ground atwixt sun-up and sun-down."

"I wish no contention of idle words with you, friend," said Heyward, curbing his dissatisfied manner, and speaking in a more gentle voice; "if you will tell me the distance to Fort Edward, and conduct me thither, your labour shall not go without its reward."

"I have heard a party was to leave the encampment this morning, for the lake shore?"

"You have heard the truth; but I preferred a nearer route, trusting to the knowledge of the Indian I mentioned."

"And he deceived you, and then deserted?"

15

"Neither, as I believe; certainly not the latter, for he is to be found in the rear."

"I should like to look at the creatur; if it is a true Iroquois I can tell him by his knavish look, and by his paint," said the scout, stepping past the charger of Heyward, and entering the path behind the mare of the singing master. After shoving aside the bushes, and proceeding a few paces, he encountered the females, who awaited the result of the conference with anxiety, and not entirely without apprehension. Behind these, again, the runner leaned against a tree, where he stood the close examination of the scout with an air unmoved, though with a look so dark and savage, that it might in itself excite fear. Satisfied with his scrutiny, the hunter soon left him. As he repassed the females, he paused a moment to gaze upon their beauty, answering to the smile and nod of Alice with a look of open pleasure. Thence he went to the side of the motherly animal, and spending a minute in a fruitless inquiry into the character of her rider, he shook his head and returned to Heyward. "A Mingo is a Mingo, and God having made him so, neither the Mohawks nor any other tribe can alter him," he said, when he had regained his former position. "If we were alone, and you would leave that noble horse at the mercy of the wolves to-night, I could show you the way to Edward myself within an hour, for it lies only about an hour's journey hence; but with such ladies in your company, 'tis impossible!"

"And why?—they are fatigued, but are quite equal to a ride of a few more miles."

"'Tis a natural impossibility!" repeated the scout, with a determined air. "I wouldn't walk a mile in these woods after night gets into them, in company with that runner, for the best rifle in the colonies. They are full of outlying Iroquois, and your mongrel Mohawk knows where to find them too well, to be my companion."

"Think you so," said Heyward, leaning forward in the saddle, and dropping his voice nearly to a whisper; "I confess I have not been without my own suspicions, though I have endeavoured to conceal them, and effected a confidence I have not always felt, on account of my companions. It was because I suspected him, that I would follow no longer; making him, as you see, follow me."

"I knew he was one of the cheats as soon as I laid eyes on him!" returned the scout, placing his fingers on his nose in sign of caution. "The thief is leaning against the foot of the sugar sapling that you can see over them bushes; his right leg is in a line with the bark of the tree, and," tapping his rifle, "I can take him, from where I stand, between the ankle and the knee, with a single shot, putting an end to his trampling through the woods for at least a month to come. If I should go back to him, the cunning varmint would suspect something, and be dodging through the trees like any frightened deer."

"It will not do. He may be innocent, and I dislike the act. Though, if I felt confident of his treachery——"

The hunter, who had already abandoned his intention to maim the runner, at the orders of his superior, mused a moment and then made a gesture which instantly brought his two red companions to his side. They spoke together earnestly in the Delaware language, though in an under tone, and by the gestures of the white man, which were frequently directed towards the top of the sapling, it was evident he pointed out the situation of their hidden enemy. His companions were not long in comprehending his wishes, and laying aside their firearms, they parted, taking opposite sides of the path, and burying themselves in the thicket, with such cautious movements, that their steps were inaudible.

"Now, go you back," said the hunter, speaking again to Heyward, "and hold the imp in talk; these Mohicans here will take him, without breaking his paint."

"Nay," said Heyward, proudly, "I will seize him myself."

"Hist! what could you do, mounted, against an Indian in the bushes?"

"But I will dismount."

"And, think you, when he saw one of your feet out of the stirrup, he would wait for the other to be free? Whoever comes into the woods to deal with the natives, must use Indian fashions, if he would wish to prosper in his undertakings. Go, then; talk openly to the miscreant, and seem to believe him the truest friend you have on 'arth."

Heyward prepared to comply, though with strong disgust at the nature of the office he was compelled to execute. Each moment, however, pressed upon him a conviction of the critical situation in which he had suffered his invaluable trust to be involved, through his own fearless confidence. The sun had already disappeared, and the woods, suddenly deprived of his light, were assuming a dusky hue, which keenly reminded him, that the hour the savage usually chose for his most barbarous and remorseless acts of vengeance or hostility, was speedily drawing at hand.

"You may see, Magua," he said, endeavouring to assume an air of freedom and confidence, "that the night is closing around us, and yet we are no nearer to William Henry than when we left the encampment of Webb, with the sun. You have missed the way, nor have I been more fortunate. But, happily, we have fallen in with a hunter, he whom you hear talking to the singer, that is acquainted with the deer-paths and byways of the woods, and who promises to lead us to a place where we may rest securely till the morning."

The Indian riveted his glowing eyes on Heyward as he asked, in his imperfect English, "Is he alone?"

"Alone!" hesitatingly answered Heyward, to whom deception was too new to be assumed without embarrassment. "Oh! not alone, surely, Magua, for you know that we are with him."

"Then le Renard Subtil will go," returned the runner, coolly raising his little wallet from the place where it had lain at his feet; "and the pale faces will see none but their own colour."

"Go! Whom call you le Renard?"

"'Tis the name his Canada fathers have given to Magua," returned the runner, with an air that manifested his pride at the distinction, though probably quite ignorant of the character conveyed by the appellation. "Night is the same as day to le Subtil when Munro waits for him."

"And what account will le Renard give the chief of William Henry concerning his daughters? Will he dare to tell the hot-blooded Scotsman that his children are left without a guide, though Magua promised to be one?"

"The Grayhead has a loud voice, and a long arm, but will le Renard hear him or feel him in the woods?" returned the wary runner.

"But what will the Mohawks say? They will make him petticoats, and bid him stay in the wigwam with the women, for he is no longer to be trusted with the business of a man."

"Le Subtil knows the path to the great lakes, and can find the bones of his fathers," was the answer of the unmoved runner.

"Enough, Magua," said Heyward; "are we not friends? why should there be bitter words between us? Munro has promised you a gift for your services when performed, and I shall be your debtor for another. Rest your weary limbs, then, and open your wallet to eat. We have a few moments to spare; let us not waste them in talk like wrangling women. When the ladies are refreshed will we proceed."

The Indian then fastened his eyes keenly on the open countenance of Heyward, but meeting his glance, he turned them quickly away, and seating himself deliberately on the ground, he drew forth the remnant of some former repast, and began to eat, though not without first bending his looks slowly and cautiously around him.

"This is well," continued Heyward; "and le Renard will have strength and sight to find the path in the morning;"—he paused, for sounds like the snapping of a dried stick, and the rustling of leaves, rose from the adjacent bushes, but, recollecting himself, instantly continued—"We must be moving before the sun is seen, or Montcalm may lie in our path, and shut us out from the fortress."

The hand of Magua dropped from his mouth to his side, and though his eyes were fastened on the ground, his head was turned aside, his nostrils expanded, and his ears seemed even to stand more erect than usual, giving to him the appearance of a statue that was made to represent intense attention.

Heyward, who watched his movements with a vigilant eye, carelessly extricated one of his feet from the stirrup, while he passed a hand towards the bear-skin covering of his holsters. Every effort to detect the point most regarded by the runner, was completely frustrated by the tremulous glances of his organs, which seemed not to rest a single instant on any particular object, and which, at the same time, could be hardly said to move. While he hesitated how to proceed, le Subtil cautiously raised himself to his feet, though with a motion so slow and guarded, that not the

18

slightest noise was produced by the change. Heyward felt it had now become incumbent on him to act; throwing his leg over the saddle, he dismounted, with a determination to advance and seize his treacherous companion, trusting the result to his own manhood. In order, however, to prevent unnecessary alarm, he still preserved an air of calmness and friendship.

"Le Renard Subtil does not eat," he said, using the appellation he had found most flattering to the vanity of the Indian. "His corn is not well parched, and seems dry. Let me examine; perhaps something may be found among my own provisions that will help his appetite."

Magua held out the wallet to meet the proffer of the other. He even suffered their hands to meet, without betraying the least emotion, or varying his riveted attitude of attention. But when he felt the fingers of Heyward moving gently along his own naked arm, he struck up the limb of the young man, and uttering a piercing cry, as he darted beneath it, plunged, at a single bound, into the opposite thicket. At the next instant, the form of Chingachgook appeared from the bushes, looking like a spectre in its paint, and glided across the path in swift pursuit. Next followed the shout of Uncas, when the woods were lighted by a sudden flash, that was accompanied by the sharp report of the hunter's rifle.

Chapter 5

— In such a night,
Did Thisbe fearfully o'ertrip the dew;
And saw the lion's shadow ere himself.
Merchant of Venice.

THE suddenness of the flight of his guide, and the wild cries of the pursuers, caused Heyward to remain fixed for a few moments in inactive surprise. Then recollecting the importance of securing the fugitive, he dashed aside the surrounding bushes, and pressed eagerly forward to lend his aid in the chase. Before he had, however, proceeded a hundred yards, he met the three foresters already returning from their unsuccessful pursuit.

"Why so soon disheartened?" he exclaimed; "the scoundrel must be concealed behind some of these trees, and may yet be secured. We are not safe while he goes at large."

"Would you set a cloud to chase the wind?" returned the disappointed scout; "I heard the imp brushing over the dry leaves like a black snake, and blinking a glimpse of him, just over ag'in yon big pine, I pulled as it might be on the scent; but 'twouldn't do! and yet for a reasoning aim, if anybody but myself had touched the trigger, I should call it a quick sight; and I may be accounted to have experience in these matters, and one who ought to know. Look at this sumach; its leaves are red, though every body knows the fruit is in the yellow blossom in the month of July!"

"'Tis the blood of le Subtil! he is hurt, and may yet fall!"

"No, no," returned the scout, in decided disapprobation of this opinion. "I rubbed the bark off a limb, perhaps, but the creatur leaped the longer for it. A rifle bullet acts on a running animal, when it barks him, much the same as one of your spurs on a horse; that is, it quickens motion, and puts life into the flesh, instead of taking it away. But when it cuts the ragged hole, after a bound or two, there is commonly a stagnation of further leaping, be it Indian, or be it deer!"

"We are four able bodies, to one wounded man!"

"Is life grievous to you?" interrupted the scout. "Yonder red devil would draw you within swing of the tomahawks of his comrades, before you were heated in the chase. It was an unthoughtful act, in a man who has so often slept with the war-whoop ringing in the air, to let off his piece, within sound of an ambushment! But then it was a natural temptation! 'twas very natural! Come, friends, let us move our station, and in such a fashion too, as will throw the cunning of a Mingo on a wrong scent, or our scalps will be drying in the wind in front of Montcalm's marquee, ag'in this hour to-morrow's sundown."

This appalling declaration, which the scout uttered with the cool assurance of a man who fully comprehended, while he did not fear to face the danger, served to remind Heyward of the importance of the charge with which he himself had been intrusted. Looking upward, he found that the thin fleecy clouds, which evening had painted on the blue sky, were already losing their faintest tints of rose colour, while the imbedded stream which glided past the spot where he stood, was to be traced only by the dark boundary of its wooded banks.

"What is then to be done?" he said, feeling the utter helplessness of doubt in such a pressing strait; "desert me not, for God's sake! remain to defend those I escort, and freely name your own reward!"

"Offer your prayers to Him, who can give us wisdom to carcumvent the cunning of the devils who fill these woods," calmly interrupted the scout; "but spare your offers of money, which neither you may live to realize, nor I to profit by. These Mohicans and I will do what man's thoughts can invent to keep such flowers (which though so sweet, were never made for the wilderness) from harm, and that without hope of any other recompense but such as God always gives to upright dealings. First, you must promise two things, both in your own name and for your friends, or, without serving you, we shall only injure ourselves!"

"Name them."

"The one is to be still as these sleeping woods, let what will happen: and the other is to keep the place where we shall take you for ever a secret from all mortal men."

"I will do my utmost to see both these conditions fulfilled."

"Then follow, for we are losing moments that are as precious as the heart's blood to a stricken deer!"

Heyward could distinguish the impatient gesture of the scout, through the increasing shadows of the evening, and moved in his footsteps swiftly towards the place where he had left the remainder of his party. When they rejoined the expecting and anxious females, he briefly acquainted them with the conditions of their new guide, and with the necessity that existed for their hushing every apprehension in instant and serious exertions. Although his alarming communication was not received without much secret terror by the listeners, his earnest and impressive manner, aided perhaps by the nature of their danger, succeeded in bracing their nerves to undergo some unlooked-for and unusual trail. Silently, and without a moment's delay, they permitted him to assist them from their saddles, when they descended quickly to the water's edge, where the scout had collected the rest of the party, more by the agency of his expressive gestures than by any use of words.

"What to do with these dumb creatures!" muttered the white man, on whom the sole control of their future movements appeared to devolve; "it would be time lost to cut their throats, and cast them into the river; and to leave them here, would be to tell the Mingoes that they have not far to seek to find their owners!"

"Then give them their bridles, and let them range the woods!" Heyward ventured to suggest.

"No; it would be better to mislead the imps, and make them believe they must equal a horse's speed to run down their chase. Ay, ay, that will blind their fire-balls of eyes!"

The Indians, however, hesitated not a moment, but taking the bridles, they led the frightened and reluctant horses down into the bed of the river.

At a short distance from the shore they turned, and were soon concealed by the projection of the bank, under the brow of which they moved, in a direction opposite to the course of the waters. In the meantime, the scout drew a canoe of bark from its place of concealment beneath some low bushes, whose branches were waving with the eddyings of the current, into which he silently motioned the females to enter. They complied without hesitation, though many a fearful and anxious glance was thrown behind them, towards the thickening gloom, which now lay like a dark barrier along the margin of the stream.

So soon as Cora and Alice were seated, the scout, without regarding the element, directed Heyward to support one side of the frail vessel, and posting himself at the other, they bore it up against the stream. In this manner they proceeded for many rods, in a silence that was only interrupted by the rippling of the water, as its eddies played around them, or the low dash made by their own cautious footsteps. At length they reached a point in the river, where the roving eye of Heyward became riveted on a cluster of black objects which had collected at a spot where the high bank threw a deeper shadow than usual on the dark waters. Hesitating to advance, he pointed out the place to the attention of his companion.

"Ay," returned the composed scout, "the Indians have hid the beasts with the judgment of natives! Water leaves no trail, and an owl's eye would be blinded by the darkness of such a hole."

The horses had been secured to some scattering shrubs that grew in the fissures of the rocks, where, standing in the water, they were left to pass the night. The scout directed Heyward and his disconsolate fellow travellers to seat themselves in the forward end of the canoe, and took possession of the other himself, as erect and steady as if he floated in a vessel of much firmer materials. The Indians warily retraced their steps towards the place they had left, when the scout, placing his pole against a rock, by a powerful shove, sent his frail bark directly into the centre of the turbulent stream. For many minutes the struggle between the light bubble in which they floated, and the swift current, was severe and doubtful. Forbidden to stir even a hand, and almost afraid to breathe, lest they should expose the frail fabric to the fury of the stream, the anxious passengers watched the glancing waters in feverish suspense. Twenty times they thought the whirling eddies were sweeping them to destruction, when the master-hand of their pilot would bring the bows of the canoe to stem the rapid, and their eyes glanced over a confused mass of the murmuring element—so swift was the passage between it and their little vessel. A long, a vigourous, and, as it appeared to the females, a desperate effort, closed the scene. Just as Alice veiled her eyes in horror, under the impression that they were about to be swept within the vortex at the foot of the cataract, the canoe floated stationary at the side of a flat rock, that lay on a level with the water.

"Where are we? and what is next to be done?" demanded Heyward, perceiving that the exertions of the scout had ceased.

"You are at the foot of Glenn's," returned the other, speaking aloud, without fear of consequences, within the roar of the cataract; "and the next thing is to make a steady landing, lest the canoe upsets, and you should go down again the hard road we have travelled, faster than you came up it; 'tis a hard rift to stem, when the river is a little swelled; and five is an unnatural number to keep dry in the hurry-skurry, with a little birchen bark and gum. There, go you all on the rock, and I will bring up the Mohicans with the venison. A man had better sleep without his scalp, than famish in the midst of plenty."

His passengers gladly complied with these directions. As the last foot touched the rock, the canoe whirled from its station, when the tall form of the scout was seen for an instant gliding above the waters, before it disappeared in the impenetrable darkness that rested on the bed of the river. Left by their guide, the travellers remained a few minutes in helpless ignorance, afraid even to move along the broken rocks, lest a false step should precipitate them down some one of the many deep and roaring caverns, into which the water seemed to tumble, on every side of them. Their suspense, however, was soon relieved; for, aided by the skill of the natives, the canoe shot back into the eddy, and floated again at the side of the low rock, before they thought the scout had even time to rejoin his companions.

"We are now fortified, garrisoned, and provisioned," cried Heyward, cheerfully, "and may set Montcalm and his allies at defiance. I know full well that your two companions are brave and cautious warriors! Have they then heard or seen any thing of our enemies?"

"I should be sorry to think they had, though this is a spot that stout courage might hold for a smart skrimmage. I will not deny, however, but the horses cowered when I passed them, as though they scented the wolves; and a wolf is a beast that is apt to hover about an Indian ambushment, craving the offals of the deer the savages kill."

The scout, whilst making his remarks, was busied in collecting certain necessary implements; as he concluded, he moved silently by the group of travellers, accompanied by the Mohicans, who seemed to comprehend his intentions with instinctive readiness, when the whole three disappeared in succession, seeming to vanish against the dark face of a perpendicular rock, that rose to the height of a few yards within as many feet of the water's edge.

Chapter 6

Those strains that once did sweet in Zion glide.
He wales a portion with judicious care;
And "Let us worship God," he says, with solemn air.
Burns.

HEYWARD and his female companions witnessed this mysterious movement with secret uneasiness; for, though the conduct of the white man had hitherto been above reproach, his rude equipments, blunt address, and strong antipathies, together with the character of his silent associates, were all causes for exciting distrust in minds that had been so recently alarmed by Indian treachery. The stranger alone disregarded the passing incidents. He seated himself on a projection of the rocks, whence he gave no other signs of consciousness than by the struggles of his spirit, as manifested in frequent and heavy sighs. Smothered voices were next heard, as though men called to each other in the bowels of the earth, when a sudden light flashed upon the vision of those without, and laid bare the much prized secret of the place.

At the farther extremity of a narrow, deep cavern in the rock, whose length appeared much extended by the perspective and the nature of the light by which it was seen, was seated the scout, holding a blazing knot of pine. The strong glare of the fire fell full upon his sturdy weather-beaten countenance and forest attire, lending an air of romantic wildness to the aspect of an individual, who, seen by the sober light of day, would have exhibited the peculiarities of a man remarkable for the strangeness of his dress, the iron-like inflexibility of his frame, and the singular compound of quick vigilant sagacity, and of exquisite simplicity, that by turns usurped the possession of his muscular features.

"Are we quite safe in this cavern?" demanded Heyward of Hawk-eye. "Is there no danger of surprise? A single armed man, at its entrance, would hold us at his mercy."

A spectral looking figure stalked from out the darkness behind the scout, and seizing a blazing brand, held it towards the further extremity of their place of retreat. Alice uttered a faint shriek, and even Cora rose to her feet, as this appalling object moved into the light; but a single word from Heyward calmed them, with the assurance it was only their attendant, Chingachgook, who, lifting another blanket, discovered that the cavern had two outlets. Then, holding the brand, he crossed a deep narrow chasm in the rocks, which ran at right angles with the passage they were in, but which, unlike that, was open to the heavens, and entered another cave, answering to the description of the first, in every essential particular.

"Such old foxes as Chingachgook and myself are not often caught in a burrow with one hole," said Hawk-eye, laughing; "you can easily see the cunning of the place—the rock is black limestone, which every body knows is soft; it makes no uncomfortable pillow, where brush and pine wood is scarce; well, the fall was once a few yards below us, and I dare to say was, in its time, as regular and as handsome a sheet of water as any along the Hudson. But old age is a great injury to good looks, as these sweet young ladies have yet to larn! The place is sadly changed! These rocks are full of cracks, and in some places, they are softer than at other some, and the water has worked out deep hollows for itself, until it has fallen back, ay, some hundred feet, breaking here, and wearing there, until the falls have neither shape nor consistency."

"We are then on an island?"

"Ay! there are the falls on two sides of us, and the river above and below. If you had daylight it would be worth the trouble to step up on the height of this rock, and look at the preversity of the water."

The repast, which was greatly aided by the addition of a few delicacies that Heyward had the precaution to bring with him when they left their horses, was exceedingly refreshing to the wearied party. Uncas acted as attendant to the females, performing all the little offices within his power, with a mixture of dignity and anxious grace that served to amuse Heyward, who well knew that it was an utter innovation on the Indian customs, which forbid their warriors to descend to any menial employment, especially in favour of their women. Once or twice he was compelled to speak, to command the attention of those he served. In such cases, he made use of English, broken and imperfect, but sufficiently intelligible, and which he rendered so mild and musical by his deep guttural voice, that it never failed to cause both ladies to look up in admiration and astonishment. In the course of these civilities a few sentences were exchanged, that served to establish the appearance of an amicable intercourse between the parties.

"Come, friend," said Hawk-eye, drawing out a keg from beneath a cover of leaves, towards the close of the repast, and addressing the stranger who sat at his elbow, doing great justice to his culinary skill, "try a little spruce; 'twill quicken the life in your bosom. I drink to our better friendship. How do you name yourself?"

"Gamut—David Gamut," returned the singing-master, mechanically wiping his mouth, preparatory to washing down his sorrows in a powerful draught of the woodman's high flavoured and well laced compound. "I teach singing to the youths of the Connecticut levy."

"You might be better employed. The young hounds go laughing and singing too much already through the woods when they ought not to breathe louder than a fox in his cover. Can you use the smooth bore, or handle the rifle?"

"Praised be God, I have never had occasion to meddle with such murderous implements!"

"Perhaps you understand the compass, and lay down the water courses and mountains of the wilderness on paper, in order that they who follow may find places by their given names?"

"I practise no such employment."

"You have a pair of legs that might make a long path seem short! you journey sometimes, I fancy, with tidings for the general?"

"Never; I follow no other than my own high vocation, which is instruction in sacred music!"

" 'Tis a strange calling!" muttered Hawk-eye, with an inward laugh, "to go through life like a cat-bird, mocking all the ups and downs that may happen to come out of other men's throats. Well, friend, I suppose it is your gift, and mustn't be denied, any more than if 'twas shooting, or some other better inclination. Let us hear what you can do in that way; 'twill be a friendly manner of saying good night, for 'tis time these ladies should be getting strength for a hard and a long push, in the pride of the morning, afore the Maquas are stirring."

"With joyful pleasure do I consent," said David, adjusting his iron-rimmed spectacles again, and producing his beloved little volume, which he immediately tendered to Alice. "What can be more fitting and consolatory, then to offer up evening praise after a day of such exceeding jeopardy?"

Alice smiled; but regarding Heyward, she blushed and hesitated.

"Indulge yourself," he whispered; "ought not the suggestion of the worthy namesake of the Psalmist to have its weight at such a moment?"

The singers were dwelling on one of those low, dying chords, which the ear devours with such greedy rapture, as if conscious that it is about to lose them, when a cry, that seemed neither human nor earthly, rose in the outward air, penetrating not only the recesses of the cavern, but to the inmost hearts of all who heard it. It was followed by a stillness apparently as deep as if the waters had been checked in their furious progress at such a horrid and unusual interruption.

"What is it?" murmured Alice, after a few moments of terrible suspense.

"What is it?" repeated Heyward aloud.

Neither Hawk-eye nor the Indians made any reply. They listened as if expecting the sound would be repeated, with a manner that expressed their own astonishment. At length, they spoke together, earnestly, in the Delaware language, when Uncas, passing by the inner and most concealed aperture, cautiously left the cavern. When he had gone, the scout first spoke English.

"What is it, or what it is not, none here can tell; though two of us have ranged the woods for more than thirty years!"

"Was it not then the shout the warriors make when they wish to intimidate their enemies?" asked Cora.

"No, no; this was bad and shocking! and had a sort of inhuman sound; but when you once hear the war-whoop, you will never mistake it for anything else. Well, Uncas!" speaking in the Delaware to the young chief, as he re-entered, "what see you? do our lights shine through the blankets?"

The answer was short and apparently decided, being given in the same tongue.

"There is nothing to be seen without," continued Hawk-eye, shaking his head in discontent, "and our hiding-place is still in darkness! Pass into the other cave, you that need it, and seek for sleep; we must be afoot long before the sun, and make the most of our time to get to Edward, while the Mingoes are taking their morning nap."

"Leave us not, Duncan," said Alice; "we cannot sleep in such a place as this, with that horrid cry still ringing in our ears!"

He approached the farther end of the cavern, to an outlet, which like the others, was concealed by blankets, and, removing the thick screen, breathed the fresh and reviving air from the cataract. One arm of the river flowed through a deep narrow ravine, which its current had worn in the soft rock, directly beneath his feet, forming an effectual defence, as he believed, against any danger from that quarter; the water a few rods above them, plunging, glancing, and sweeping along in its most violent and broken manner.

"Nature has made an impenetrable barrier on this side," he continued, pointing down the perpendicular declivity, into the dark current, before he dropped the blanket; "and as you know that good men, and true, are on guard in front, I see no reason why the advice of our honest host should be disregarded. I am certain Cora will join me in saying, that sleep is necessary to you both."

Duncan ceased speaking; for while his eyes were riveted on those of Alice, who had turned towards him with the eagerness of filial affection, to catch his words, the same strong, horrid cry, as before, filled the air, and rendered him mute. A long, breathless silence succeeded, during which, each looked to the others in fearful expectation of hearing the sound repeated. At length, the blanket was slowly raised, and the scout stood in the aperture with a countenance whose firmness evidently began to give way, before a mystery that seemed to threaten some unknown danger, against which all his cunning and experience might prove of no avail.

Chapter 7

> They do not sleep.
> On yonder cliffs, a grisly band,
> I see them sit.   *Gray.*

"'Twould be neglecting a warning that is given for our good, to lie hid any longer," said Hawk-eye, "when such sounds are raised in the forest! These gentle ones may keep close, but the Mohicans and I will watch upon the rock, where I suppose a major of the 60th would wish to keep us company. I have listened to all the sounds of the woods for thirty years, as a man will listen whose life and death depends so often on the quickness of his ears. There is no whine of the panther, no whistle of the cat-bird, nor any invention of the devilish Mingoes, that can cheat me! But neither the Mohicans, nor I, who am a white man without a cross, can explain the cry just heard. We, therefore, believe it a sign given for our good."

"It is extraordinary!" exclaimed Heyward, taking his pistols from the place where he had laid them on entering; "be it a sign of peace, or a signal of war, it must be looked to. Lead the way, my friend; I follow."

On issuing from their place of confinement, the whole party instantly experienced a grateful renovation of their spirits, by exchanging the pent air of their hiding place, for the cool and invigorating atmosphere, which played around the whirlpools and pitches of the cataract.

"Here is nothing to be seen but the gloom and quiet of a lovely evening," whispered Duncan; "how much should we prize such a scene, and all this breathing solitude, at any other moment, Cora! Fancy yourselves in security, and what now, perhaps, increases your terror, may be made conducive to enjoyment——"

"Listen!" interrupted Alice.

The caution was unnecessary. Once more the same sound arose, as if from the bed of the river, and having broken out of the narrow bounds of the cliffs, was heard undulating through the forest, in distant and dying cadences.

"Can any here give a name to such a cry?" demanded Hawk-eye, when the last echo was lost in the woods; "if so, let him speak: for myself, I judge it not to belong to 'arth!"

"Here, then, is one who can undeceive you," said Duncan; "I know the sound full well, for often have I heard it on the field of battle, and in situations which are frequent in a soldier's life. 'Tis the horrid shriek that a horse will give in his agony; oftener drawn from him in pain, though sometimes in his terror. My charger is either a prey to the beasts of the forest, or he sees his danger without the power to avoid it. The sound might deceive me in the cavern, but in the open air I know I cannot be wrong."

The scout and his companions listened to this simple explanation, with the interest of men who imbibe new ideas, at the same time that they get rid of old ones, which had proved disagreeable inmates. The two latter uttered their usual and expressive explanation, "hugh!" as the truth first glanced upon their minds, while the former, after a short musing pause, took on himself to reply.

"I cannot deny your words," he said; "for I am little skilled in horses, though born where they abound. The wolves must be hovering above their heads on the bank, and the timersome creatures are calling on man for help, in the best manner they are able. Uncas"—he spoke in Delaware—"Uncas, drop down in the canoe, and whirl a brand among the pack; or fear may do what the wolves can't get at to perform, and leave us without horses in the morning, when we shall have so much need to journey swiftly."

The young native had already descended to the water, to comply, when a long howl was raised on the edge of the river, and was borne swiftly off into the depths of the forest, as though the beasts, of their own accord, were abandoning their prey, in sudden terror. Uncas, with instinctive quickness, receded, and the three foresters held another of their low, earnest conferences.

"We have been like hunters, who have lost the points of the heavens, and from whom the sun has been hid for days," said Hawk-eye, turning away from his companions; "now we begin again to know the signs of our course, and the paths are cleared from briars! Seat yourselves in the shade, which the moon throws from yonder beech—'tis thicker than that of the pines—and let us wait for that which the Lord may choose to send next. Let all your conversation be in whispers; though it would be better, and perhaps, in the end, wiser, if each one held discourse with his own thoughts for a time."

In this manner hours passed by without further interruption. All but Hawk-eye and the Mohicans lost every idea of consciousness, in uncontrollable drowsiness. But the watchfulness of these vigilant protectors neither tired nor slumbered. It was continued without any apparent consequences, until the moon had set, and a pale streak above the tree tops, at a bend of the river a little below, announced the approach of day.

Then, for the first time, Hawk-eye was seen to stir. He crawled along the rock, and shook Duncan from his heavy slumbers.

"Now is the time to journey," he whispered; "awake the gentle ones, and be ready to get into the canoe when I bring it to the landing place."

"Have you had a quiet night," said Heyward; "for myself, I believe sleep has gotten the better of my vigilance."

"All is yet still as midnight. Be silent, but be quick."

By this time Duncan was thoroughly awake, and he immediately lifted the shawl from the sleeping fair ones. The motion caused Cora to raise

28

her hand as if to repulse him, while Alice murmured in her soft, gentle voice, "No, no, dear father, we were not deserted; Duncan was with us."

"Yes, sweet innocence," whispered the delighted youth; "Duncan is here, and while life continues, or danger remains, he will never quit thee. Cora! Alice! awake! The hour has come to move."

While the words were still on the lips of Heyward, there had arisen such a tumult of yells and cries, as served to drive the swift currents of his own youthful blood back from its bounding course into the fountains of his heart. It seemed, for near a minute, as if the demons of hell had possessed themselves of the air about them, and were venting their savage humours in barbarous sounds. The cries came from no particular direction, though it was evident they filled the woods, and, as the appalled listeners easily imagined, the caverns of the falls, the rocks, the bed of the river, and the upper air. David raised his tall person in the midst of the infernal din, with a hand on either ear, exclaiming—

"Whence comes this discord? Has hell broke loose, that man should utter sounds like these?"

The bright flashes, and the quick reports of a dozen rifles, from the opposite banks of the stream, followed this incautious exposure of his person, and left the unfortunate singing master senseless on that rock where he had been so long slumbering. The Mohicans boldly sent back the intimidating yell of their enemies, who raised a shout of savage triumph as they witnessed the fall of Gamut. The flash of rifles was then quick and close between them, but either party was too well skilled to leave even a limb exposed to the hostile aim. Duncan listened with intense anxiety for the strokes of the paddle, believing that flight was now their only refuge. The river glanced by with its ordinary velocity, but the canoe was no where to be seen on its dark waters. He had just fancied they were cruelly deserted by the scout, as a stream of flame issued from the rock beneath him, and a fierce yell, blended with a shriek of agony, announced that the messenger of death, hurled from the fatal weapon of Hawk-eye, had found a victim. At this slight repulse the assailants instantly withdrew, and gradually, the place became still as before the sudden tumult.

Duncan seized the favourable moment to spring to the body of Gamut, which he bore within the shelter of the narrow chasm that protected the sisters. In another minute the whole party was collected in this spot of comparative safety.

"The poor fellow has saved his scalp," said Hawk-eye, coolly passing his hand over the head of David; "but he is a proof that a man may be born with too long a tongue! 'Twas downright madness to show six feet of flesh and blood on a naked rock to the raging savages; and I only wonder he has escaped with life."

"Is he not dead?" demanded Cora, in a voice whose husky tones showed how powerfully natural horror struggled with her assumed firmness. "Can we do aught to assist the wretched man?"

"No, no! the life is in his heart yet, and after he has slept awhile he will come to himself, and be a wiser man for it, till the hour of his real time shall come," returned Hawk-eye, casting another oblique glance at the insensible body, while he filled his charger with admirable nicety. "Carry him in, Uncas, and lay him on the saxafrax. The longer his nap lasts, the better it will be for him; as I doubt whether he can find a proper cover for such a shape on these rocks; and singing won't do any good with the Iroquois."

At that moment the woods were filled with a burst of cries, and, at the signal, four savages sprang from the cover of the drift wood. Heyward felt a burning desire to rush forward to meet them, so intense was the delirious anxiety of the moment, but he was restrained by the deliberate examples of the scout and Uncas. When their foes, who leaped over the black rocks that divided them, with long bounds, uttering the wildest yells, were within a few rods, the rifle of Hawk-eye slowly rose among the shrubs, and poured out its fatal contents. The foremost Indian bounded like a stricken deer, and fell headlong among the clefts of the island.

A single yell burst from the woods, and all was again still.

"'Twas the last charge in my horn, and the last bullet in my pouch," he said. "Uncas, lad, go down to the canoe, and bring up the big horn; it is all the powder we have left, and we shall need it to the last grain, or I am ignorant of the Mingo nature."

The young Mohican instantly complied, leaving the scout turning over the useless contents of his pouch, and shaking the empty horn with renewed discontent. From this unsatisfactory examination, however, he was soon called by a loud and piercing exclamation from Uncas, that sounded even to the unpractised ears of Duncan, as the signal of some new and unexpected calamity. Every thought filled with apprehension for the precious treasure he had concealed in the cavern, the young man started to his feet, totally regardless of the hazard he incurred by such an exposure. As if actuated by a common impulse, his movement was imitated by his companions, and, together, they rushed down the pass to the friendly chasm, with a rapidity that rendered the scattering fire of their enemies perfectly harmless. The unwonted cry had brought the sisters, together with the wounded David, from their place of refuge, and the whole party, at a single glance, was made acquainted with the nature of the disaster, that had disturbed even the practised stoicism of their youthful Indian protector.

Chapter 8

They linger yet,
Avengers of their native land.
Gray.

AT a short distance from the rock, their little bark was to be seen floating across the eddy, towards the swift current of the river, in a manner which proved that its course was directed by some hidden agent.

The instant this unwelcome sight caught the eye of the scout, his rifle was levelled, as by instinct, but the barrel gave no answer to the bright sparks of the flint.

"'Tis too late, tis too late!" Hawk-eye exclaimed, dropping the useless piece, in bitter disappointment; "the miscreant has struck the rapid, and had we powder, it could hardly send the lead swifter than he now goes!"

As he ended, the adventurous Huron raised his head above the shelter of the canoe, and while it glided swiftly down the stream, waved his hand and gave forth the shout, which was the known signal of success. His cry was answered by a yell, and a laugh from the woods, as tauntingly exulting as if fifty demons were uttering their blasphemies at the fall of some Christian soul.

"Well may you laugh, ye children of the devil!" said the scout, seating himself on a projection of the rock, and suffering his gun to fall neglected at his feet, "for the three quickest and truest rifles in these woods, are no better than so many stalks of mullen, or the last year's horn of a buck!"

"What then is to be done?" demanded Duncan, losing the first feeling of disappointment, in a more manly desire for exertion; "what will become of us?"

"It may be a minute, or it may be an hour, afore the wily sarpents steal upon us, and it is quite in natur for them to be lying within hearing at this very moment," said Hawk-eye; "but come they will, and in such a fashion as will leave us nothing to hope. It is befitting that I should die as becomes my colour, with no words of scoffing in my mouth, and without bitterness at the heart!"

"Why die at all?" said Cora, advancing from the place where natural horror had, until this moment, held her riveted to the rock; "the path is open on every side: fly, then, to the woods, and call on God for succour! Go, brave men, we owe you too much already; let us no longer involve you in our hapless fortunes!"

"You but little know the craft of the Iroquois, lady, if you judge they have left the path open to the woods!" returned Hawk-eye, who, however, immediately added to his simplicity, "the down stream current, it is certain, might soon sweep us beyond the reach of their rifles, or the sound of their voices."

"Then try the river. Why linger, to add to the number of the victims of our merciless enemies?"

"Why," repeated the scout, looking about him proudly, "because it is better for a man to die at peace with himself, than to live haunted by an evil conscience! What answer could we give to Munro, when he asked us where and how we left his children?"

"Go to him, and say, that you left them with a message to hasten to their aid," returned Cora, advancing nigher to the scout, in her generous ardour; "that the Hurons bear them into the northern wilds, but that by vigilance and speed they may yet be rescued; and if, after all, it should please Heaven, that his assistance come too late, bear to him," she continued, the firm tones of her voice gradually lowering, until they seemed nearly choked, "the love, the blessings, the final prayers of his daughters, and bid him not to mourn their early fate, but to look forward with humble confidence to the Christian's goal to meet his children."

The hard weather-beaten features of the scout began sensibly to work, as he listened, and when she had ended, he dropped his chin to his hand, like a man musing profoundly on the nature of her proposal.

"There is reason in her words!" at length broke from his compressed and trembling lips; "ay, and they bear the spirit of Christianity. Chingachgook! Uncas! hear you the talk of the dark-eyed woman!"

He now spoke in Delaware to his companions, and his address, though calm and deliberate, seemed very decided. The elder Mohican heard him with deep gravity, and appeared to ponder on his words, as though he felt the importance of their import. After a moment of hesitation, he waved his hand in assent, and uttered the English word "good," with the peculiar emphasis of his people. Then, replacing his knife and tomahawk in his girdle, the warrior moved silently to the edge of the rock most concealed from the hostile banks of the river. Here he paused a moment, pointed significantly to the woods below, and saying a few words in his own language, as if indicating his intended route, he dropped into the water, and sunk from before the eyes of the anxious witnesses of his movements.

The scout delayed his departure to speak to the generous maiden, whose breathing became lighter as she saw the success of her remonstrance.

"Wisdom is sometimes given to the young, as well as the old," he said; "and what you have spoken is wise, not to call it by a better word. If you are led into the woods, that is, such of you as may be spared for a while, break the twigs on the bushes as you pass, and make the marks of your trail as broad as you can, when, if mortal eyes can see them, depend on having a friend who will follow to the ends of the 'arth afore he deserts you."

He gave Cora an affectionate shake of the hand, lifted his rifle, and after regarding it a moment with melancholy solicitude, laid it carefully aside, and descended to the place where Chingachgook had just disappeared. For an instant he hung suspended by the rock; and looking about him, with a countenance of peculiar care, he added bitterly, "Had the powder held out, this disgrace could never have befallen!" then, loosening his hold, the water closed above his head, and he also became lost to view.

All eyes were now turned on Uncas, who stood leaning against the ragged rock, in immovable composure. After waiting a short time Cora pointed down the river, and said—

"Your friends, as you perceive, have not been seen, and are now, most probably, in safety; is it not time for you to follow?"

"Uncas will stay," the young Mohican calmly answered, in his imperfect English.

"To increase the horror of our capture, and to diminish the chances of our release! Go, generous young man," Cora continued, lowering her eyes under the ardent gaze of the Mohican, and perhaps with an intuitive consciousness of her power; "go to my father, as I have said, and be the most confidential of my messengers. Tell him to trust you with the means to buy the freedom of his daughters. Go; 'tis my wish, 'tis my prayer, that you will go!"

The settled, calm look of the young chief changed to an expression of gloom, but he no longer hesitated. With a noiseless step he crossed the rock and dropped into the troubled stream. Hardly a breath was drawn by those he left behind until they caught a glimpse of his head emerging for air, far down the current, when he again sunk, and was seen no more.

These sudden and apparently successful experiments had all taken place in a few minutes of that time which had now become so precious. After the last look at Uncas, Cora returned, and, with a quivering lip, addressed herself to Heyward:

"I have heard of your boasted skill in the water, too, Duncan," she said; "follow, then, the wise examples set you by these simple and faithful beings."

"Is such the faith Cora Munro would exact from her protector," said the young man, smiling mournfully, but with bitterness.

"This is not a time for idle subtleties and false opinions," she answered; "but a moment when every duty should be equally considered. To us you can be of no further service here, but your precious life may be saved for other and nearer friends."

He made no reply, though his eyes fell wistfully on the beautiful form of Alice, who was clinging to his arm with the dependency of an infant.

"Consider, after all," continued Cora, after a pause of a moment, during which she seemed to struggle with a pang, even more acute than any that her fears had excited, "the worst to us can be but death; a tribute that all must pay at the good time of God's appointment."

"There are evils even worse than death," said Duncan, speaking hoarsely, and as if fretful at her importunity, "but which the presence of one who would die on your behalf may avert."

Cora instantly ceased her entreaties, and veiling her face in her shawl, drew the nearly insensible Alice after her into the deepest recess of the inner cavern.

Chapter 9

Be gay securely;
Dispel, my fair, with smiles, the tim'rous clouds,
That hang on thy clear brow.
Death of Agrippina.

THE sudden and almost magical change from the stirring incidents of the combat, to the stillness that now reigned around him, acted on the heated imagination of Heyward like some exciting dream. While all the images and events he had witnessed remained deeply impressed on his memory, he felt a difficulty in persuading himself of their truth. Still ignorant of the fate of those who had trusted to the aid of the swift current, he at first listened intently to any signal, or sounds of alarm, which might announce the good or evil fortune of their hazardous undertaking. His attention was, however, bestowed in vain; for, with the disappearance of Uncas, every sign of the adventurers had been lost, leaving him total uncertainty of their subsequent fate.

"The Hurons are not to be seen," he said, addressing David, whose faculties had by no means recovered from the effects of the stunning blow he had received; "let us conceal ourselves in the cavern, and trust the rest to Providence."

"There is melody in the fall of the cataract, and the rushing of many waters is sweet to the senses!" said David, pressing his hand confusedly on his brow. "Is not the air yet filled with shrieks and cries, as though the departed spirits of the damned——"

"Not now, not now," interrupted the impatient Heyward, "they have ceased; and they who raised them, I trust in God, they are gone too! every thing but the water is still and at peace; in, then, where you may create those sounds you love so well to hear."

David smiled sadly, though not without a momentary gleam of pleasure lighting his countenance at this allusion to his beloved vocation. He no longer hesitated to be led to a spot, which promised such unalloyed gratification to his wearied senses; and, leaning on the arm of his companion, he entered the narrow mouth of the cave. Duncan seized a pile of the sassafras, which he drew before the passage, studiously concealing every appearance of an aperture. Within this fragile barrier he arranged the blankets abandoned by the foresters, darkening the inner extremity of the cavern, while its outer received a chastened light from the narrow ravine, through which one arm of the river rushed, to form the junction with its sister branch, a few rods below. He then seated himself in the centre of the cavern, grasping his remaining pistol with a hand firmly clenched, while his contracted and frowning eye announced the sullen desperation of his purpose. "The Hurons, if they come, may not gain our position so easily as they think," he lowly muttered; and, dropping his head back against the rock, he seemed to await the result in patience, though his gaze was unceasingly bent on the open avenue to their place of retreat.

With the last sound of his voice, a deep, a long, and almost breathless silence succeeded. The fresh air of the morning had penetrated the recess, and its influence was gradually felt on the spirits of its inmates. As minute after minute passed by, leaving them in undisturbed security, the insinuating feeling of hope was gradually gaining possession of every bosom, though each one felt reluctant to give utterance to expectations that the next moment might so fearfully destroy.

David alone formed an exception to these varying emotions. A gleam of light from the opening crossed his wan countenance, and fell upon the pages of the little volume, whose leaves he was again occupied in turning, as if searching for some song more fitted to their condition than any that had yet met his eye. He was most probably acting all this time under a confused recollection of the promised consolation of Duncan. At length, it would seem, his patient industry found its reward; for, without explanation or apology, he pronounced aloud the characteristic appellation of "Isle of Wight," drew a long, sweet sound from his pitch-pipe, and then ran through the preliminary modulations of the air, whose name he had just mentioned, with the sweeter tones of his own musical voice.

"May not this prove dangerous?" asked Cora, glancing her dark eyes at Major Heyward.

"Poor fellow! his voice is too feeble to be heard amid the din of the falls," was the answer; "besides, the cavern will prove his friend. Let him, then, indulge his passion, since it may be done without hazard."

The open sympathy of the listeners soon stirred the spirit of the votary of music, whose voice regained its richness and volume, without losing that touching softness which proved its secret charm. Exerting his renovated powers to the utmost, he was filling the arches of the cave with long and full tones, when a yell burst into the air without, that instantly stilled his pious strains, choking his voice suddenly, as though his heart had literally bounded into the passage of his throat.

"We are lost!" exclaimed Alice, throwing herself into the expanded arms of Cora.

"Not yet, not yet," returned the agitated, but undaunted Heyward; "the sound came from the centre of the island, and it has been produced by the sight of their dead companions. We are not yet discovered, and there is still hope."

Faint and almost despairing as was the prospect of escape, the words of Duncan were not thrown away, for it awakened the powers of the sisters in such a manner, that they awaited the result in silence. A second yell soon followed the first when a rush of voices was heard pouring down the island, from its upper to its lower extremity, until they reached the naked rock above the caverns, where, after a shout of savage triumph, the air continued full of horrible cries and screams, such as man alone can utter, and he only when in a state of the fiercest barbarity.

In the midst of this tumult a triumphant yell was raised within a few feet of the hidden entrance to the cave. Heyward abandoned every hope, with the belief it was the signal that they were discovered. Again the impression passed away, as he heard the voices collect near the spot where the white man had so reluctantly abandoned his rifle. Amid the jargon of the Indian dialects that he now plainly heard, it was easy to distinguish not only words, but sentences, in the patois of the Canadas. A burst of voices had shouted, simultaneously, "la Longue Carabine!" causing the opposite woods to re-echo with a name which Heyward well remembered to have heard, had been given by his enemies to a celebrated hunter and scout of the English camp, and who he now learned for the first time had been his late companion.

"La Longue Carabine! la Longue Carabine!" passed from mouth to mouth, until the whole band appeared to be collected round the trophy, which would seem to announce the death of its formidable owner. After a vociferous consultation, which was, at times, deafened by bursts of savage joy, they again separated, filling the air with the name of a foe, whose body Heyward could collect from their expressions, they hoped to find concealed in some crevice of the island.

"Now," he whispered to the trembling sisters, "now is the moment of uncertainty! If our place of retreat escape this scrutiny, we are still safe! In every event, we are assured, by what has fallen from our enemies, that our friends have escaped, and in two short hours we may look for succour from Webb."

A shout was at that moment heard, as if issuing from the centre of the rock, announcing that the neighbouring cavern had at length been entered. In a minute, the number and loudness of the voices indicated that the whole party were collected in and around that secret place.

As the inner passages to the two caves were so close to each other, Duncan, believing that escape was no longer possible, passed David and the sisters, to place himself between the latter and the first onset of the terrible meeting. Grown desperate by his situation, he drew nigh the slight barrier which separated him only by a few feet from his relentless pursuers, and placing his face to the casual opening, he even looked out, with a sort of appalling indifference on their movements.

Within reach of his arm was the brawny shoulder of a gigantic Indian, whose deep and authoritative voice appeared to give directions to the proceedings of his fellows. Beyond him again, Duncan could look into the deep vault opposite, which was filled with savages, upturning and rifling the humble furniture of the scout. The wound of David had dyed the leaves of sassafras with a colour, that the natives well knew was anticipating the season. Over this sign of their success, they set up a howl, like an opening from so many hounds who had recovered their lost trail. After this yell of victory, they tore up the fragrant bed of the cavern, and bore the branches into the chasm, scattering the boughs, as if they suspected them of concealing the person of the man they had so long hated and feared. One fierce and wild looking warrior approached the chief, bearing a load of the brush, and, pointing exultingly to the deep red stains with which it was sprinkled, uttered his joy in Indian yells, whose meaning Heyward was only enabled to comprehend by the frequent repetition of the name of "la Longue Carabine!" When this triumph had ceased he cast the bush on the slight heap that Duncan had made before the entrance of the second cavern, and closed the view. His example was followed by others; who as they drew the branches from the cave of the scout, threw them into one pile, adding unconsciously to the security of those they sought. The very slightness of the defence was its chief merit, for no one thought of disturbing a mass of brush, which all of them believed, in that moment of hurry and confusion, had been accidentally raised by the hands of their own party.

As the blankets yielded before the outward pressure, and the branches settled into the fissure of the rock by their own weight, forming a compact body, Duncan once more breathed freely. With a light step, and lighter heart, he returned to the centre of the cave, and took the place he had left, where he could command a view of the opening next the river. While he was in the act of making this movement, the Indians, as if changing their purpose by a common impulse, broke away from the chasm in a body, and were heard rushing up the island again, towards the point whence they had originally descended. Here another wailing cry betrayed that they were again collected around the bodies of their dead comrades.

Duncan now ventured to look at his companions; for, during the most critical moments of their danger, he had been apprehensive that the anxiety of his countenance might communicate some additional alarm to those who were so little able to sustain it.

"They are gone, Cora!" he whispered; "Alice, they are returned whence they came, and we are saved! To heaven, that has alone delivered us from the grasp of so merciless an enemy, be all the praise!"

"Then to Heaven will I return my thanks!" exclaimed the younger sister, rising from the encircling arms of Cora, and easing herself, with enthusiastic gratitude, on the naked rock to her knees; "to that Heaven who has spared the tears of a grey-headed father—has saved the lives of those I so much love——"

Both Heyward, and the more tempted Cora, witnessed the act of involuntary emotion with powerful sympathy, the former secretly believing that piety had never worn a form so lovely as it had now assumed in the youthful person of Alice. Her eyes were radiant with the glow of her grateful feelings; the flush of her beauty was again seated on her cheeks, and her whole soul seemed ready and anxious to pour out its thanksgiving, through the medium of her eloquent features. But when her lips moved, the words they should have uttered appeared frozen by some new and sudden chill. Her bloom gave place to the paleness of death; her soft and melting eyes grew hard, and seemed contracting with horror; while those hands which she had raised clasped in each other, towards heaven, dropped in horizontal lines before her, the fingers pointing forward in convulsed motion. Heyward turned the instant she gave a direction to his suspicions, and, peering just above the ledge which formed the threshold of the open outlet of the cavern, he beheld the malignant, fierce, and savage features of le Renard Subtil.

In that moment of horrid surprise, the self-possession of Heyward did not desert him. He observed by the vacant expression of the Indian's countenance, that his eye accustomed to the open air, had not yet been able to penetrate the dusky light which pervaded the depth of the cavern. He had even thought of retreating beyond a curvature in the natural wall, which might still conceal him and his companions when, by the sudden gleam of intelligence that shot across the features of the savage, he saw it was too late, and that they were betrayed.

The look of exultation and brutal triumph which announced this terrible truth, was irresistibly irritating. Forgetful of every thing but the impulse of his hot blood, Duncan levelled his pistol and fired. The report of the weapon made the cavern bellow like the eruption of a volcano, and when the smoke it vomited had driven away before the current of air which issued from the ravine, the place so lately occupied by the features of his treacherous guide was vacant. Rushing to the outlet, Heyward caught a glimpse of his dark figure, stealing around a low and narrow ledge, which soon hid him entirely from his sight.

Among the savages, a frightful stillness succeeded the explosion, which had just been heard bursting from the bowels of the rock. But when le Renard raised his voice in a long and intelligible whoop, it was answered by a spontaneous yell from the mouth of every Indian within hearing of the sound. The clamorous noises again rushed down the island, and before Duncan had time to recover from the shock, his feeble barrier of brush was scattered to the winds, the cavern was entered at both its extremities, and he and his companions were dragged from their shelter, and borne into the day, where they stood surrounded by the whole band of the triumphant Hurons.

Chapter 10

I fear we shall outsleep the coming morn,
As much as we this night have overwatched.
Midsummer-Night's Dream.

THE instant the first shock of this sudden misfortune had abated, Duncan began to make his observations on the appearance and proceedings of their captors. Contrary to the usages of the natives, in the wantonness of their success, they had respected not only the persons of the trembling sisters, but his own. The rich ornaments of his military attire had indeed been repeatedly handled by different individuals of the tribe, with eyes expressing a savage longing to possess the baubles; but before the customary violence could be resorted to, a mandate in the authoritative voice of the larger warrior already mentioned, stayed the uplifted hand, and convinced Heyward that they were to be reserved for some object of particular moment.

Magua then summoned his warriors to himself in council. Their deliberations were short, and, it would seem, by the silence of most of the party, the decision unanimous. By the frequency with which the few speakers pointed in the direction of the encampment of Webb, it was apparent they dreaded the approach of danger from that quarter. This consideration probably hastened their determination, and quickened the subsequent movements.

During this short conference, Heyward, finding a respite from his greatest fears, had leisure to admire the cautious manner in which the Hurons had made their approaches, even after hostilities had ceased.

It had already been stated, that the upper half of the island was a naked rock, and destitute of any other defences than a few scattering logs of drift wood. They had selected this point to make their descent, having borne the canoe through the wood, around the cataract, for that purpose. Placing their arms in the little vessel, a dozen men, clinging to its sides, had trusted themselves to the direction of the canoe, which was controlled by two of the most skilful warriors, in attitudes, that enabled them to command a view of the dangerous passage. Favoured by this arrangement, they touched the head of the island, at that point which had proved so fatal to their first adventurers, but with the advantages of superior numbers, and the possession of fire-arms. That such had been the manner of their descent, was rendered quite apparent to Duncan, for they now bore the light bark from the upper end of the rock, and placed it in the water near the mouth of the outer cavern. As soon as this change was made, the leader made signs to the prisoners to descend and enter.

As resistance was impossible, and remonstrance useless, Heyward set the example of submission by leading the way into the canoe, where he was soon seated with the sisters, and the still wondering David. Notwithstanding the Hurons were necessarily ignorant of the little channel among the eddies and rapids of the stream, they knew the common signs of such a navigation too well, to commit any material blunder. When the pilot chosen for the task of guiding the canoe had taken his station, the whole band plunged again into the river, the vessel glided down the current, and in a few moments the captives found themselves on the south bank of the stream, nearly opposite to the point where they had struck it the preceding evening.

Here was held another short but earnest consultation, during which, the horses, to whose panic their owners ascribed their heaviest misfortune, were led from the cover of the woods and brought to the sheltered spot.

When all were prepared Magua made the signal to proceed, advancing in front, to lead the party in his own person. Next followed David, who was gradually coming to a true sense of his condition, as the effects of the wound became less and less apparent. The sisters rode in his rear, with Heyward at their side, while the Indians flanked the party, and brought up the close of their march, with a caution that seemed never to tire.

Cora alone remembered the parting injunctions of the scout, and whenever an opportunity offered, she stretched forth her arm to bend aside the twigs that met her hands. But the vigilance of the Indians rendered this act of precaution both difficult and dangerous. She was often defeated in her purpose by encountering the dark glances of their watchful eyes, when it became necessary to feign an alarm she did not feel, and occupy the limb, by some gesture of feminine apprehension. Once, and once only, was she completely succesful; when she broke down the bough of a large sumach, and by a sudden thought, let her glove fall at the same instant. This sign, intended for those that might follow, was observed by one of her conductors, who restored the glove, broke the remaining branches of the bush in such a manner, that it appeared to proceed from the struggling of some beast in its branches, and then laid his hand on his tomahawk, with a look so significant, that it put an effectual end to these stolen memorials of their passage.

As there were horses, to leave the prints of their footsteps, in both bands of the Indians, this interruption cut off any probable hopes of assistance being conveyed through the means of their trail.

Heyward would have called out twenty times to their leader, and ventured a remonstrance, had there been any thing encouraging in the gloomy reserve of the savage. But Magua, during all this time, seldom turned to look at his followers, and never spoke. With the sun for his only guide, or aided by such blind marks as are only known to the sagacity of a native, he held his way along the barrens of pine, through occasional little fertile vales, across brooks and rivulets, and over undulating hills, with the accuracy of instinct, and nearly with the directness of a bird. He never seemed to hesitate. Whether the path was hardly distinguishable, whether it disappeared, or whether it lay beaten and plain before him, made no sensible difference in his speed or certainty. It seemed as though fatigue could not affect him. Whenever the eyes of the wearied travellers rose from the decayed leaves over which they trode, his dark form was to be seen glancing among the stems of the trees in front, his head immoveably fastened in a forward position, with the light plume on its crest, fluttering in a current of air, made solely by the swiftness of his own motion.

But all this diligence and speed was not without an object. After crossing a low vale, through which a gushing brook meandered, he suddenly rose a hill, so steep and difficult of ascent, that the sisters were compelled to alight, in order to follow. When the summit was gained, they found themselves on a level spot, but thinly covered with trees, under one of which Magua had thrown his dark form, as if willing and ready to seek that rest, which was so much needed by the whole party.

Chapter 11

—Cursed be my tribe,
If I forgive him.—
Shylock.

THE Indian had selected for this desirable purpose, one of those steep, pyramidal hills, which bear a strong resemblance to artificial mounds, and which so frequently occur in the valleys of the American states. The one in question was high and precipitous; its top flattened, as usual; but with one of its sides more than ordinarily irregular. It possessed no other apparent advantages for a resting-place, than in its elevation and form, which might render defence easy, and surprise nearly impossible. As Heyward, however, no longer expected that rescue, which time and distance now rendered so improbable, he regarded these little peculiarities with an eye devoid of interest, devoting himself entirely to the comfort and condolence of his feebler companions. The Narragansets were suffered to browse on the branches of the trees and shrubs, that were thinly scattered over the summit of the hill, while the remains of their provisions were spread under the shade of a beech, that stretched its horizontal limbs like a vast canopy above them.

Duncan left the beech, and straggled, as if without an object, to the spot where le Renard was seated. He was anxious to persuade the Indian that a reward awaited him if he returned the girls unharmed to their father. "Will not the chief of William Henry be better pleased to see his daughters before another night may have hardened his heart to their loss, and will make him less liberal in his reward?" he finished.

Heyward paused, for he knew not how to construe the remarkable expression that gleamed across the swarthy features of the attentive Indian. At first it seemed as if the remembrance of the promised reward grew vivid in his mind, as he listened to the sources of parental feeling which were to assure its possession; but as Duncan proceeded, the expression of joy became so fiercely malignant, that it was impossible not to apprehend it proceeded from some passion even more sinister than avarice.

"Go," said the Huron, suppressing the alarming exhibition, in an instant, in a death-like calmness of countenance; "go to the dark haired daughter, and say, Magua waits to speak. The father will remember what the child promises."

Duncan, who interpreted this speech to express a wish for some additional pledge that the promised gifts should not be withheld, slowly and reluctantly repaired to the place where the sisters were now resting from their fatigue, to communicate its purport to Cora.

"You understand the nature of an Indian's wishes," he concluded, as he led her towards the place where she was expected, "and must be prodigal of your offers of powder and blankets. Ardent spirits are, however, the most prized by such as he; nor would it be amiss to add some boon from your own hand, with that grace you so well know how to practice. Remember, Cora, that on your presence of mind and ingenuity, even your life, as well as that of Alice, may in some measure depend."

The Indian rose slowly from his seat, and stood for near a minute silent and motionless. He then signed with his hand for Heyward to retire, saying coldly—

"When the Huron talks to the women, his tribe shut their ears."

Cora waited until he had departed, and then turning to the native, with all the dignity of her sex, in her voice and manner, she added: "What would le Renard say to the daughter of Munro?"

"Listen," said the Indian, laying his hand firmly upon her arm, as if willing to draw her utmost attention to his words; a movement that Cora as firmly, but quietly repulsed, by extricating the limb from his grasp— "Magua was born a chief and a warrior among the red Hurons of the lakes; he saw the suns of twenty summers make the snows of twenty winters run off in the streams, before he saw a paleface, and he was happy! Then his Canada fathers came into the woods, and taught him to drink the fire-water, and he became a rascal. The Hurons drove him from the graves of his fathers, as they would chase the hunted buffalo. He ran down the shores of the lakes, and followed their outlet to the 'city of cannon.' There he hunted and fished, till the people chased him again through the woods into the arms of his enemies. The chief, who was born a Huron, was at last a warrior among the Mohawks!"

"What then have I to do or say in the matter of your misfortunes, not to say of your errors?"

"Listen," repeated the Indian, resuming his earnest attitude; "when his English and French fathers dug up the hatchet, le Renard struck the war-post of the Mohawks, and went out against his own nation. The pale faces have driven the red skins from their hunting grounds, and now, when they fight, a white man leads the way. The old chief of Horican, your father, was the great captain of our war party. He said to the Mohawks, do this, and do that, and he was minded. He made a law that if an Indian swallowed the fire-water, and came into the cloth wigwams of his warriors, it should not be forgotten. Magua foolishly opened his mouth, and the hot liquor led him into the cabin of Munro. What did the grey-head?—let his daughter say."

"He forgot not his words, and did justice by punishing the offender," said the undaunted maiden.

"Justice!" repeated the Indian, casting an oblique glance of the most ferocious expression at her unyielding countenance: "is it justice to make evil, and then punish for it! Magua was not himself; it was the fire-water that spoke and acted for him, but Munro did not believe it. The Huron chief was tied up before all the pale-face warriors, and whipped with sticks like a dog."

"You would then revenge the injury inflicted by Munro, on his helpless daughters. Would it not be more like a man to go before his face, and take the satisfaction of a warrior?"

"The arms of the pale-faces are long, and their knives sharp!" returned the savage, with a malignant laugh; "why should le Renard go among the muskets of his warriors, when he holds the spirit of the grey-head in his hand?"

"Name your intention, Magua," said Cora, struggling with herself to speak with steady calmness. "Is it to lead us prisoners to the woods, or do you contemplate even some greater evil? Is there no reward, no means of palliating the injury, and of softening your heart? At least, release my gentle sister, and pour out all your malice on me. Purchase wealth by her safety, and satisfy your revenge with a single victim. The loss of both his daughters might bring the aged man to his grave, and where then would be the satisfaction of le Renard?"

"Listen," said the Indian again. "The light eyes can go back to the Horican and tell the old chief what has been done, if the dark-haired woman will swear by the Great Spirit of her fathers to tell no lie."

"What must I promise?" demanded Cora, still maintaining a secret ascendancy over the fierce passions of the native by the collected and feminine dignity of her presence.

"When Magua left his people, his wife was given to another chief; he has now made friends with the Hurons, and will go back to the graves of his tribe on the shores of the great lake. Let the daughter of the English chief follow, and live in his wigwam for ever."

However revolting a proposal of such a character might prove to Cora, she retained, notwithstanding her powerful disgust, sufficient self-command to reply, without betraying the least weakness.

"And what pleasure would Magua find in sharing his cabin with a wife he did not love; one who would be of a nation and colour different from his own! It would be better to take the gold of Munro, and buy the heart of some Huron maid with his gifts and generosity."

The Indian made no reply for near a minute, but bent his fierce looks on the countenance of Cora in such wavering glances, that her eyes sunk with shame, under an impression that, for the first time, they had encountered an expression that no chaste female might endure. While she was shrinking within herself, in dread of having her ears wounded by some proposal still more shocking than the last, the voice of Magua answered in its tones of deepest malignancy—

"When the blows scorched the back of the Huron, he would know where to find a woman to feel the smart. The daughter of Munro would draw his water, hoe his corn, and cook his venison. The body of the grey-head would sleep among his cannon, but his heart would lie within reach of the knife of le Subtil."

"Monster! well dost thou deserve thy treacherous name!" cried Cora, in an ungovernable burst of filial indignation. "None but a fiend could meditate such a vengeance! But thou overratest thy power. You shall find it is, in truth, the heart of Munro you hold, and that it will defy your utmost malice!"

The Indian answered this bold defiance by a ghastly smile that showed an unaltered purpose, while he motioned her away, as if to close their conference for ever. Heyward flew to the side of the agitated maiden, and demanded the result of a dialogue that he had watched at a distance with so much interest. But unwilling to alarm the fears of Alice, she evaded a direct reply, betraying only by her countenance her utter want of success, and keeping her anxious looks fastened on the slightest movements of their captors. To the reiterated and earnest questions of her sister concerning her probable destination, she made no other answer than by pointing towards the dark group with an agitation she could not control, and murmuring, as she folded Alice to her bosom—

"There, there! read our fortunes in their faces; we shall see! we shall see!"

The action and the choked utterance of Cora, spoke more impressively than any words, and' quickly drew the attention of her companions on that spot, where her own was riveted with an intenseness that nothing but the importance of the stake could create.

When Magua reached the cluster of savages, he commenced speaking with the utmost dignity of an Indian chief. The first syllables he uttered had the effect to cause his listeners to raise themselves in attitudes of respectful attention.

He enumerated the warriors of the party; their several merits; their frequent services to the nation; their wounds, and the number of the scalps they had taken. He described the cataract of Glenn's; the impregnable position of its rocky island, with its caverns and its numerous encircling rapids and whirlpools: he named the name of "la Longue Carabine," and paused until the forest beneath them had sent up the last echo of a loud and long yell, with which the hated appellation was received. He pointed toward the youthful military captive, and described the death of a favourite warrior who had been precipitated into the deep ravine by his hand. When this recital of events was ended, his voice once more changed and became plaintive, and even musical, in its low, soft, guttural sounds. Then suddenly lifting his voice to a pitch of terrific energy, he concluded by demanding—

"Are the Hurons dogs, to bear this? There is a dark spot on the name of the Hurons, and it must be hid in blood!"

When he pointed out their means of vengeance, he struck a chord which never failed to thrill in the breast of an Indian. With the first intimation that it was within their reach, the whole band sprang upon their feet, as one man, and giving utterance to their rage for a single instant, in the most frantic cries, they rushed upon their prisoners in a body, with drawn knives and uplifted tomahawks. Heyward threw himself between the sisters and their enemies, the foremost of whom he grappled with a desperate strength that for a moment checked his violence. This unexpected resistance gave Magua time to interpose, and with rapid enunciation and animated gestures, he drew the attention of the band again to himself.

Two powerful warriors cast themselves together on Heyward, while another was occupied in securing the less active singing-master. Neither of the captives, however, submitted without a desperate though fruitless struggle. Even David hurled his assailant to the earth; nor was Heyward secured, until the victory over his companion enabled the Indians to direct their united force to that object. When the young soldier regained his recollection, he had the painful certainty before his eyes, that a common fate was intended for the whole party. On his right was Cora, in a durance similar to his own, pale and agitated, but with an eye whose steady look still read the proceedings of their enemies. On his left, the withes which bound her to a pine, performed that office for Alice which her trembling limbs refused, and alone kept her lovely but fragile form from sinking to the ground.

The vengeance of the Hurons had now taken a new direction, and they prepared to execute it with all that barbarous ingenuity with which they were familiarized by the practice of centuries. Some sought knots, to raise the blazing pile; one was riving the splinters of pine, in order to pierce the flesh of their captives with the burning fragments; and others bent the tops of two saplings to the earth, in order to suspend Heyward by the arms between the recoiling branches. But the vengeance of Magua sought a deeper and a more malignant enjoyment.

While the less refined monsters of the band prepared, before the eyes of those who were to suffer, these well known and vulgar means of torture, he approached Cora, and pointed out, with the most malign expression of countenance, the speedy fate that awaited her—

"Ha!" he added, "what says the daughter of Munro? Shall I send the yellow hair to her father, and will you follow Magua to the great lakes, to carry his water and feed him with corn?"

The savage continued, pointing, with taunting irony, towards Alice.

"Look! the child weeps! She is young to die! Send her to Munro, to comb his grey hairs, and keep the life in the heart of the old man."

"No, no, no; better that we should die as we have lived—together!"

"Then die!" shouted Magua, hurling his tomahawk with violence at the unresisting speaker, and gnashing his teeth with a rage that could no longer be bridled, at this sudden exhibition of firmness in the one he believed the weakest of the party. The axe cleaved the air in front of Heyward, and cutting some of the flowing ringlets of Alice, buried itself, and quivered in the tree above her head. The sight maddened Duncan to desperation. Collecting all his energies in one effort, he snapped the twigs which bound him, and rushed upon another savage, who was preparing, with loud yells, and a more deliberate aim, to repeat the blow. They encountered, grappled, and fell to the earth together. The naked body of his antagonist, afforded Heyward no means of holding his adversary, who glided from his grasp, and rose again with one knee on his chest, pressing him down with the weight of a giant. Duncan already saw the knife gleaming in the air, when a whistling sound swept past him, and was rather accompanied than followed, by the sharp crack of a rifle. He felt his breast relieved from the load it had endured; he saw the savage expression of his adversary's countenance change to a look of vacant wildness, and then the Indian fell prostrate and dead, on the faded leaves by his side.

Chapter 12

Clo—I am gone, Sir,
And anon, Sir,
I'll be with you again.
Twelfth Night.

THE Hurons stood aghast at this sudden visitation of death on one of their band. But, as they regarded the fatal accuracy of an aim, which had dared to immolate an enemy, at so much hazard to a friend, the name of "La Longue Carabine" burst simultaneously from every lip, and was succeeded by a wild and sort of plaintive howl. The cry was answered by a loud shout from a little thicket, where the incautious party had piled their arms; and, at the next moment, Hawk-eye, too eager to load the rifle he had regained, was seen advancing upon them, brandishing the clubbed weapon, and cutting the air with wide and powerful sweeps. Bold and rapid as was the progress of the scout, it was exceeded by that of a light and vigorous form, which bounding past him, leaped, with incredible activity and daring, into the very centre of the Hurons where it stood, whirling a tomahawk, and flourishing a glittering knife, with fearful menaces, in front of Cora. Quicker than the thoughts could follow these unexpected and audacious movements, an image, armed in the emblematic panoply of death, stole, with the imaginary glidings of a spectre, before their eyes, and assumed a threatening attitude at the other side. The savage tormentors recoiled before these warlike intruders, and uttered, as they appeared in such quick succession, the often repeated and peculiar exclamation of surprise, followed by the well known and dreaded appellations of—

"Le Cerf Agile! le Gros Serpent!"

But the wary and vigilant leader of the Hurons was not so easily disconcerted. Casting his keen eyes around the little plain, he comprehended the nature of the assault at a glance, and encouraging his followers by his voice, as well as by his example, he unsheathed his long and dangerous knife, and rushed, with a loud whoop, upon the expecting Chingachgook. It was the signal for a general combat. Neither party had firearms, and the contest was to be decided in the deadliest manner; hand to hand, with weapons of offence, and none of defence.

When Uncas had brained his first antagonist, he turned, like a hungry lion, to seek another. The fifth and only Huron disengaged at the first onset, had paused a moment, and then seeing that all around him were employed in the deadly strife, he had sought, with hellish vengeance, to complete the baffled work of revenge. Raising a shout of triumph, he had sprung towards the defenceless Cora, sending his keen axe, as the dreadful precursor of his approach. The tomahawk grazed her shoulder, and cutting the withes which bound her to the tree, left the maiden at liberty to fly. She eluded the grasp of the savage, and reckless of her own safety, threw herself on the bosom of Alice, striving, with convulsed and ill-directed fingers, to tear asunder the twigs which confined the person of her sister.

It was just then the sight caught the eye of Uncas. Bounding from his footsteps he appeared for an instant darting through the air, and descending in a ball, he fell on the chest of his enemy, driving him for many yards from the spot headlong and prostrate. The violence of the exertion cast the young Mohican at his side. They arose together, fought, and bled, each in his turn. But the conflict was soon decided; the tomahawk of Heyward, and the rifle of Hawk-eye, descending on the skull of the Huron, at the same moment that the knife of Uncas reached his heart.

The battle was now entirely terminated with the exception of the protracted struggle between "le Renard Subtil" and "le Gros Serpent." Well did these barbarous warriors prove that they deserved those significant names, which had been bestowed for deeds in former wars. When they engaged, some little time was lost in eluding the quick and vigorous thrusts which had been aimed at their several lives. Suddenly darting on each other, they closed, and came to the earth, twisted together, like twining serpents, in pliant and subtle folds. In this manner, the scene of the combat was removed from the centre of the little plain to its verge. The Mohican now found an opportunity to make a powerful thrust with his knife; Magua suddenly relinquished his grasp, and fell backwards without motion, and seemingly, without life. His adversary leaped on his feet, making the arches of the forest ring with the sounds of his shout of triumph.

"Well done for the Delawares! victory to the Mohican!" cried Hawk-eye, once more elevating the butt of the long and fatal rifle; "a finishing blow from a man without a cross, will never tell against his honour, nor rob him of his right to the scalp!"

But, at that very moment when the dangerous weapon was in the act of descending, the subtle Huron rolled swiftly from beneath the danger over the edge of the precipice, and falling on his feet, was seen leaping with a single bound into the centre of a thicket of low bushes, which clung along its sides. The Delawares, who had believed their enemy dead, uttered their exclamation of surprise, and were following with speed and clamour, like hounds in open view of the deer, when a shrill and peculiar cry from the scout, instantly changed their purpose, and recalled them to the summit of the hill.

When the foresters had made their selection from the captured arsenal of the Hurons and distributed their prizes, the scout announced, openly, that the hour had arrived when it was necessary to move. By this time the sisters had learned to still the exhibition of their emotions. Aided by Duncan and the young Mohican, the two descended the precipitous sides of that hill which they had so lately ascended under such very different auspices, and whose summit had so nearly proved the scene of their horrible massacre. At the foot they found their Narragansets browsing the herbage of the bushes and having mounted, they followed the movements of a guide, who, in the most deadly straits, had so often proved himself their friend. Their journey was, however, short. Hawk-eye, leaving the blind path that the Hurons had followed, turned short to his right, and entering the thicket, he crossed a babbling brook, and halted in a narrow dell, under the shade of a few water elms. Their distance from the base of the fatal hill was but a few rods, and the steeds had been serviceable to the maidens only in crossing the shallow stream.

The scout and the Indians seemed to be familiar with the sequestered place where they now were; for, leaning their rifles against the trees, they commenced throwing aside the dried leaves, and opening the blue clay, out of which a clear and sparkling spring of bright, glancing water, quickly bubbled. The white man then looked about him, as though seeking for some object which was not to be found as readily as he expected.

"Them careless imps, the Mohawks, with their Tuscarora and Onondaga brethren, have been here slaking their thirst," he muttered, "and the vagabonds have thrown away the gourd! This is the way with benefits, when they are bestowed upon such disremembering hounds! Here has the Lord laid his hand, in the midst of the howling wilderness, for their good, and raised a fountain of water from the bowels of the 'arth, that might laugh at the richest shop of apothecary's ware in all the colonies; and see! the knaves have trodden in the clay, and deformed the cleanliness of the place, as though they were brute beasts, instead of human men!"

Uncas silently extended towards him the desired gourd, which the spleen of Hawk-eye had hitherto prevented him from observing, suspended, with sufficient care, on the branch of an elm. Filling it with water, he retired a short distance to a place where the ground was more firm and dry; here he coolly seated himself, and after taking a long, and, apparently, a grateful draught, he commenced a very strict examination of the fragments of food left by the Hurons, which had hung in a wallet on his arm.

"Thank you, lad," he continued, returning the empty gourd to Uncas, "now we will see how these rampaging Hurons lived when outlying in ambushments. Look at this! The varlets know the better pieces of the deer, and one would think they might carve and roast a saddle equal to the best cook in the land! But everything is raw, for them Iroquois are thorough savages. Uncas, take my steel, and kindle a fire; a mouthful of a tender broil will give natur a helping hand after so long a trail."

Heyward, perceiving that their guides now set about their repast in sober earnest, assisted the maidens to alight, and placed himself at their side, not unwilling to enjoy a few moments of grateful rest after the bloody scene he had just gone through. While the culinary process was in hand, curiosity induced him to inquire into the circumstances which had led to their timely and unexpected rescue.

"How is it that we see you so soon, my generous friend," he asked, "and without aid from the garrison of Edward?"

"Had we gone to the bend in the river, we might have been in time to rake the leaves over your bodies, but too late to have saved your scalps," coolly answered the scout. "No, no; instead of throwing away strength and opportunity by crossing to the fort, we lay by, under the bank of the Hudson, waiting to watch the movements of the Hurons."

"You then were witnesses of all that passed!"

"Not of all, for Indian sight is too keen to be easily cheated, and we kept close. A difficult matter it was, too, to keep this Mohican boy snug in the ambushment! Ah! Uncas, Uncas, your behaviour was more like that of a curious woman, than of a warrior on his scent!"

"You saw our capture?" Heyward next demanded.

"We heard it," was the significant answer. "An Indian yell is plain language to men who have passed their days in the woods. But when you landed, we were driven to crawl, like sarpents, beneath the leaves; and then we lost sight of you entirely, until we placed eyes on you again, trussed to the trees, and ready bound for an Indian massacre."

"Our rescue was the deed of Providence! It was nearly a miracle that you took not the wrong path, for the Hurons divided, and each band of them had its horses!"

"Ay! there we were thrown off the scent, and might indeed have lost the trail, had it not been for Uncas," returned the scout, with the tone and manner of a man who recalled all the embarrassment of the past moment; "we took the path, however, that led into the wilderness; for we judged, and judged rightly, that the savages would hold that course with their prisoners. But when we had followed it for many miles, without finding a single twig broken, as I had advised, my mind misgave me, especially as all the footsteps had the prints of moccasins."

"Our captors had the precaution to see us shod like themselves," said Duncan, raising a foot, and exhibiting the gaily ornamented buskin he wore.

"Ay! 'twas judgmatical, and like themselves, though we were too ex-part to be thrown from a trail by so common an invention."

"To what then are we indebted for our safety?"

"Uncas was bold enough to say that the beasts ridden by the gentle ones," continued Hawk-eye, glancing his eyes, not without curious interest, on the sorrel fillies of the ladies, "planted the legs of one side on the ground at the same time, which is contrary to the movements of all trotting four-footed animals of my knowledge, except the bear! And yet here are horses that always journey in this manner, as my own eyes have seen, and as their trail has shown for twenty long miles."

"'Tis the merit of the animal! They come from the shores of Narraganset Bay, in the small province of Providence Plantations, and are celebrated for their hardihood, and the ease of this peculiar movement, though other horses are not unfrequently trained to the same."

The Mohicans had suspended their operations about the glimmering fire to listen, and when Duncan had done, they looked at each other significantly, the father uttering the never-failing exclamation of surprise. The scout ruminated, like a man digesting his newly acquired knowledge, and once more stole a curious glance at the horses, before he continued—

"I dare to say there are even stranger sights to be seen in the settlements!" he said at length; "natur is sadly abused by man when he once gets the mastery. But, go sideling, or go straight, Uncas had seen the movement, and their trail led us on to the broken bush. The outer branch, near the prints of one of the horses, was bent upward, as a lady breaks a flower from its stem, but all the rest were ragged and broken down, as if the strong hand of a man had been tearing them! So I concluded that the cunning varments had seen the twig bent, and had torn the rest, to make us believe a buck had been feeling the boughs with his antlers."

"I do believe your sagacity did not deceive you, for some such thing occurred!"

"That was easy to see", added the scout, in no degree conscious of having exhibited any extraordinary sagacity: "and a very different matter it was from a waddling horse! It then struck me the Mingoes would push for this spring, for the knaves well know the vartue of its waters."

"Is it then so famous?" demanded Heyward, examining with a more curious eye the secluded dell, with its bubbling fountain, surrounded, as it was, by earth of a deep dingy brown.

"Few red skins who travel south and east of the great lakes but have heard of its qualities. Will you taste for yourself?"

Heyward took the gourd, and after swallowing a little of the water, threw it aside with violent grimaces of discontent. The scout laughed, in his silent, but heartfelt manner, and shook his head with vast satisfaction, as he continued—

"Ah! you want the flavour that one gets by habit: the time was when I liked it as little as yourself, but I have come to my taste, and I now crave it as a deer does the licks. Your high spiced wines are not better liked than a red skin relishes this water, especially when his natur is ailing. But Uncas has made his fire, and it is time we think of eating, for our journey is long and all before us."

When this necessary, and, happily, grateful duty had been performed, each of the foresters stooped and took a long and parting draught at that solitary and silent spring, around which and its sister fountains, within fifty years, the wealth, beauty, and talents of a hemisphere were to assemble in such throngs, in pursuit of health and pleasure. Then Hawk-eye announced his determination to proceed. The sisters resumed their saddles; Duncan and David grasped their rifles, and followed on their footsteps, the scout leading the advance, and the Mohicans bringing up the rear. The whole party moved swiftly through the narrow path towards the north, leaving the healing waters to mingle unheeded with the adjacent brook.

Chapter 13

Guard.—Qui est là?
Puc.—Païsans, pouvres gens de France.
King Henry VI.

WHEN the banks of a little stream were gained, Hawk-eye made halt; and, taking the moccasins from his feet, he invited Heyward and Gamut to follow his example. He then entered the water, and for near an hour they travelled in the bed of the brook, leaving no dangerous trail. The moon had already sunk into an immense pile of black clouds, which lay impending above the western horizon, when they issued from the low and devious water-course, to rise again to the light and level of the sandy but wooded plain. Here the scout seemed to be at home, for he held on his way with the certainty and diligence of a man who moved in the security of his own knowledge. The path soon became more uneven, and the travellers could plainly perceive that the mountains drew nigher to them on each hand, and that they were, in truth, about entering one of the wildest gorges. Suddenly Hawk-eye made a pause, and waiting until he was joined by the whole party, he spoke; though in tones so low and cautious, that they added to the solemnity of his words, in the quiet and darkness of the place.

"It is easy to know the path-ways, and to find the licks and water-courses of the wilderness," he said; "but who that saw this spot could venture to say that a mighty army was at rest among yonder silent trees and barren mountains?"

"We are then at no great distance from William Henry!" said Heyward, advancing with interest, nigher to the scout.

"It is yet a long and weary path," was the answer, "and when and where to strike it, is now our greatest difficulty. The French have gathered around the fort in good earnest, and we have a delicate needle to thread in passing them."

"And but little time to do it in," added Heyward, glancing his eyes upward, towards the bank of vapour that concealed the setting moon.

Further words were unnecessary; for Hawk-eye, merely uttering the mandate to "follow," moved along the route by which they had just entered their present critical and even dangerous situation. Their progress, like their late dialogue, was guarded and without noise; for none knew at what moment a passing patrol, or a crouching piquet, of the enemy, might rise upon their path.

Hawk-eye soon deviated from the line of their retreat, and striking off towards the mountains which form the western boundary of the narrow plain, he led his followers, with swift steps, deep within the dense shadows, that were cast from their high and broken summits. Their route was now painful; lying over ground ragged with rocks, and intersected with ravines, and their progress proportionately slow. Bleak and black hills lay on every side of them, compensating, in some degree, for the additional toil of the march, by the sense of security they

51

imparted. At length the party began slowly to rise a steep and rugged ascent, by a path that curiously wound among rocks and trees, avoiding the one, and supported by the other, in a manner that showed it had been devised by men long practised in the arts of the wilderness. As they gradually rose from the level of the valleys, the thick darkness which usually precedes the approach of day began to disperse, and objects were seen in the plain and palpable colours with which they had been gifted by nature. When they issued from the stinted woods which clung to the barren sides of the mountain, upon a flat and mossy rock, that formed its summit, they met the morning, as it came blushing above the green pines of a hill, that lay on the opposite side of the valley of the Horican.

The scout now told the sisters to dismount, and taking the bridles from the mouths, and the saddles off the backs of the jaded beasts, he turned them loose, to glean a scanty subsistence among the shrubs and meagre herbage of that elevated region.

"Go," he said, "and seek your food where nature gives it you; and beware that you become not food to ravenous wolves yourselves among these hills."

"Have we no further need of them?" demanded Heyward.

"See and judge with your own eyes," said the scout, advancing towards the eastern brow of the mountain, whither he beckoned for the whole party to follow. "If it was as easy to look into the heart of man, as it is to spy out the nakedness of Montcalm's camp from this spot, hypocrites would grow scarce, and the cunning of a Mingo might prove a losing game, compared to the honesty of a Delaware."

When the travellers had reached the verge of the precipice, they saw, at a glance, the truth of the scout's declaration, and the admirable foresight with which he had led them to their commanding station.

Directly on the shore of the lake, and nearer to its western than to its eastern margin, lay the extensive earthen ramparts and low buildings of William Henry.—Two of the sweeping bastions appeared to rest on the water, which washed their bases, while a deep ditch and extensive morasses, guarded its other sides and angles. The land had been cleared of wood for a reasonable distance around the work, but every other part of the scene lay in the green livery of nature, except where the limpid water mellowed the view, or the bold rocks thrust their black and naked heads about the undulating outlines of the mountain ranges. In its front might be seen the scattered sentinels, who held a weary watch against their numerous foes, and within the walls themselves the travellers looked down upon men still drowsy with a night of vigilance. Towards the south-east, but in immediate contact with the fort, was an intrenched camp, posted on a rocky eminence, that would have been far more eligible for the work itself, in which Hawk-eye pointed out the presence of those auxiliary regiments that had so recently left the Hudson in their company. From the woods a little farther to the south rose numerous dark and lurid smokes, that were easily to be distinguished from the purer exhalations of the springs, and which the scout also showed to Heyward, as evidences that the enemy lay in force in that direction.

But the spectacle which most concerned the young soldier, was on the western bank of the lake, though quite near to its southern termination. On a stripe of land, which appeared, from its stand, too narrow to contain such an army, but which, in truth, extended many hundreds of yards from the shores of the Horican to the base of the mountain, were to be seen the white tents and military engines for an encampment of ten thousand men. Batteries were already thrown up in their front, and even while the spectators above them were looking down, with such different emotions, on a scene which lay like a map beneath their feet, the roar of artillery rose from out the valley, and passed off, in thundering echoes, along the eastern hills.

"See!" exclaimed the scout, unconsciously directing the attention of Cora to the quarters of her own father, "how that shot has made the stone fly from the side of the commandant's house! Ay! these Frenchers will pull it to pieces faster than it was put together, solid and thick though it be!"

"Heyward, I sicken at the sight of danger that I cannot share," said the undaunted but anxious daughter. "Let us go to Montcalm, and demand admission; he dare not deny a child the boon!"

"You would scarce find the tent of the Frenchman with the hair on your head!" said the blunt scout. "If I had but one of the thousand boats which lie empty along that shore, it might be done. Ha! here will soon be an end of the firing, for yonder comes a fog that will turn day to night, and make an Indian arrow more dangerous than a moulded cannon. Now, if you are equal to the work and will follow, I will make a push; for I long to get down into that camp, if it be only to scatter some Mingo dogs that I see lurking in the skirts of yonder thicket of birch."

"We are equal!" said Cora, firmly; "on such an errand we will follow to any danger!"

The scout turned to her with a smile of honest and cordial approbation, as he answered—

"I would I had a thousand men of brawny limbs and quick eyes that feared death as little as you! I'd send them jabbering Frenchers back into their den again, afore the week was ended, howling like so many fettered hounds, or hungry wolves. But stir," he added, turning from her to the rest of the party, "the fog comes rolling down so fast, we shall have but just the time to meet it on the plain, and use it as a cover. Remember, if any accident should befall me, to keep the air blowing on your left cheeks—or, rather, follow the Mohicans; they'd scent their way, be it in day or be it at night."

The direction taken by Hawk-eye soon brought the travellers to the level of the plain nearly opposite to a sallyport, in the western curtain of the fort, which lay, itself, at the distance of about half a mile from the point where he halted, to allow Duncan to come up with his charge. In their eagerness, and favoured by the nature of the ground, they had anticipated the fog, which was rolling heavily down the lake, and it became necessary to pause, until the mist had wrapped the camp of the enemy in their fleecy mantle. The Mohicans profited by the delay, to steal out of the woods, and to make a survey of surrounding objects. They were followed at a little distance, by the scout, with a view to profit early by their report, and to obtain some faint knowledge for himself of the more immediate localities.

In a very few moments he returned, his face reddened with vexation, while he muttered forth his disappointment in words of no very gentle import.

"Here has the cunning Frenchman been posting a piquet directly in our path," he said: "red skins and whites; and we shall be as likely to fall into their midst, as to pass them in the fog!"

"Cannot we make a circuit to avoid the danger," asked Heyward; "and come into our path again when it is past?"

"Who that once bends from the line of his march, in a fog, can tell when or how to turn to find it again? The mists of Horican are not like the curls from a peace-pipe, or the smoke which settles above a mosquetoe fire!"

Heyward perceiving that, in fact, a crisis had arrived, when acts were more required than words, placed himself between the sisters, and drew them swiftly forward, keeping the dim figure of their leader in his eyes. It was soon apparent that Hawk-eye had not magnified the power of the fog, for before they had proceeded twenty yards, it was difficult for the different individuals of the party to distinguish each other, in the vapour.

They had made their little circuit to the left, and were already inclining again towards the right, having as Heyward thought, got over nearly half the distance to the friendly works, when his ears were saluted with the fierce summons, in French, apparently within twenty feet of them, of—

"Who goes there?"

"Push on!" whispered the scout, once more bending to the left.

"Push on!" repeated Heyward, when the summons was renewed by a dozen voices, each of which seemed charged with threatening menaces.

"It is I," cried Duncan, dragging, rather than leading, those he supported, swiftly onward.

"Fool! Who? I!"

"A friend of France."

"You have more the air of an enemy of France. Stop or I swear I will make you a friend of the devil. No! Fire, comrades, fire!"

The order was instantly obeyed, and the fog was stirred by the explosion of fifty muskets. Happily the aim was bad, and the bullets cut the air in a direction a little different from that taken by the fugitives though still so nigh them, that to the unpractised ears of David and the two maidens, it appeared as if they whistled within a few inches of the organs. The outcry was renewed, and the order, not only to fire again, but to pursue, was too

54

plainly audible. When Heyward briefly explained the meaning of the words they heard, Hawk-eye halted, and spoke with quick decision and great firmness.

"Let us deliver our fire," he said; "they will believe it a sortie, and give way, or will wait for reinforcements."

The scheme was well conceived, but failed in its effect. The instant the French heard their pieces, it seemed as if the plain was alive with men, muskets rattling along its whole extent, from the shores of the lake to the farthest boundary of the woods.

"We shall draw their entire army upon us, and bring on a general assault," said Duncan. "Lead on my friend, for your own life and ours!"

Cries, oaths, voices calling to each other and the reports of muskets, were now quick and incessant, and apparently on every side of them. Suddenly a strong glare of light flashed across the scene, the fog rolled upwards in thick wreaths, and several cannon belched across the plain, and the roar was thrown heavily back from the bellowing echoes of the mountain.

"'Tis from the fort!" exclaimed Hawk-eye, turning short on his tracks; "and we, like stricken fools, were rushing to the woods, under the very knives of the Maquas."

The instant their mistake was rectified, the whole party retraced the error with the utmost diligence. Duncan willingly relinquished the support of Cora to the offered arm of Uncas, and Cora as readily accepted the welcome assistance. Men, hot and angry in the pursuit, were evidently on their footsteps, and each instant threatened their capture, if not their destruction.

"Point de quartier, aux coquins!" cried an eager pursuer, who seemed to direct the operations of the enemy.

"Stand firm, and be ready, my gallant 60ths!" suddenly exclaimed a voice above them, in the deep tones of authority; "wait to see the enemy, fire low, and sweep the glacis."

"Father! father!" exclaimed a piercing female cry from out the mist; "it is I! Alice! thy own Elsie! spare, oh! save your daughters!"

"Hold!" shouted the former speaker, in the awful tones of parental agony, the sound reaching even to the woods, and rolling back in solemn echo. "'Tis she! God has restored me my children! Throw open the sally-port; to the field, 60ths, to the field; pull not a trigger, lest ye kill my lambs! Drive off these dogs of France with your steel."

Duncan heard the grating of the rusty hinges, and darting to the spot, directed by the sound, he met a long line of dark-red warriors, passing swiftly towards the glacis. He knew them for his own battalion of the royal Americans, and flying to their head, soon swept every trace of his pursuers from before the works.

For an instant, Cora and Alice had stood trembling and bewildered by this unexpected desertion; but, before either had leisure for speech, or even thought, an officer of gigantic frame, whose locks were bleached with years and service, but whose air of military grandeur had been rather softened than destroyed by time, rushed out of the body of the mist, and folded them to his bosom, while large scalding tears rolled down his pale and wrinkled cheeks, and he exclaimed, in the peculiar accent of Scotland—

"For this I thank thee, Lord! Let danger come as it will, thy servant is prepared!"

Chapter 14

> Then go we in, to know his embassy;
> Which I could, with a ready guess, declare,
> Before the Frenchman speak a word of it.
> *King Henry V.*

THE few succeeding days were passed amid all the privations, the uproar, and the dangers of the siege, which was vigorously pressed by a power, against whose approaches Munro possessed no competent means of resistance. It appeared as if Webb, with his army, which lay slumbering on the banks of the Hudson, had utterly forgotten the strait to which his brethren were reduced. Montcalm had filled the woods of the portage with his savages, every yell and whoop from whom rang through the British encampment, chilling the hearts of men, who were already but too much disposed to magnify the danger, with additional terror.

It was on the afternoon of the fifth day of the siege, and the fourth of his own service in it, that Major Heyward profited by a parley that had just been beaten, by repairing to the ramparts of one of the water bastions, to breathe the cool air from the lake, and to take a survey of the progress of the siege.

Duncan had stood in a musing attitude a few minutes, when his eyes were directed to the glacis in front of the sally-port already mentioned, by the sounds of approaching footsteps.—He walked to an angle of the bastion, and beheld the scout advancing, under the custody of a French officer, to the body of the fort. The countenance of Hawk-eye was haggard and care-worn, and his air dejected, as though he felt the deepest degradation at having fallen into the power of his enemies. He was without his favourite weapon, and his arms were even bound behind him with thongs, made of the skin of a deer. The arrival of flags, to cover the messengers of summons, had occurred so often of late, that when Heyward first threw his careless glance on this group, he expected to see another of the officers of the enemy, charged with a similar office; but the instant he recognised the tall person, and still sturdy, though downcast, features of his friend, the woodsman, he started with surprise, and turned to descend from the bastion into the bosom of the work.

Munro was pacing his narrow apartment, with a disturbed air, and gigantic strides, as Duncan entered.

"You have anticipated my wishes, Major Heyward," he said; "I was about to request—this favour."

"I am so sorry to see, sir, that the messenger I so warmly recommended, has returned in custody of the French! I hope there is no reason to distrust his fidelity?"

"The fidelity of the 'Long Rifle' is well known to me," returned Munro, "and is above suspicion; though his usual good fortune seems, at last, to have failed. Montcalm has got him, and with the accursed politeness of his nation, he has sent him in with a doleful tale of 'knowing how I valued the fellow, he could not think of retaining him.' A jesuitical way, that, Major Duncan Heyward, of telling a man of his misfortunes!"

"But the general and his succour?——"

"Did ye look to the south as ye entered and could ye not see them?" said the old soldier, laughing bitterly. "Hoot! hoot! you're an impatient boy, sir, and cannot give the gentlemen leisure for their march!"

"But what says the scout? he has eyes and ears, and a tongue! what verbal report does he make?"

"Oh! sir, he is not wanting in natural organs, and he is free to tell all that he has seen and heard. The whole amount is this: there is a fort of his majesty's on the banks of the Hudson, called Edward, in honour of his gracious highness of York, you'll know, and it is well filled with armed men, as such a work should be!"

"And can I be of service in the matter?"

"Sir, you can; the Marquis of Montcalm has, in addition to his other civilities, invited me to a personal interview between these works and his own camp; in order, as he says, to impart some additional information. Now, I think it would not be wise to show any undue solicitude to meet him, and I would employ you, an officer of rank, as my substitute; for it would but ill comport with the honour of Scotland, to let it be said one of her gentlemen was outdone in civility, by a native of any country on earth!"

Without assuming the supererogatory task of entering into a discussion of the comparative merits of national courtesy, Duncan cheerfully assented to supply the place of the veteran, in the approaching interview. A long and confidential communication now succeeded, during which the young man received some additional insight into his duty, from the experienced and native acuteness of his commander, and then the former took his leave.

The general of the enemy received the youthful messenger, surrounded by his principal officers, and by a swarthy band of the native chiefs, who had followed him to the field, with the warriors of their several tribes. Heyward paused short, when, in glancing his eyes rapidly over the dark group of the latter, he beheld the malignant countenance of Magua, regarding him with the calm but sullen attention which marked the expression of that subtle savage. A slight exclamation of surprise even burst from the lips of the young man; but instantly recollecting his errand, and the presence in which he stood, he suppressed every appearance of emotion, and turned to the hostile leader, who had already advanced a step to receive him.

"Monsieur," said the latter, "J'ai beaucoup de plaisir à—bah!—où est cet interprète?"

"I do not think an interpreter will be necessary, monsieur," Heyward modestly replied; "I speak a little French."

"Ah, I am very pleased to hear it," said Montcalm, taking Duncan familiarly by the arm, and leading him deep into the marquee, a little out of earshot: "I detest those rogues there; one never knows what horse one is on with them. Eh bien! Monsieur," he continued, still speaking in French; "though I should have been proud of receiving your commandant, I am very happy that he has seen proper to employ an officer so distinguished, and who, I am sure, is so amiable as yourself."

Duncan bowed low, pleased with the compliment, in spite of a most heroic determination to suffer no artifice to allure him into a forgetfulness of the interests of his prince; and Montcalm, after a pause of a moment, as if to collect his thoughts, proceeded—

"Your commandant is a brave man, and well qualified to repel my assaults. Mais, Monsieur, is it not time to begin to take more counsel of humanity, and less of your own courage? The one as strongly characterises the hero as the other!"

"We consider the qualities as inseparable", returned Duncan, smiling; "but while we find in the vigour of your excellency every motive to stimulate the one, we can, as yet, see no particular call for the exercise of the other."

Montcalm, in his turn, slightly bowed; but it was with the air of a man too practised to remember the language of flattery. After musing a moment, he added:

"It is possible my glasses have deceived me, and that your works resist our cannon better than I had supposed. You know our force?"

"Our accounts vary," said Duncan, carelessly; "the highest, however, has not exceeded twenty thousand men."

The Frenchman bit his lip, and fastened his eyes keenly on the other, as if to read his thoughts; then with a readiness peculiar to himself, he continued, as if assenting to the truth of an enumeration, which he knew was not credited by his visitor.

"It is a poor compliment to the vigilance of us soldiers, Monsieur, that do what we will, we never can conceal our numbers. If it were to be done at all, one would believe it might succeed in these woods. Though you think it too soon to listen to the calls of humanity," he added, smiling archly, "I may be permitted to believe that gallantry is not forgotten by one so young as yourself. The daughters of the commandant, I learn, have passed into the fort since it was invested?"

"It is true, Monsieur; but so far from weakening our efforts, they set us an example of courage in their own fortitude. Were nothing but resolution necessary to repel so accomplished a soldier as M. de Montcalm, I would gladly trust the defence of William Henry to the elder of those ladies."

"I should be sorry to have the defence protracted in such a manner as to irritate my red friends there," continued Montcalm, glancing his eyes at the group of grave and attentive Indians, without attending to the other's question; "I find it difficult, even now, to limit them to the usages of war."

Heyward was silent, for a painful recollection of the dangers he had so recently escaped, came over his mind, and recalled the images of those defenceless beings who had shared in all his sufferings.

"Those men there," said Montcalm, following up the advantage which he conceived he had gained, "are most formidable when baffled; and it is unnecessary to tell you with what difficulty they are restrained in their anger. Eh bien, Monsieur! shall we speak of the terms of the surrender!"

"I fear your excellency has been deceived as to the strength of William Henry, and the resources of its garrison!"

"I have not sat down before Quebec, but an earthenwork, that is defended by twenty-three hundred gallant men," was the laconic, though polite reply.

"Our mounds are earthen certainly—nor are they seated on the rocks of Cape Diamond; but they stand on that shore which proved so destructive to Dieskau and his brave army. There is also a powerful force within a few hours' march of us, which we account upon as part of our means of defence."

"Some six or eight thousand men," returned Montcalm, with much apparent indifference, "whom their leader wisely judges to be safer in their works than in the field."

It was now Heyward's turn to bite his lip with vexation, as the other so coolly alluded to a force which the young man knew to be overrated. Both mused a little while in silence, when Montcalm renewed the conversation in a way that showed he believed the visit of his guest was, solely, to propose terms of capitulation. After a protracted and fruitless interview, Duncan took his leave, favourably impressed with an opinion of the courtesy and talents of the enemy's captain, but as ignorant of what he came to learn as when he arrived. Montcalm followed him as far as the entrance of the marquee, renewing his invitations to the commandant of the fort to give him an immediate meeting in the open ground between the two armies.

There they separated, and Duncan returned to the advanced post of the French, accompanied as before; whence he instantly proceeded to the fort, and to the quarters of his own commander.

Chapter 15

Edg.—Before you fight the battle, ope this letter.
Lear.

MUNRO listened to the lengthened detail of Duncan, at first calmly, then swelling with the wounded feelings of a soldier.

"You have said enough, Major Heyward!" exclaimed the angry old man; "enough to make a volume of commentary on French civility! Here has this gentleman invited me to a conference, and when I send him a capable substitute, for ye're all that, Duncan, though your years are but few, he answers me with a riddle!"

"He may have thought less favourably of the substitute, my dear sir," returned Duncan, smiling; "and you will remember that the invitation, which he now repeats, was to the commandant of the works, and not to his second."

"Well, sir, is not a substitute clothed with all the power and dignity of him who grants the commission? He wishes to confer with Munro! Faith, sir, I have much inclination to indulge the man, if it should only be to let him behold the firm countenance we maintain, in spite of his numbers and his summons! There might be no bad policy in such a stroke, young man. I will meet the Frenchman, and that without fear or delay; promptly, sir, as becomes a servant of my royal master. Go, Major Heyward, and give them a flourish of the music, and send out a messenger to let them know who is coming. We will follow with a small guard, for such respect is due to one who holds the honour of his king in keeping; and hark'ee, Duncan," he added, in a half whisper, though they were alone, "it may be prudent to have some aid at hand, in case there should be treachery at the bottom of it all."

The young man availed himself of this order to quit the apartment; and, as the day was fast coming to a close, he hastened without delay to make the necessary arrangements. A very few minutes only were necessary to parade a few files, and to despatch an orderly with a flag to announce the commandant of the fort. When Duncan had done both these, he led the guard to the sally-port, near which he found his superior already waiting his appearance. As soon as the usual ceremonials of a military departure were observed, the veteran, and his more youthful companion, left the fortress, attended by the escort.

They had proceeded only a hundred yards from the works, when the little array which attended the French general to the conference was seen issuing from the hollow way which formed the bed of a brook that ran between the batteries of the besiegers and the fort. From the moment that Munro left his own works to appear in front of his enemies, his air had been grand, and his step and countenance highly military. The instant he caught a glimpse of the white plume that waved in the hat of Montcalm, his eye lighted with the consciousness of his own daring, and age no longer appeared to posses any influence over his vast and still muscular person.

"Speak to the boys to be watchful, sir," he said, in an under tone, to Duncan; "and to look well to their flints and steel, for one is never safe with a servant of these Louis; at the same time, we will show them the front of men in deep security. Ye'll understand me, Major Heyward!"

He was interrupted by the clamour of a drum from the approaching Frenchmen, which was immediately answered, when each party pushed an orderly in advance, bearing a white flag, and the wary Scotsman halted, with his guard close at his back. As soon as this slight salutation had passed, Montcalm moved towards them with a quick but graceful step, baring his head to the veteran, and dropping his spotless plume nearly to the earth in courtesy. If the air of Munro was more commanding and manly, it wanted both the ease and insinuating polish of the Frenchman. Neither spoke for a few moments, each regarding the other with curious and interested eyes. Then, as became his superior rank, and the nature of the interview, Montcalm first broke the silence. After uttering the usual words of greeting to Munro, he turned to Duncan, and continued, with a smile of recognition, speaking always in French—

"I am rejoiced, Monsieur, that you have given us the pleasure of your company on this occasion. There will be no necessity to employ an ordinary interpreter, for in your hands I feel the same security as if I spoke your language myself."

Duncan acknowledged the compliment, when Montcalm, turning to his guard, which, in imitation of that of their enemies, pressed close upon him, continued—

"Back, my children—you make us feel hot; retire a little."

Before Major Heyward would imitate this proof of confidence, he glanced his eyes around the plain, and beheld, with uneasiness, the numerous dusky groups of savages, who looked out from the margin of the surrounding woods, curious spectators of the pending interview.

"Monsieur de Montcalm will readily acknowledge the difference of our situation," he said, with some embarrassment, pointing at the same time towards those dangerous foes who were to be seen in almost every direction. "Were we to dismiss our guard, we should stand here at the mercy of our enemies."

"Monsieur, you have the plighted faith of a French gentleman, for your safety," returned Montcalm, laying his hand impressively on his heart, "and it should suffice."

"It shall. Fall back," Duncan added to the officer who led the escort; "fall back, sir, beyond hearing, and wait for orders."

Munro witnessed this movement with manifest uneasiness, nor did he fail to demand an instant explanation.

"Is it not your interest, sir, to betray no distrust?" retorted Duncan. "Monsieur de Montcalm pledges his word for our safety, and I have ordered the men to withdraw a little, in order to prove how much we depend on his assurance."

The old man made a gesture of resignation, though his rigid features still betrayed his obstinate adherence to a distrust which he derived from a sort of hereditary contempt of his enemy, rather than from any present signs, which might warrant so uncharitable a feeling. Montcalm waited patiently until this little dialogue in demivoice was ended, when he drew nigher, and opened the subject of their conference.

"I have solicited this interview from your superior, Monsieur," he said, "because I believe he will allow himself to be persuaded, that he has already done every thing which is necessary for the honour of his prince, and will now listen to the admonitions of humanity. I will for ever bear testimony that his resistance has been gallant, and was continued so long as there was any hope."

When this opening was translated to Munro, he answered with dignity, but with sufficient courtesy.

"However I may prize such testimony from Monsieur Montcalm, it will be more valuable when it shall be better merited."

The French general smiled, as Duncan gave him the purport of this reply, and observed—

"What is now so freely accorded to approved courage, may be refused to useless obstinacy. Monsieur would wish to see my camp, and witness, for himself, our numbers, and the impossibility of his resisting them with success."

"I know that the king of France is well served," returned the unmoved Scotsman, as soon as Duncan ended his translation; "but my own royal master has as many and as faithful troops."

"Though not at hand, fortunately for us," said Montcalm, without waiting, in his ardour, for the interpreter. "There is a destiny in war, to which a brave man knows how to submit with the same courage that he faces his foes."

"Had I been conscious that Monsieur Montcalm was master of the English, I would have spared myself the trouble of so awkward a translation," said the vexed Duncan, drily; remembering instantly his recent by-play with Munro.

"Your pardon, Monsieur," rejoined the Frenchman, suffering a slight colour to appear on his dark check. "There is a vast difference between understanding and speaking a foreign tongue; you will, therefore, please to assist me still." Then, after a short pause, he added, "These hills afford us every opportunity of reconnoitring your works, Messieurs, and I am possibly as well acquainted with their weak condition as you can be yourselves."

"Ask the French general if his glasses can reach to the Hudson," said Munro, proudly; "and if he knows when and where to expect the army of Webb."

"Let General Webb be his own interpreter," returned the polite Montcalm, suddenly extending an open letter towards Munro, as he spoke; "you will there learn, Monsieur, that his movements are not likely to prove embarrassing to my army."

The veteran seized the offered paper without waiting for Duncan to translate the speech, and with an eagerness that betrayed how important he deemed its contents. As his eye passed heavily over the words, his countenance gradually changed from its look of military pride, to one of deep chagrin; his lips began to quiver; and, as he suffered the paper to fall from his hand, his head dropped upon his chest, like that of a man whose hopes were all withered at a single blow. Duncan caught the letter from the ground, and, without apology for the liberty he took, he read, at a glance, its cruel purport. Their common superior, so far from encouraging them to resist, advised a speedy surrender, urging, in the plainest language, as a reason, the utter impossibility of his sending a single man to their rescue.

"The man has betrayed me!" Munro at length bitterly exclaimed, "he has brought dishonour to the door of one where disgrace was never before known to dwell, and shame has he heaped heavily on my grey hairs!"

"Say not so!" cried Duncan; "we are yet masters of the fort, and of our honour! Let us then sell our lives at such a rate, as shall make our enemies believe the purchase too dear!"

"Boy, I thank thee!" exclaimed the old man, rousing himself from his stupor; "you have, for once, reminded Munro of his duty. We will go back, and dig our graves behind those ramparts!"

"Messieurs," said Montcalm, advancing towards them a step, in his generous interest; "you little know Louis de St. Veran, if you believe him capable of profiting by this letter, to humble brave men, or to build up a dishonest reputation for himself. Listen to my terms before you leave me."

"What says the Frenchman?" demanded the veteran, sternly; "does he make a merit of having captured a scout, with a note from headquarters? Sir, he had better raise this siege, and go to sit down before Edward, if he wishes to frighten his enemies with words!"

Duncan explainted the other's meaning.

"Monsieur de Montcalm, we will hear you," the veteran added, more calmly, as Duncan ended.

"To retain the fort is now impossible," said his liberal enemy; "it is necessary to the interest of my master that it should be destroyed; but, as for yourselves, and your brave comrades, there is no privilege dear to a soldier that shall be denied."

"Our colours?" demanded Heyward.

"Carry them to England, and show them to your king."

"Our arms?"

"Keep them; none can use them better!"

"Our march; the surrender of the place?"

"Shall all be done in a way most honourable to yourselves."

Duncan now turned to explain these proposals to his commander, who heard him with amazement, and a sensibility that was deeply touched by such unusual and unexpected generosity.

"Go you, Duncan," he said; "go with this marquess, as indeed marquess he should be; go to his marquee, and arrange it all. I have lived to see two things in my old age, that never did I expect to behold: an Englishman afraid to support a friend, and a Frenchman too honest to profit by his advantage!"

So saying, the veteran again dropped his head to his chest, and returned slowly towards the fort, exhibiting in the dejection of his air, to the anxious garrison, a harbinger of evil tidings.

Chapter 16

Weave we the woof. The thread is spun.
The web is wove. The work is done.
Gray.

THE hostile armies, who lay in the wilds of the Horican, passed the night of the ninth of August, 1757, much in the manner that would have prevailed, had they encountered on the fairest field of Europe. While the conquered were still, sullen and dejected, the victors triumphed.

In the morning, the first tap of the French drums was echoed from the bosom of the fort; and presently the valley was filled with the strains of martial music, rising long, thrilling, and lively, above the rattling accompaniment. The horns of the victors sounded merry and cheerful flourishes, until the last laggard of the camp was at his post; but the instant the British fifes had blown their shrill signal, they became mute. In the mean time the day had dawned, and when the line of the French army was ready to receive its general, the rays of a brilliant sun were glancing along its glittering array. Then, that success which was already so well known, was officially announced; the favoured band, who were selected to guard the gates of the fort, were detailed, and defiled before their chief; the signal of their approach was given, and all the usual preparations for a change of masters were ordered and executed directly under the guns of the contested works.

A very different scene presented itself within the lines of the Anglo-American army. As soon as the warning signal was given, it exhibited all the signs of a hurried and forced departure. The sullen soldiers shouldered their empty tubes, and fell into their places, like men whose blood had been heated by the past contest, and who only desired the opportunity to revenge an indignity, which was still wounding to their pride, concealed, as it was, under all the observances of military etiquette. Women and children ran from place to place, some bearing the scanty remnants of their baggage, and others searching, in the ranks, for those countenances they looked up to for protection.

Munro appeared among his silent troops, firm, but dejected. It was evident that the unexpected blow had struck deep into his heart, though he struggled to sustain his misfortune with the port of a man.

Duncan was touched at the quiet and impressive exhibition of his grief. He had discharged his own duty, and he now pressed to the side of the old man, to know in what particular he might serve him.

"My daughters," was the brief but expressive reply.

"Good heavens! Are not arrangements already made for their convenience!"

64

"To-day I am only a soldier, Major Heyward," said the veteran. "All that you see here claim alike to be my children."

Duncan had heard enough. Without losing one of those moments which had now become so precious, he flew towards the quarters of Munro, in quest of the sisters. He found them on the threshold of the low edifice, already prepared to depart, and surrounded by a clamorous and weeping assemblage of their own sex, that had gathered about the place, with a sort of instinctive consciousness, that it was the point most likely to be protected. Though the cheeks of Cora were pale, and her countenance anxious, she had lost none of her firmness; but the eyes of Alice were inflamed, and betrayed how long and bitterly she had wept. They both, however, received the young man with undisguised pleasure; the former, for a novelty, being the first to speak.

"The fort is lost," she said, with a melancholy smile; "though our good name, I trust, remains!"

"'Tis brighter than ever! But, dearest Miss Munro, it is time to think less of others, and to make some provision for yourself. Military usage—pride—that pride on which you so much value yourself— demands that your father and I should, for a little while, continue with the troops. Then where to seek a proper protector for you, against the confusion and chance of such a scene!"

"None is necessary," returned Cora; "who will dare to injure or insult the daughter of such a father, at a time like this?"

"I would not leave you alone," continued the youth, looking about him in a hurried manner, "for the command of the best regiment in the pay of the king! Remember, our Alice is not gifted with all your firmness, and God only knows the terror she might endure."

"You may be right," Cora replied, smiling again, but far more sadly than before. "Listen; chance has already sent us a friend when he is most needed."

Duncan did listen, and on the instant comprehended her meaning. The low and serious sounds of the sacred music, so well known to the eastern provinces, caught his ear, and instantly drew him to an apartment in an adjacent building, which had already been deserted by its customary tenants. There he found David pouring out his pious feelings, through the only medium in which he ever indulged. Duncan waited, until by the cessation of the movement of the hand he believed the strain was ended, when, by touching his shoulder, he drew the attention of the other to himself, and in a few words explained his wishes.

"Even so," replied the single-minded disciple of the King of Israel, when the young man had ended; "I have found much that is comely and melodious in the maidens, and it is fitting that we, who have consorted in so much peril, should abide together in peace."

"It will be your duty to see that none dare to approach the ladies with any rude intention, or to offer insult or taunt at the misfortune of their brave father. In this task you will be seconded by the domestics of their household."

"Even so."

"It is possible, that the Indians and stragglers of the enemy may intrude; in which case, you will remind them of the terms of the capitulation, and threaten to report their conduct to Montcalm. A word will suffice."

Gamut cheerfully assented, and together they immediately sought the maidens. Cora received her new, and somewhat extraordinary protector, courteously at least; and even the pallid features of Alice lighted again with some of their native archness, as she thanked Heyward for his care. Duncan took occasion to assure them he had done the best that circumstances permitted, and, as he believed, quite enough for the security of their feelings; of danger there was none. He then spoke gladly of his intention to rejoin them the moment he had led the advance a few miles towards the Hudson, and immediately took his leave.

As the confused and timid throng left the protecting mounds of the fort, and issued on the open plain, the whole scene was at once presented to their eyes. At a little distance on the right, and somewhat in the rear, the French army stood to their arms Montcalm having collected his parties, so soon as his guards had possession of the works. They were attentive, but silent observers of the proceedings of the vanquished, failing in none of the stipulated military honours, and offering no taunt or insult, in their success, to their less fortunate foes. Living masses of the English, to the amount, in the whole, of near three thousand, were moving slowly across the plain, towards the common centre, and gradually approached each other, as they converged to the point of their march, a vista cut through the lofty trees, where the road to the Hudson entered the forest. Along the sweeping borders of the woods hung a dark cloud of savages, eyeing the passage of their enemies, and hovering at a distance, like vultures, who were only kept from swooping on their prey by the presence and restraint of a superior army. A few had straggled among the conquered columns, where they stalked in sullen discontent; attentive, though, as yet, passive observers of all that moving multitude.

The advance, with Heyward at its head, had already reached the defile, and was slowly disappearing, when the attention of Cora was drawn to a collection of stragglers, by the sounds of contention. A truant provincial was paying the forfeit of his disobedience, by being plundered of those very effects which had caused him to desert his place in the ranks. The man was of powerful frame, and too avaricious to part with his goods without a struggle. Individuals from either party interfered; the one side to prevent, and the other to aid in the robbery. Voices grew loud and angry, and a hundred savages appeared, as it were by magic, where a dozen only had been seen a few minutes before. It was then that Cora saw the form of Magua, gliding among his countrymen, and speaking with his fatal and artful eloquence.

At that dangerous moment Magua placed his hands to his mouth, and raised the fatal and appalling whoop. The scattered Indians started at the well known cry, as coursers bound at the signal to quit the goal; and directly, there arose such a yell along the plain, and through the arches of the woods, as seldom bursted from human lips before. They who heard it listened with a curdling horror at the heart, little inferior to that dread which may be expected to attend the blasts of the final summons.

More than two thousand raging savages broke from the forest at the signal, and threw themselves across the fatal plain with instinctive alacrity. We shall not dwell on the revolting horrors that succeeded. Death was every where, and in his most terrific and disgusting aspects. Resistance only served to inflame the murderers, who inflicted their furious blows long after their victims were beyond the power of their resentment. The flow of blood might be likened to the outbreaking of a gushing torrent.

In such a scene, none had leisure to note the fleeting moments. It might have been ten minutes, (it seemed an age), that the sisters had stood riveted to one spot, horror-stricken, and nearly helpless. When the first blow was struck, their screaming companions had pressed upon them in a body, rendering flight impossible; and now that fear or death had scattered most, if not all, from around them, they saw no avenue open, but such as conducted to the tomahawks of their foes. On every side arose shrieks, groans, exhortations, and curses. At this moment, Alice caught a glimpse of the vast form of her father, moving rapidly across the plain, in the direction of the French army. He was in truth proceeding to Montcalm, fearless of every danger, to claim the tardy escort, for which he had before conditioned. Fifty glittering axes and barbed spears were offered unheeded at his life, but the savages respected his rank and calmness, even in their greatest fury. The dangerous weapons were brushed aside by the still nervous arm of the veteran, or fell of themselves, after menacing an act that it would seem no one had courage to perform. Fortunately the vindictive Magua was searching his victim in the very band the veteran had just quitted.

"Father—father—we are here!" shrieked Alice, as he passed at no great distance, without appearing to heed them. "Come to us, father, or we die!"

The cry was repeated, and in terms and tones that might have melted a heart of stone, but it was unanswered. Once, indeed, the old man appeared to catch the sounds, for he paused and listened; but Alice had dropped senseless on the earth, and Cora had sunk at her side, hovering, in untiring tenderness, over her lifeless form. Munro shook his head in disappointment, and proceeded, bent on the high duty of his responsible station.

"Lady," said Gamut, who, helpless and useless as he was, had not yet dreamed of deserting his trust, "it is the jubilee of the devils, and this not a meet place for Christians to tarry in. Let us up and fly!"

"Go," said Cora, still gazing at her unconscious sister; "save thyself. To me thou canst not be of further use."

David comprehended the unyielding character of her resolution, by the simple, but expressive gesture, that accompanied her words. He gazed for a moment at the dusky forms that were acting their hellish rites on every side of him, and his tall person grew more erect, while his chest heaved, and every feature swelled, and seemed to speak with the power of the feelings by which he was governed.

"If the Jewish boy might tame the evil spirit of Saul by the sound of his harp, and the words of sacred song, it may not be amiss," he said, "to try the potency of music here."

Then raising his voice to its highest tones, he poured out a strain so powerful as to be heard, even amid the din of that bloody field. More than one savage rushed towards them, thinking to rifle the unprotected sisters of their attire, and bear away their scalps; but when they found this strange and unmoved figure riveted to his post, they paused to listen. Astonishment soon changed to admiration, and they passed on to other and less courageous victims, openly expressing their satisfaction at the firmness with which the white warrior sung his death song. Encouraged and deluded by his success, David exerted all his powers to extend what he believed so holy an influence. The unwonted sounds caught the ears of a distant savage, who flew, raging, from group to group, like one who, scorning to touch the vulgar herd, hunted for some victim more worthy of his renown.

It was Magua, who uttered a yell of pleasure when he beheld his ancient prisoners again at his mercy.

"Come," he said, laying his soiled hand on the dress of Cora, "the wigwam of the Huron is open. Is it not better than this place?"

"Away!" cried Cora, veiling her eyes from his revolting aspect.

He hesitated a moment; and then catching the light and senseless form of Alice in his arms, the subtle Indian moved swiftly across the plain towards the woods.

"Hold!" shrieked Cora, following wildly on his footsteps, "release the child! wretch! what is't you do?"

But Magua was deaf to her voice; or rather he knew his power, and was determined to maintain it.

"Stay—lady—stay," called Gamut, after the unconscious Cora. "The holy charm is beginning to be felt, and soon shalt thou see this horrid tumult stilled."

Perceiving that in his turn, he was unheeded, the faithful David followed the distracted sister, raising his voice again in sacred song, and sweeping the air to the measure with his long arm in diligent accompaniment. In this manner they traversed the plain, through the flying, the wounded and the dead. The fierce Huron was at any time sufficient for himself, and the victim that he bore, though Cora would have fallen more than once under the blows of her savage enemies, but for the extraordinary being who stalked in her rear, and who now appeared to the astonished natives gifted with the protecting spirit of madness.

68

Magua, who knew how to avoid the more pressing dangers, and also to elude pursuit, entered the woods through a low ravine, where he quickly found the Narragansets, which the travellers had abandoned so shortly before, awaiting his appearance, in custody of a savage as fierce and as malign in his expression as himself. Laying Alice on one of the horses, he made a sign for Cora to mount the other.

Notwithstanding the horror excited by the presence of her captor, there was a present relief in escaping from the bloody scene enacting on the plain, to which the maiden could not be altogether insensible. She took her seat, and held forth her arms for her sister, with an air of entreaty and love, that even the Huron could not deny. Placing Alice then on the same animal with Cora, he seized the bridle, and commenced his route by plunging deeper into the forest. David, perceiving that he was left alone utterly disregarded, as a subject too worthless even to destroy, threw his long limb across the saddle of the beast they had deserted, and made such progress in the pursuit, as the difficulties of the path permitted.

They soon began to ascend; but, as the motion had a tendency to revive the dormant faculties of her sister, the attention of Cora was too much divided between the tenderest solicitude in her behalf and in listening to the cries which were still too audible on the plain to note the direction in which they journeyed. When, however, they gained the flattened surface of the mountain top, and approached the eastern precipice, she recognised the spot to which she had once before been led, under the more friendly auspices of the scout. Here Magua suffered them to dismount, and, notwithstanding their own captivity, the curiosity which seemed inseparable from horror, induced them to gaze at the sickening sight below.

The cruel work was still unchecked. On every side the captured were flying before their relentless persecutors, while the armed columns of the Christian king stood fast, in an apathy which has never been explained, and which has left an immovable blot on the otherwise fair escutcheon of their leader. Nor was the sword of death stayed until cupidity got the mastery of revenge. Then, indeed, the shrieks of the wounded, and the yells of their murderers, grew less frequent, until finally, the cries of horror were lost to their ear, or were drowned in the loud, long, and piercing whoops of the triumphant savages.

Chapter 17

Why, any thing;
An honourable murderer, if you will;
For nought I did in hate, but all in honour.
Othello.

THE third day from the capture of the fort was drawing to a close, but the business of the narrative must still detain the reader on the shores of the "holy lake." When last seen, the environs of the works were filled with violence and uproar. They were now emphatically possessed by stillness and death. The blood-stained conquerors had departed; and their camp, which had so lately rung with the merry rejoicings of a victorious army, lay a silent and deserted city of huts. The fortress was a smouldering ruin; charred rafters, fragments of exploded artillery, and rent mason work, covering its earthen mounds in confused and negligent disorder.

About an hour before the setting of the sun, on the day already mentioned, the forms of five men might have been seen issuing from the narrow vista of trees, where the path to the Hudson entered the forest, and advancing in the direction of the ruined works. At first their progress was slow and guarded, as though they entered with reluctance amid the horrors of the spot, or dreaded the renewal of some of its frightful incidents. A light figure preceded the rest of the party with all the caution and activity of a native, ascending every hillock to reconnoitre, and indicating by gestures to his companions the route he deemed it most prudent they should pursue. Nor were those in the rear wanting in every caution and foresight known to forest warfare. One among them, and he also was an Indian, moved a little on one flank, and watched the neighbouring margin of the woods with eyes long accustomed to read the smallest sign of approaching danger. The remaining three were white, though clad in vestments strikingly adapted, both in quality and colour, to their present hazardous pursuit, that of hanging on the skirts of a retiring army in the wilderness.

The reader will perceive at once in these respective characters, the Mohicans, and their white friend the scout: together with Munro and Heyward. It was in truth the father in quest of his children, attended by the youth who felt so deep a stake in their happiness, and those brave and trusty foresters who had already proved their skill and fidelity through the trying scenes related.

When Uncas, who moved in front, had reached the centre of the plain, he raised a cry that drew his companions in a body to the spot. The young warrior had halted over a group of females, who lay in a cluster, a confused mass of dead. Notwithstanding the revolting horrors of the exhibition, Munro and Heyward flew towards the festering heap, endeavouring, with a love that no unseemliness could extinguish, to discover whether any vestiges of those they sought were to be seen among the tattered and many coloured garments. The father and the lover found instant relief in the search; though each was condemned again to experience the misery of an uncertainty that was hardly less insupportable than the most revolting truth. They were standing silent and thoughtful around the melancholy pile when the scout approached. Eyeing the sad spectacle with an angry and flushed countenance, the sturdy woodsman, for the first time since entering the plain, spoke intelligibly and aloud—

"I have been on many a shocking field, and have followed a trail of blood for weary miles," he said, "but never have I found the hand of the devil so plain as it is here to be seen! Revenge is an Indian feeling, and

70

all who know me know that there is no cross in my veins; but this much will I say—here, in the face of Heaven, and with the power of the Lord so manifest in this howling wilderness, that should these Frenchers ever trust themselves again within the range of a ragged bullet, there is one rifle shall play its part, so long as flint will fire or powder burn!—I leave the tomahawk and knife to such as have a natural gift to use them. What say you, Chingachgook," he added in Delaware; "shall the red Hurons boast of this to their women when the deep snows come?"

Uncas was gazing intently in his front. Then he bounded away from the spot, and in the next instant was seen tearing from a bush and waving in triumph a fragment of the green riding veil of Cora. The movement, the exhibition, and the cry, which burst from the lips of the young Mohican, instantly drew the whole party once more about him.

"Here are no dead!" said Heyward, in a voice that was hollow and nearly stifled by apprehension; "the storm seems not to have passed this way."

"That's manifest, and clearer than the heavens above our heads," returned the cool and undisturbed scout; "but either she or they that have robbed her have passed the bush; for I remember the rag she wore to hide a face that all did love to look upon. Uncas, you are right; the dark hair has been here, and she has fled, like a frighted fawn, to the wood: none who could fly would remain to be murdered! Let us have a search for the marks she left; for to Indian eyes I sometimes think even a humming-bird leaves his trail in the air!"

The young Mohican darted away at the suggestion, and the scout had hardly done speaking before the former raised a cry of success from the margin of the forest. On reaching the spot, the anxious party perceived another portion of the veil fluttering on the lower branch of a beech.

"Softly, softly," said the scout, extending his long rifle in front of the eager Heyward; "we now know our work, but the beauty of the trail must not be deformed. A step too soon may give us hours of trouble. We have them, though; that much is beyond denial."

"Hugh!" exclaimed Chingachgook, who had been occupied in examining an opening that had been evidently made through the low underbush which skirted the forest; and who now stood erect, as he pointed downwards, in the attitude and with the air of a man who beheld a disgusting serpent.

"Here is the palpable impression of the footsteps of a man!" cried Heyward, bending over the indicated spot; "he has trod in the margin of this pool, and the mark cannot be mistaken. They are captives!"

"Better so than left to starve in the wilderness," returned the scout; "and they will leave a wider trail. I would wager fifty beaver skins to as many flints, that the Mohicans and I enter their wigwams within the month! Stoop to it, Uncas, and try what you can make of that moccasin: for moccasin it plainly is, and no shoe."

The young Mohican bent over the track, and removing the scattered leaves from around the place, he examined it with much of that sort of scrutiny that a money-dealer in these days of pecuniary doubts, would bestow on a suspected due-bill. At length, he arose from his knees, as if satisfied with the result of the examination.

"Well, boy," demanded the attentive scout, "what does it say? can you make anything of the tell-tale?"

"Le Renard Subtil."

Said the woodsman, "here then have passed the dark hair and Magua."

"And not Alice?" demanded the startled Heyward.

"Of her we have not yet seen the signs," returned the scout, looking closely around at the trees, the bushes, and the ground. "What have we there! Uncas, bring hither the thing you see dangling from yonder thorn-bush."

When the youthful Indian warrior had complied, the scout received the prize, and holding it on high, he laughed in his silent but heartfelt manner, before he said—

"'Tis the tooting we'pon of the singer! now we shall have a trail a priest might travel. Uncas, look for the marks of a shoe that is long enough to uphold six feet two of tottering human flesh. I begin to have some hopes of the fellow, since he has given up squalling, to follow, perhaps, some better trade."

"Here is something like the footsteps of one who has worn a shoe," said Heyward, gladly changing the discourse from the abuse of David, to whom he now felt the strongest tie of gratitude; "can it be that of our friend?"

"Touch the leaves lightly, or you will disconcert the formation. That! that is the print of a foot, but 'tis the dark hair's; and small it is, too, for one of such a noble height and grand appearance! The singer would cover it with his heel!"

Before they had proceeded many rods, the Indians stopped, and appeared to gaze at some signs on the earth, with more than their usual keenness. Both father and son spoke quick and loud, now looking at the object of their mutual admiration, and now regarding each other with the most unequivocal pleasure.

"They have found the little foot!" exclaimed the scout, moving forward, without attending further to his own portion of the duty. "What have we here! An ambushment has been planted in this spot! No, by the truest rifle on the frontiers, here have been them one-sided horses again! Now the whole secret is out, and all is plain as the north-star at midnight. Yes, here they have mounted. There the beasts have been bound to a sapling, in waiting; and yonder runs the broad path away to the north, in full sweep for the Canadas."

"But still there are no signs of Alice—of the younger Miss Munro," said Duncan.

"Unless the shining bauble Uncas has just lifted from the ground, should prove one. Pass it this way, lad that we may look at it."

Heyward instantly knew it for a trinket that Alice was fond of wearing, and which he recollected, with the tenacious memory of a lover, to have seen on the fatal morning of the massacre, dangling from the fair neck of his mistress. He seized the highly prized jewel, and as he proclaimed the fact, it vanished from the eyes of the wondering scout, who in vain looked for it on the ground, long after it warmly pressed against the beating heart of Duncan.

"Pshaw!" said the disappointed Hawk-eye, ceasing to rake the leaves with the breech of his rifle; "'tis a certain sign of age when the sight begins to weaken. Such a glittering gewgaw, and not to be seen! Well, well, I can squint along a clouded Larrel yet, and that is enough to settle all disputes between me and the Mingoes. I should like to find the thing too, if it were only to carry it to the right owner, and that would be bringing the two ends of what I call a long trail together—for by this time the broad St. Lawrence, or perhaps, even the Great Lakes, are atwixt us."

"So much the more reason why we should not delay our march," returned Heyward; "let us proceed."

"Young blood and hot blood, they say, are much the same thing. We are not about to start on a squirrel hunt, or to drive a deer into the Horican, but to outlie for days and nights, and to stretch across a wilderness where the feet of men seldom go, and where no bookish knowledge would carry you through harmless. An Indian never starts on such an expedition without smoking over his council fire; and though a man of white blood, I honour their customs in this particular, seeing that they are deliberate and wise. We will therefore go back, and light our fire to-night in the ruins of the old fort, and in the morning we shall be fresh, and ready to undertake our work like men, and not like babbling women, or eager boys."

Heyward instantly saw, by the manner of the scout, that altercation would be useless. Munro had again sunk into that sort of apathy which had beset him since his last overwhelming misfortunes, and from which he was, apparently, to be roused only by some new and powerful excitement. Making a merit of necessity, the young man took the veteran by the arm, and followed in the footsteps of the Indians and the scout, who had already begun to retrace the path which conducted them to the plain.

Chapter 18

"Land of Albania; let me bend mine eyes
On thee, thou rugged nurse of savage men!"
Childe Harold.

THE heavens were still studded with stars when Hawk-eye came to arouse the sleepers. Casting aside their cloaks, Munro and Heyward were on their feet, while the woodsman was still making his low calls at the entrance of the rude shelter where they had passed the night. When they issued from beneath its concealment, they found the scout awaiting their appearance nigh by, and the only salutation between them was the significant gesture for silence made by their sagacious leader.

"Think over your prayers," he whispered, as they approached him; "for He, to whom you make them, knows all tongues; that of the heart as well as those of the mouth. But speak not a syllable; it is rare for a white voice to pitch itself properly in the woods, as we have seen by the example of that miserable devil, the singer. Come," he continued, turning towards a curtain of the works; "let us get into the ditch on this side, and be regardful to step on the stones and fragments of wood as you go."

His companions complied, though to one of them the reasons of all this extraordinary precaution were yet a mystery. When they were in the low cavity that surrounded the earthen fort on three of its sides, they found the passage nearly choked by the ruins. With care and patience, however, they succeeded in clambering after the scout, until they reached the sandy shore of the Horican.

"That's a trail that nothing but a nose can follow," said the satisfied scout, looking back along their difficult way; "grass is a treacherous carpet for a flying party to tread on, but wood and stone take no print from a moccasin. Had you worn your armed boots, there might, indeed, have been something to fear! but with the deer-skin suitably prepared, a man may trust himself generally on rocks with safety. Shove in the canoe nigher to the land, Uncas; this sand will take a stamp as easily as the butter of the Dutchers on the Mohawk. Softly, lad, softly; it must not touch the beach, or the knaves will know by what road we have left the place."

The young man observed the precaution; and the scout laying a board from the ruins to the canoe, made a sign for the two officers to enter. When this was done, everything was studiously restored to its former disorder; and then Hawk-eye succeeded in reaching his little birchen vessel, without leaving behind him any of those marks which he appeared so much to dread.

Just as the day dawned they entered the narrows of the lake, and stole swiftly and cautiously among their numberless little islands.

Their route lay along a wide reach that was lined by high and ragged mountains. Here the islands were few, and easily avoided.

When they had reached a bay nigh the northern termination of the lake, the canoe was driven upon the beach, and the whole party landed.

The canoe was lifted from the water, and borne on the shoulders of the party. They proceeded into the wood, making as broad and obvious a trail as possible. They soon reached a water-course, which they crossed, and continued onward, until they came to an extensive and, naked rock. At this point, where their footsteps might be expected to be no longer visible, they retraced their route to the brook, walking backwards with the utmost care. They now followed the bed of the little stream to the lake, into which they immediately launched their canoe again. A low point concealed them from the headland, and the margin of the lake was fringed for some distance with dense and overhanging bushes. Under the cover of these natural advantages, they toiled their way, with patient industry, until the scout pronounced that he believed it would be safe once more to land.

The halt continued until evening rendered objects indistinct and uncertain to the eye. Then they resumed their route, and, favoured by the darkness, pushed silently and vigorously towards the western shore. Although the rugged outline of mountain, to which they were steering, presented no distinctive marks to the eyes of Duncan, the Mohican entered the little haven he had selected with the confidence and accuracy of an experienced pilot.

The boat was again lifted and borne into the woods, where it was carefully concealed under a pile of brush. The adventurers assumed their arms and packs, and the scout announced to Munro and Heyward that he and the Indians were at last in readiness to proceed.

Chapter 19

If you find a man there, he shall die a flea's death.
Merry Wives of Windsor.

THE party had landed on the border of a region that is, even to this day, less known to the inhabitants of the states than the deserts of Arabia, or the steppes of Tartary. It was the sterile and rugged district which separates the tributaries of Champlain from those of the Hudson, the Mohawk, and of the St. Lawrence. Since the period of our tale, the active spirit of the country has surrounded it with a belt of rich and thriving settlements, though none but the hunter or the savage is ever known, even now, to penetrate its rude and wild recesses.

After proceeding a few miles, the progress of Hawk-eye, who led the advance, became more deliberate and watchful. He often stopped to examine the trees; nor did he cross a rivulet, without attentively considering the quantity, the velocity, and the colour of its waters. Distrusting his own judgment, his appeals to the opinion of Chingachgook were frequent and earnest. During one of these conferences, Heyward observed that Uncas stood a patient and silent, though, as he imagined, an interested listener. He was strongly tempted to address the young chieftain, and demand his opinion of their progress; but the calm and dignified demeanour of the native induced him to believe that, like himself, the other was wholly dependent on the sagacity and intelligence of the seniors of the party. At last the scout spoke in English, and at once explained the embarrassment of their situation.

"When I found that the home path of the Hurons run north," he said, "it did not need the judgment of many long years to tell me that they would follow the valleys, and keep atween the waters of the Hudson and the Horican, until they might strike the springs of the Canada streams, which would lead them into the heart of the country of the Frenchers.

Yet here are we within a short range of the Scaroon, and not a sign of a trail have we crossed! Human nature is weak, and it is possible we may not have taken the proper scent."

"Heaven protect us from such an error!" exclaimed Duncan. "Let us retrace our steps, and examine, as we go, with keener eyes. Has Uncas no counsel to offer in such a strait?"

The young Mohican cast a quick glance at his father, but instantly recovering his quiet and reserved mien, he continued silent. Chingachgook had caught the look, and motioning with his hand, he bade him speak. The moment this permission was accorded, the countenance of Uncas changed from its grave composure to a gleam of intelligence and joy. Bounding forward like a deer, he sprang up the side of a little acclivity, a few rods in advance, and stood exultingly over a spot of fresh earth, that looked as though it had been recently upturned by the passage of some heavy animal. The eyes of the whole party followed the unexpected movement and read their success in the air of triumph that the youth assumed.

"See!" said Uncas, pointing north and south, at the evident marks of the broad trail on either side of him; "the dark hair has gone towards the frost."

"Hound never ran on a more beautiful scent," responded the scout, dashing forward at once on the indicated route; "we are favoured, greatly favoured, and can follow with high noses. Ay, here are both your waddling beasts; this Huron travels like a white general! The fellow is stricken with a judgment, and is mad! Look sharp for wheels, Sagamore," he continued, looking back and laughing, in his newly awakened satisfaction; "we shall soon have the fool journeying in a coach, and that with three of the best pair of eyes on the borders in his rear."

By the middle of the afternoon they had passed the Scaroon, and were following the route of the declining sun. After descending an eminence to a low bottom, through which a swift stream glided, they suddenly came to a place where the party of le Renard had made a halt. Extinguished brands were lying around a spring, the offals of a deer were scattered about the place, and the trees bore evident marks of having been browsed long and closely by the horses. At a little distance, Heyward discovered, and contemplated with tender emotion, the small bower under which, he was fain to believe, that Cora and Alice had reposed. But while the earth was trodden, and the footsteps of both men and beasts were so plainly visible around the place, the trail appeared to have suddenly ended.

It was easy to follow the tracks of the Narragansets, but they seemed only to have wandered without guides, or any other object than the pursuit of food. At length Uncas, who, with his father, had endeavoured to trace the route of the horses, came upon a sign of their presence, that was quite recent. Before following the clue, he communicated his success to his companions, and while the latter were consulting on the circumstance, the youth reappeared, leading the two fillies, with their saddles broken, and the housings soiled, as though they had been permitted to run at will for several days.

"What should this prove?" said Duncan, turning pale, and glancing his eyes around him, as if he feared the brush and leaves were about to give up some horrid secret.

"That our march is come to a quick end, and that we are in an enemy's country," returned the scout. "It is true that the horses are here, but the Hurons are gone; let us then hunt for the path by which they are departed."

Hawk-eye and the Mohicans now applied themselves to the task in good earnest. A circle of a few hundred feet in circumference was drawn, and each of the party took a segment for his portion. The examination, however, resulted in no discovery. The impressions of footsteps were numerous, but they all appeared like those of men who had wandered about the spot without any design to quit it. Again the scout and his companions made the circuit of the halting-place, each slowly following the other, until they assembled in the centre once more, no wiser than they started.

"Such cunning is not without its devilry!" exclaimed Hawk-eye, when he met the disappointed looks of his assistants. "We must get down to it, Sagamore, beginning at the spring, and going over the ground by inches. The Huron shall never brag in his tribe that he has a foot which leaves no print!"

Setting the example himself, the scout engaged in the scrutiny with renewed zeal. Not a leaf was left unturned. The sticks were removed and the stones lifted—for Indian cunning was known frequently to adopt those objects as covers, labouring with the utmost patience and industry to conceal each footstep as they proceeded. Still no discovery was made. At length Uncas, whose activity had enabled him to achieve his portion of the task the soonest, raked the earth across the turbid little rill which ran from the spring and diverted its course into another channel. So soon as its narrow bed below the dam was dry, he stooped over it with keen and curious eyes. A cry of exultation immediately announced the success of the young warrior.

"The lad will be an honour to his people!" said Hawk-eye, regarding the trail with as much admiration as a naturalist would expend on the tusk of the mammoth, or the rib of a mastodon; "ay, and a thorn in the sides of the Hurons. Yet that is not the footstep of an Indian! the weight is too much on the heel, and the toes are squared, as though one of the French dancers had been in pigeon-winging his tribe! Run back, Uncas, and bring me the size of the singer's foot. You will find a beautiful print of it just opposite yon rock, ag'in in the hill side."

While the youth was engaged in this commission, the scout and Chingachgook were attentively considering the impression. The measurements agreed, and the former unhesitantly pronounced that the footstep was that of David, who had once more been made to exchange his shoes for moccasins.

"I can now read the whole of it, as plainly as if I had seen the arts of le Subtil," he added; "the singer being a man whose gifts lay chiefly in his throat and feet, was made to go first, and the others have trod in his steps, imitating their formation."

"But," cried Duncan, "I see no signs of——"

"The gentle ones," interrupted the scout; "the varlet has found a way to carry them, until he supposed he had thrown any followers off the scent. My life on it we see their pretty little feet again before many rods go by."

The whole party now proceeded following the course of the rill, keeping anxious eyes on the regular impressions. The water soon flowed into its bed again, but watching the ground on either side, the foresters pursued their way, content with knowing that the trail lay beneath. More than half a mile was passed before the rill rippled close around the base of an extensive and dry rock. Here they paused to make sure that the Hurons had not quitted the water.

It was fortunate they did so. For the quick and active Uncas soon found the impression of a foot on a bunch of moss, where it would seem an Indian had inadvertently trodden. Pursuing the direction given by this discovery, he entered the neighbouring thicket, and struck the trail as fresh and obvious as it had been before they reached the spring. Another shout announced the good fortune of the youth to his companions, and at once terminated the search.

"Ay, it has been planned with Indian judgment," said the scout, when the party was assembled around the place; "and would have blinded white eyes."

"Shall we proceed?" demanded Heyward.

"Softly, softly; we know our path, but it is good to examine the formation of things. This is my schooling, Major, and if one neglects the book, there is no better chance of learning from the hand of Providence, than yon idle boy has with an old gal. All is plain but one thing, which is the manner that the knave contrived to get the gentle ones along the blind trail. Even a Huron would be too proud to let their tender feet touch the water."

"Will this assist in explaining the difficulty?" said Heyward, pointing towards the fragments of a sort of hand-barrow, that had been rudely constructed of boughs, and bound together with withes, and which now seemed carelessly cast aside as useless.

"'Tis all explained!" cried the delighted Hawk-eye. "If them varlets have passed a minute, they have spent hours in striving to fabricate a lying end to their trail! Well, I've known them waste a day in the same manner to as little purpose. Here we have three pair of moccasins, and two little feet. Now the singer was beginning to be footsore and leg-weary, as is plain by his trail. There you see he slipped; here he has travelled wide and tottered; and there, again, it looks as though he journeyed on snow-shoes. Ay, ay, a man who uses his throat altogether, can hardly give his legs a proper training!"

Before an hour had elapsed, however, the speed of Hawk-eye sensibly abated, and his head, instead of maintaining its former direct and forward look, began to turn suspiciously from side to side, as if he were conscious of approaching danger. He soon stopped again, and awaited for the whole party to come up.

"I scent the Hurons," he said, speaking to the Mohicans; "yonder is open sky through the tree tops, and we are getting too nigh their encampment. Sagamore, you will take the hill side, to the right; Uncas will bend along the brook to the left, while I will try the trail. If any thing should happen, the call will be three croaks of a crow. I saw one of the birds fanning himself in the air, just beyond the dead oak—another sign that we are touching an encampment."

The Indians departed their several ways, without deeming any reply necessary, while Hawk-eye cautiously proceeded with the two gentlemen. Heyward soon pressed to the side of their guide, eager to catch an early glimpse of those enemies he had pursued with so much toil and anxiety. His companion told him to steal to the edge of the wood, which as usual was fringed with a thicket, and wait his coming, for he wished to examine certain suspicious signs a little on one side. Duncan obeyed, and soon found himself in a situation to command a view which he found as extraordinary as it was novel.

The trees of many acres had been felled, and the glow of a mild summer's evening had fallen on the clearing, in beautiful contrast to the gray light of the forest. A short distance from the place where Duncan stood, the stream had seemingly expanded into a little lake, covering most of the low land from mountain to mountain. The water fell out of this wide basin in a cataract so regular and gentle, that it appeared rather to be the work of human hands, than fashioned by nature. A hundred earthern dwellings stood on the margin of the lake, and even in its waters, as though the latter had overflowed its usual banks. Their rounded roofs, admirably moulded for defence against the weather, denoted more of industry and foresight than the natives were wont to bestow on their regular habitations, much less on those they occupied for the temporary purposes of hunting and war. In short, the whole village or town, whichever it might be termed, possessed more of method and neatness of execution than the white man had been accustomed to believe belonged ordinarily to the Indian habits. It appeared, however, to be deserted: at least, so thought Duncan for many minutes; but at length he fancied he discovered several human forms advancing towards him on all fours, and apparently dragging in their train some heavy, and as he was quick to apprehend, some formidable engine. Just then a few dark looking heads gleamed out of the dwellings, and the place seemed suddenly alive with beings, which, however, glided from cover to cover so swiftly as to allow no opportunity of examing their humours or pursuits. Alarmed at these suspicious and inexplicable movements, he was about to attempt the signal of the crows, when the rustling of the leaves at hand drew his eyes to another direction.

The young man started and recoiled a few paces instinctively, when he found himself within a hundred yards of a stranger Indian. Recovering his recollection on the instant, instead of sounding an alarm, which might have proved fatal to himself, he remained stationary, an attentive observer of the other's motions.

An instant of calm observation served to assure Duncan that he was undiscovered. The native, like himself, seemed occupied in considering the low dwellings of the village, and the stolen movements of its inhabitants. It was impossible to discover the expression of his features through the grotesque mask of paint under which they were concealed; though Duncan fancied it was rather melancholy than savage. His head was shaved as usual, with the exception of the crown, from whose tuft three or four faded feathers from a hawk's wing were loosely dangling. A ragged calico mantle half encircled his body, while his nether garment was composed of an ordinary shirt, the sleeves of which were made to perform the office that is usually executed by a much more commodious arrangement. His legs were bare and sadly cut and torn by briars. The feet were, however, covered with a pair of good bearskin moccasins. Altogether the appearance of the individual was forlorn and miserable.

Duncan was still curiously observing the person of his neighbour, when the scout stole silently and cautiously to his side.

"You see we have reached their settlement, or encampment," whispered the young man; "and here is one of the savages himself in a very embarrassing position for our further movements."

Hawk-eye started, and dropped his rifle, when directed by the finger of his companion, the stranger came under his view. Then lowering the dangerous muzzle, he stretched forward his long neck, as if to assist a scrutiny that was already intensely keen.

"The imp is not a Huron," he said, "nor of any of the Canada tribes! and yet you see by his clothes the knave has been plundering a white. Ay, Montcalm has raked the woods for his inroad, and a whooping murdering set of varlets has he gathered together! Can you see where he has put his rifle or his bow?"

"He appears to have no arms; nor does he seem to be viciously inclined. Unless he communicate the alarm to his fellows, who, as you see, are dodging about the water, we have but little to fear from him."

The scout turned to Heyward, and regarded him with unconcealed amazement. Then opening wide his mouth, he indulged in unrestrained and heartfelt laughter, though in that silent and peculiar manner which danger had so long taught him to practise.

Repeating the words, "fellows who are dodging about the water!" he added, "so much for schooling and passing a boyhood in the settlements! The knave has long legs though, and shall not be trusted. Do you keep him under your rifle, while I creep in behind through the bush, and take him alive. Fire on no account!"

Heyward had already permitted his companion to bury part of his person in the thicket, when, stretching forth his arm, he arrested him in order to ask—

"If I see you in danger, may I not risk a shot?"

Hawk-eye regarded him a moment, like one who knew just how to take the question; then, nodding his head, he answered, still laughing, though inaudibly—

"Fire a whole platoon, Major."

In the next moment he was concealed by the leaves. Duncan waited several minutes in feverish impatience, before he caught another glimpse of the scout. Then he reappeared, creeping along the earth, from which his dress was hardly distinguishable, directly in the rear of his intended captive. Having reached within a few yards of the latter, he rose to his feet silently and slowly. At that instant several loud blows were struck on the water, and Duncan turned his eyes just in time to perceive that a hundred dark forms were plunging in a body into the troubled little sheet. Grasping his rifle, his looks were again bent on the Indian near him. Instead of taking the alarm, the unconscious savage stretched forward his neck, as if he also watched the movements about the gloomy lake, with a sort of silly curiosity. In the meantime, the uplifted hand of Hawk-eye was above him; but, without any apparent reason, it was withdrawn, and its owner indulged in another long, though still silent, fit of merriment. When the peculiar and hearty laughter of Hawk-eye was ended, instead of grasping his victim by the throat, he tapped him lightly on the shoulder, and exclaimed aloud—

"How now friend! have you a mind to teach the beavers to sing?"

"Even so," was the ready answer. "It would seem that the Being that gave them power to improve his gifts so well, would not deny them voices to proclaim his praise."

Chapter 20

"*Bot.* Are we all met?
Qui. Pat—pat; and here's a marvellous
Convenient place for our rehearsal."
Shakespeare.

THE reader may better imagine, than we describe, the surprise of Heyward. His lurking Indians were suddenly converted into fourfooted beasts; his lake into a beaver pond; his cataract into a dam, constructed by those industrious and ingenious quadrupeds; and a suspected enemy into his tried friend, David Gamut, the master of psalmody. The presence of the latter created so many unexpected hopes relative to the sisters, that, without a moment's hesitation, the young man broke out of his ambush, and sprang forward to join the two principal actors in the scene.

The merriment of Hawk-eye was not easily appeased. Without ceremony, and with a rough hand, he twirled the supple Gamut around on his heel, and more than once affirmed that the Hurons had done themselves great credit in the fashion of his costume. Then, seizing the hand of the other, he squeezed it with a gripe that brought the tears into the eyes of the placid David, and wished him joy of his new condition.

"You were about opening your throat-practysings among the beavers, were ye?" he said. "The cunning devils know half the trade already, for they beat the time with their tails, as you heard just now; and in good time it was too, or 'kill-deer' might have sounded the first note among them. I have known greater fools, who could read and write, than an experienced old beaver; but as for squalling, the animals are born dumb! —What think you of such a song as this?"

David shut his sensitive ears, and even Heyward, apprised as he was of the nature of the cry, looked upward in quest of the bird, as the cawing of a crow rang in the air about them.

"See," continued the laughing scout, as he pointed towards the remainder of the party, who, in obedience to the signal, were already approaching; "this is music which has its natural virtues; it brings two good rifles to my elbow, to say nothing of the knives and tomahawks. But we see that you are safe; now tell us what has become of the maidens."

"They are captives to the heathen," said David; "and, though greatly troubled in spirit, enjoying comfort and safety in the body."

"Both?" demanded the breathless Heyward.

"Even so. Though our wayfaring has been sore, and our sustenance scanty, we have had little other cause of complaint except the violence done our feelings by being thus led in captivity into a far land."

"Bless ye for these very words!" exclaimed the trembling Munro; "I shall then receive my babes spotless and angel-like as I lost them!"

"I know not that their delivery is at hand," returned the doubting David; "the leader of these savages is possessed of an evil spirit, that no power short of Omnipotence can tame. I have tried him sleeping and waking, but neither sounds nor language seem to touch his soul."

"Where is the knave?" bluntly interrupted the scout.

"He hunts the moose to-day with his young men; and to-morrow, as I hear, they pass further into these forests, and nigher to the borders of Canada. The elder maiden is conveyed to a neighbouring people, whose lodges are situate beyond yonder black pinnacle of rock; while the younger is detained among the women of the Hurons, whose dwellings are but two short miles hence, on a table land, where the fire has done the office of the axe, and prepared the place for their reception."

"Alice, my gentle Alice!" murmured Heyward; "she has lost the consolation of her sister's presence!"

"Even so. But as far as praise and thanksgiving in psalmody can temper the spirit in affliction, she has not suffered."

"Has she then a heart for music?"

"Of the graver and more solemn character; though it must be acknowledged, that in spite of all my endeavours, the maiden weeps oftener than she smiles. At such moments I forbear to press the holy songs; but there are many sweet and comfortable periods of satisfactory communication, when the ears of the savages are astounded with the upliftings of our voices!"

"And why are you permitted to go at large, unwatched?"

David composed his features into what he intended should express an air of modest humility, before he meekly replied—

"Little be the praise to such a worm as I. But though the power of psalmody was suspended in the terrible business of that field of blood through which we passed, it has recovered its influence, even over the souls of the heathen, and I am suffered to go and come at will."

The scout laughed, and tapping his own forehead significantly, he perhaps explained the single indulgence more satisfactorily, when he said—

"The Indians never harm a non-composser. But why, when the path lay open before your eyes, did you not strike back on your own trail, (it is not so blind as that which a squirrel would make,) and bring in the tidings to Edward?"

The scout, remembering only his own sturdy and iron nature, had probably exacted a task, that David, under no circumstances, could have performed. But, without entirely losing the meekness of his air, the latter was content to answer—

"Though my soul would rejoice to visit the habitations of Christendom once more, my feet would rather follow the tender spirits intrusted to my keeping, even into the idolatrous province of the Jesuits, than take one step backward while they pined in captivity and sorrow."

Though the figurative language of David was not very intelligible to all who heard him, the sincere and steady expression of his eye, and the glow on his honest countenance, were not easily mistaken. Uncas pressed close to his side, and regarded the speaker with a look of grave commendation, while his father expressed his satisfaction by the ordinary pithy exclamation of approbation. The scout shook his head, as he rejoined—

"The Lord never intended that the man should place all his endeavours in his throat, to the neglect of other and better gifts. But he has fallen into the hands of some silly woman, when he should have been gathering his education under a blue sky, and among the beauties of the forest. Here, friend, I did intend to kindle a fire with this tooting whistle of thine, but as you value the thing, take it, and blow your best on it!"

Gamut received his pitch-pipe with as strong an expression of pleasure, as he believed it compatible with the grave functions he exercised to exhibit. After essaying his virtues, repeatedly, in contrast with his own voice, and satisfying himself that none of its melody was lost, he made a very serious demonstration towards achieving a few stanzas of one the longest effusions in the little volume so often mentioned.

Heyward, however, hastily interrupted his pious purpose, by continuing questions concerning the past and present condition of his fellow captives, and in a manner more methodical than had been permitted by his feelings in the opening of their interview. The narrative of David was simple, and the facts few.

Magua had waited on the mountain until a safe moment to retire presented itself, when he had descended and taken the route along the western side of the Horican, in the direction of the Canadas. As the subtle Huron was familiar with the paths, and well knew there was no immediate danger of pursuit, their progress had been moderate, and far from fatiguing. It appeared, from the unembellished statement of David, that his own presence had been rather endured than desired: though even Magua had not been entirely exempt from that veneration with which the Indians regard those whom the Great Spirit has visited in their intellects. At night, the utmost care had been taken of the captives, both to prevent injury from the damps of the woods, and to guard against an escape. At the spring, the horses were turned loose, as has been seen; and notwithstanding the remoteness and length of their trail, the artifices already named were resorted to, in order to cut off every clue to their place of retreat. On their arrival at the encampment of his people, Magua, in obedience to a policy seldom departed from, separated his prisoners. Cora had been sent to a tribe that temporarily occupied an adjacent valley, though David was far too ignorant of the customs and history of the natives, to be able to declare any thing satisfactory concerning their name or character. He only knew that they had not engaged in the late expedition against William Henry; that, like the Hurons themselves, they were allies of Montcalm; and that they maintained an amicable, though a watchful, intercourse with the warlike and savage people, whom chance had for a time, brought in such close and disagreeable contact with themselves.

The Mohicans and the scout listened to his interrupted and imperfect narrative, with an interest that obviously increased as he proceeded, and it was while attempting to explain the pursuits of the community, in which Cora was detained, that the latter abruptly demanded—

"Did you see the fashion of their knives? were they of English or French formation?"

"My thoughts were bent on no such vanities, but rather mingled in consolation with those of the maidens."

"The time may come when you will not consider the knife of a savage such a despicable vanity," returned the scout, with a strong expression of contempt for the other's dullness. "Had they held their corn-feasts—or can you say any thing of the totems of their tribe?"

"Of corn, we had many and plentiful feasts; for the grain, being in the milk, is both sweet to the mouth and comfortable to the stomach. Of totem, I know not the meaning; but if it appertaineth in any wise to the art of Indian music, it need not be inquired after at their hands. They never join their voices in praise, and it would seem that they are among the profanest of the idolatrous."

"Therein you belie the nature of an Indian. Even the Mingo adores but the true and living God! 'Tis a wicked fabrication of the whites, and I say it to the shame of my colour, that would make the warrior bow down before images of his own creation. It is true, they endeavour to make truces with the wicked one—as who would not with an enemy he cannot conquer—but they look up for favour and assistance to the Great and Good Spirit only."

"It may be so," said David; "but I have seen strange and fantastic images drawn in their paint, of which their admiration and care, savoured of spiritual pride; especially one, and that too a foul and loathsome object."

"Was it a sarpent?" quickly demanded the scout.

"Much the same. It was in the likeness of an abject and creeping tortoise!"

"Hugh!" exclaimed both the attentive Mohicans in a breath; while the scout shook his head with the air of one, who had made an important, but, by no means pleasing discovery. Then the father spoke in the language of the Delawares, and with a calmness and dignity that instantly arrested the attention even of those to whom his words were unintelligible. His gestures were impressive, and at times energetic. Once he lifted his arm on high, and as it descended the action threw aside the folds of his light mantle, a finger resting on his breast, as if he would enforce his meaning by the attitude. Duncan's eyes followed the movement, and he perceived that the animal just mentioned was beautifully, though faintly, worked in a blue tint, on the swarthy breast of the chief. All that he had ever heard of the violent separation of the vast tribes of the Delawares, rushed across his mind, and he awaited the proper moment to speak, with a suspense that was rendered nearly intolerable, by his interest in the stake. His wish, however, was anticipated by the scout, who turned from his red friend, saying—

"We have found that which may be good or evil to us, as Heaven disposes. The Sagamore is of the high blood of the Delawares, and is the great chief of their Tortoises! That some of this stock are among the people of whom the singer tells us, is plain, by his words: and had he but spent half the breath in prudent questions, that he has blown away in making a trumpet of his throat, we might have known how many warriors they numbered. It is, altogether, a dangerous path we move in; for a friend whose face is turned from you, often bears a bloodier mind than the enemy who seeks your scalp!"

"Explain," said Duncan.

"'Tis a long and melancholy tradition, and one I little like to think of; for it is not to be denied, that the evil has been mainly done by men with white skins. But it has ended in turning the tomahawk of brother against brother, and brought the Mingo and the Delaware to travel in the same path!"

"You then suspect it is a portion of that people among whom Cora resides?"

The scout nodded his head in assent, though he seemed anxious to waive the further discussion of a subject that appeared painful. The impatient Duncan now made several hasty and desperate propositions to attempt the release of the sisters. Munro seemed to shake off his dull apathy, and listened to the wild schemes of the young man with a deference that his grey hairs and reverend years should have denied. But the scout, after suffering the ardour of the lover to expend itself a little, found means to convince him of the folly of precipitation in a matter that would require their coolest judgment and utmost fortitude.

"It would be well," he added, "to let this man go in again, as usual, and for him to tarry in the lodges, giving notice to the gentle ones of our approach, until we call him out, by signal, to consult. You know the cry of a crow, friend, from the whistle of the whip-poor-will?"

"'Tis a pleasing bird," returned David, "and has a soft and melancholy note! though the time is rather quick and ill-measured."

"He speaks of the wish-ton-wish," said the scout; "well, since you like his whistle, it shall be your signal. Remember, then, when you hear the whip-poor-will's call three times repeated, you are to come into the bushes, where the bird might be supposed—"

"Stop," interrupted Heyward. "I will accompany him."

"You!" exclaimed the astonished Hawk-eye; "are you tired of seeing the sun rise and set?"

"David is a living proof that the Hurons can be merciful."

"Ay, but David can use his throat, as no man in his senses would pervart the gift."

"I too can play the madman, the fool, the hero—in short, any or everything—to rescue her I love from such captivity. Name your objections no longer; I am resolved."

Hawk-eye regarded the young man a moment in speechless amazement. But Duncan, who, in deference to the other's skill and services, had hitherto submitted somewhat implicitly to his dictation, now assumed the superior, with a loftiness of manner that was not easily resisted. He waved his hand, in sign of his dislike to all remonstrance, and then, in more tempered language, he continued—

"You have the means of disguise; change me; paint me, too, if you will; in short, alter me to any thing—a fool."

"It is not for one like me to say that he who is already formed by so powerful a hand as Providence, stands in need of a change," muttered the discontented scout. "When you send your parties abroad in war, you find it prudent at least to arrange the marks and places of encampment, in order that they who fight on your side may know when and where to expect a friend?"

"Listen," interrupted Duncan; "you have heard from this faithful follower of the captives, that the Indians are of two tribes, if not of different nations. With one, whom you think to be a branch of the Delawares, is she you call the 'dark-hair'; the other, and younger of the ladies, is undeniably with our declared enemies, the Hurons. It becomes my youth and rank to attempt the latter adventure. While you, therefore, are negotiating with your friends for the release of one of the sisters, I will effect that of the other, or die."

The awakened spirit of the young soldier gleamed in his eyes, and his form dilated and became imposing under its influence. Hawk-eye, though too much accustomed to Indian artifices not to foresee all the danger of the experiment, knew not well how to combat this sudden resolution. Perhaps there was something in the proposal that suited his own hardy nature, and that secret love of desperate adventure, which had increased with his daily experience, until hazard and danger had become, in some measure, necessary to the enjoyment of his existence. Instead of continuing to oppose the scheme of Duncan, his humour suddenly altered, and he lent himself to its execution.

"Come," he said, with a good humoured smile; "the buck that will take to the water must be headed, and not followed; Chingachgook has as many paints as the engineer officer's wife, who takes down nature on scraps of paper, making the mountains look like cocks of rusty hay, and placing the blue sky in reach of your hand: the Sagamore can use them too! Seat yourself on the log, and, my life on it, he can soon make a natural fool of you, and that well to your liking."

Duncan complied, and the Mohican, who had been an attentive listener to the discourse, readily undertook the office. Long practised in all the subtle arts of his race, he drew, with great dexterity and quickness, the fantastic shadow that the natives were accustomed to consider as the evidence of a friendly and jocular disposition. Every line that could possibly be interpreted into a secret inclination for war, was carefully avoided: while, on the other hand, he studied those conceits that might be construed into a wish for amity. In short, he entirely sacrificed every appearance of the warrior, to the masquerade of a buffoon. Such exhibitions were not uncommon among the Indians; and, as Duncan was already sufficiently disguised in his dress, there certainly did exist some reason for believing, that, with his knowledge of French, he might pass for a juggler from Ticonderoga, straggling among the allied and friendly tribes.

When he was thought to be sufficiently painted, the scout gave him much friendly advice; concerted signals, and appointed the place where they should meet, in the event of mutual success. The parting between Munro and his young friend was more melancholy and feeling; still, the former submitted to the separation with an indifference that his warm and honest nature would never have permitted in a more healthful state of mind. The scout led Heyward aside, and acquainted him with his intention to leave the veteran in some safe encampment in charge of Chingachgook, while he and Uncas pursued their inquiries among the people they had reason to believe were Delawares. Then renewing his cautions and advice, he concluded by saying, with a solemnity and warmth of feeling with which Duncan was deeply touched—

"And now God bless you! You have shown a spirit that I like; for it is the gift of youth, more especially one of warm blood and a stout heart. But believe the warning of a man, who has reason to know all he says to be true. You will have occasion for your best manhood, and for a sharper wit, than what is to be gathered in books, afore you outdo the cunning, or get the better of the courage of a Mingo! God bless you! If the Hurons master your scalp, rely on the promise of one, who has two stout warriors to back him—they shall pay for their victory, with a life for every hair it holds! I say, young gentleman, may Providence bless our undertaking, which is altogether for good; and remember, that to outwit the knaves, it is lawful to practise things that may not be naturally the gift of a white skin."

Duncan shook his worthy and reluctant associate warmly by the hand, once more recommended his aged friend to his care, and returning his good wishes, he motioned to David to proceed. Hawk-eye gazed after the high-spirited and adventurous young man for several moments, in open admiration; then shaking his head, doubtingly, he turned, and led his own division of the party into the concealment of the forest.

The route taken by Duncan and David lay directly across the clearing of the beavers, and along the margin of their pond. When the former found himself alone with one so simple, and so little qualified to render any assistance in desperate emergencies, he first began to be sensible of the difficulties of the task he had undertaken. The faded light increased the gloominess of the bleak and savage wilderness, that stretched so far on every side of him, and there was even a fearful character in the stillness of those little huts, that he knew were so abundantly peopled. It struck him, as he gazed at the admirable structures, and the wonderful precautions of their sagacious inmates, that even the brutes of these vast wilds were possessed of an instinct nearly commensurate with his own practised reason; and he could not reflect, without anxiety, on the unequal contest that he had so rashly courted. Then came the glowing image of Alice; her distress; her actual danger; and all the peril of his situation faded before her loveliness. Cheering David with his voice, he moved more swiftly onward, with the light and vigorous step of youth and enterprise.

After making nearly a semicircle around the pond, they diverted from the water-course and began to ascend to the level of a slight elevation in that bottom land, over which they journeyed. Within half an hour they gained the margin of another opening, that bore all the signs of having been also made by the beavers, and which those sagacious animals had probably been induced, by some accident, to abandon, for the more eligible position they now occupied. A very natural sensation caused Duncan to hesitate a moment, unwilling to leave the cover of their bushy path, as a man pauses to collect his energies before he essays any hazardous experiment, in which he is secretly conscious they will all be needed. He profited by the halt, to gather such information as might be obtained from his short and hasty glances.

On the opposite side of the clearing and near the point where the brook tumbled over some rocks, from a still higher level, some fifty or sixty lodges rudely fabricated of logs, brush, and earth, intermingled, were to be discovered. They were arranged without any order, and seemed to be constructed with very little attention to their neatness or beauty. Indeed, so very inferior were they, in the two latter particulars, to the village Duncan had just seen, that he began to expect a second surprise, no less astonishing than the former. This expectation was in no degree diminished, when, by the doubtful twilight, he beheld twenty or thirty forms, rising alternately, from the cover of the tall, coarse grass, in front of the lodges, and then sinking again from the sight, as it were to burrow in the earth. By the sudden and hasty glimpses that he caught of these figures, they seemed more like dark glancing spectres, or some other unearthly beings, than creatures fashioned with the ordinary and vulgur materials of flesh and blood. A gaunt, naked form, was seen, for a single instant, tossing its arms wildly in the air, and then the spot it had filled was vacant, the figure appearing, suddenly, in some other and distant place, or being succeeded by another, possessing the same mysterious character. David observing that his companion lingered, pursued the direction of his gaze, and in some measure recalled the recollection of Heyward, by speaking—

"There is much fruitful soil uncultivated here," he said; "and I may add, without the sinful leaven of self-condemnation, that, since my short sojourn in these heathenish abodes, much good seed has been scattered by the way side."

"The tribes are fonder of the chase, than of the arts of men of labour," returned the unconscious Duncan, still gazing at the objects of his wonder.

"It is rather joy than labour to the spirit, to lift up the voice in praise; but sadly do these boys abuse their gifts! Rarely have I found any of their age, on whom nature has so freely bestowed the elements of psalmody; and surely, surely, there are none who neglect them more. Three nights have I now tarried here, and three several times have I assembled the urchins to join in sacred song, and as often have they responded to my efforts with whoopings and howlings that have chilled my inmost soul!"

"Of whom speak you?"

"Of those children of the devil, who waste their precious moments in yonder idle antics. Ah! the wholesome restraint of discipline is but little known among this self-abandoned people! In a country of birches, a rod is never seen; and it ought not to appear a marvel in my eyes, that the choicest blessings of Providence are wasted in such cries as these."

David closed his ears against the juvenile pack, whose yells just then rang shrilly through the forest; and Duncan, suffering his lip to curl in a proud smile, as in mockery at his own momentary superstition, said firmly—

"We will proceed."

Without removing the safeguard from his ears, the master of song complied, and together they pursued their way, boldly, towards what David was sometimes wont to call "the tents of the Philistines."

Chapter 21

—But though the beast of game
The privilege of chase may claim;
Though space and law the stag we lend,
Ere hound we slip, or bow we bend;
Whoever recked, where, how, or when,
The prowling fox was trapped or slain?
Lady of the Lake.

IT is unusual to find an encampment of the natives, like those of the more instructed whites, guarded by the presence of armed men. Well informed of the approach of every danger, while it is yet at a distance, the Indian generally rests secure under his knowledge of the signs of the forest, and the long and difficult paths that separate him from those he has most reason to dread. But the enemy who, by any unlucky concurrence of accidents, has found means to elude the vigilance of the scouts, will seldom meet with sentinels nearer home to sound the alarm. In addition to this general usage, the tribes friendly to the French king knew too well the weight of the blow that had just been struck, to apprehend any immediate danger from the hostile nations that were tributary to the crown of Britain.

When Duncan and David, therefore, found themselves in the centre of the busy children, who played the antics already mentioned, it was without the least previous intimation of their approach. But so soon as they were observed, the whole of the juvenile pack raised, by common consent, a single shrill and warning whoop; and then sunk, as it were by magic, from before the sight of their visitors. The naked, tawny bodies of the crouching urchins, blended so nicely, at that hour, with the withered herbage, that at first it seemed as if the earth had, in truth, swallowed up their forms; though, when surprise had permitted Duncan, to bend his own wondering looks more curiously about the spot, he found them everywhere met by dark, quick, and rolling eyeballs.

Gathering no encouragement from this startling presage of the nature of the scrutiny he was likely to undergo from the more mature judgments of the men, there was an instant when the young soldier would gladly have retreated. It was, however, too late to appear even to hesitate. The cry of the children had drawn a dozen warriors to the door of the nearest lodge, where they stood, clustered in a dark and savage group, gravely awaiting the nearer approach of those who had thus unexpectedly come among them.

David, in some measure familiarized to the scene, led the way, with a steadiness that no slight obstacle was likely to disconcert, into this very building. It was the principal edifice of the village, though roughly constructed of the bark and branches of trees; being the lodge in which the tribe held its councils and public meetings, during their temporary residence on the borders of the English province. Duncan found it difficult to assume the necessary appearance of unconcern, as he brushed the dark and powerful frames of the savages who thronged its threshold; but, conscious that his existence depended on his presence of mind, he trusted to the discretion of his companion, whose footsteps he closely followed, endeavouring, as he proceeded, to rally his thoughts for the occasion. His blood had stagnated for a moment, when he found himself in absolute contact with such fierce and implacable enemies; but he so far mastered his feelings, as to pursue his way into the centre of the lodge, with an exterior that did not betray the weakness. Imitating the example of the deliberate Gamut, he drew a bundle of fragrant brush from beneath a pile, that filled a corner of the hut, and seated himself in silence.

So soon as their visitor had passed, the observant warriors fell back from the entrance, and arranging themselves about him, they seemed patiently to wait the moment when it might comport with the dignity of the stranger to speak. By far the greater number stood leaning, in lazy, lounging attitudes, against the upright posts that supported the crazy building, while three or four of the oldest and most distinguished of the chiefs placed themselves, in their ordinary manner, on the earth, a little more in advance.

A flaring torch was burning in the place, and sent its red glare from face to face, and figure to figure, as it wavered, inconstantly, in the currents of air. Duncan profited by its light, to read, with jealous looks, the probable character of his reception, in the countenances of his hosts. But his ingenuity availed him little, against the cold artifices of the people he had encountered. The chiefs in front scarce cast a glance at his person, keeping their eyes fastened on the ground, with an air that might have been intended for respect, but which it was quite easy to construe into distrust. The men in shadow were less reserved. Duncan soon detected their searching, but stolen looks, which, in truth, scanned his person, and attire inch by inch, leaving no emotion of the countenance, no gesture, no line of the paint, nor even the fashion of a garment, unheeded, and without its secret comment.

At length, one whose hair was beginning to be sprinkled with gray, but whose sinewy limbs and firm tread announced that he was still equal to the arduous duties of manhood, advanced from out the gloom of a corner, whither he had probably posted himself to make his observations unseen, and spoke. He used the language of the Wyandots, or Hurons: his words were, consequently, unintelligible to Heyward, though they seemed, by the gestures that accompanied them, to be uttered more in courtesy than anger. The latter shook his head, and made a gesture indicative of his inability to reply.

"Do none of my brothers speak the French or the English?" he said, in the former language, looking about him, from countenance to countenance, in hopes of finding a nod of assent.

Though more than one head turned, as if to catch the meaning of his words, they remained unanswered.

"I should be grieved to think," continued Duncan, speaking slowly and using the simplest French of which he was the master, "to believe that none of this wise and brave nation understand the language that the 'Grand Monarque' uses when he talks to his children. His heart would be heavy, did he believe his red warriors paid him so little respect!"

A long and grave pause succeeded, during which no movement of a limb, nor any expression of an eye, betrayed the impression produced by his remark. Duncan, who knew that silence was a virtue amongst his hosts, gladly had recourse to the custom, in order to arrange his ideas. At length, the same warrior, who had before addressed him, replied, by drily demanding, in the slight patois of the Canadas—

"When our Great Father speaks to his people, is it with the tongue of a Huron?"

"He knows no difference in his children, whether the colour of the skin be red, or black, or white," returned Duncan, evasively; "though chiefly is he satisfied with the brave Hurons."

"In what manner will he speak," demanded the wary chief, "when the runners count to him the scalps which five nights ago grew on the heads of the Yengeese?"

"They were his enemies," said Duncan, shuddering involuntarily; "and, doubtless, he will say it is good—my Hurons are very valiant."

"Our Canada father does not think it. Instead of looking forward to reward his Indians, his eyes are turned backwards. He sees the dead Yengeese, but no Huron. What can this mean?"

"A great chief, like him, has more thoughts than tongues. He looks to see that no enemies are on his trail."

"The canoe of a dead warrior will not float on the Horican," returned the savage gloomily. "His ears are open to the Delawares, who are not our friends, and they fill them with lies."

"It cannot be. See; he has bid me, who am a man that knows the art of healing, to go to his children, the red Hurons of the Great Lakes, and ask if any are sick!"

Another long and deep silence succeeded this annunciation of the character Duncan had assumed. Every eye was simultaneously bent on his person, as if to inquire into the truth or falsehood of the declaration, with an intelligence and keenness, that caused the subject of their scrutiny to tremble for the result. He was, however, relieved again, by the former speaker.

"Do the cunning men of the Canadas paint their skins?" the Huron coldly continued; "we have heard them boast that their faces were pale."

"When an Indian chief comes among his white fathers," returned

Duncan, with great steadiness, "he lays aside his buffalo robe, to carry the shirt that is offered him. My brothers have given me paint, and I wear it."

A low murmur of applause announced that the compliment to the tribe was favourably received. The elderly chief made a gesture of commendation, which was answered by most of his companions, who each threw forth a hand, and uttered the usual brief exclamation of pleasure. Duncan began to breathe more freely, believing that the weight of his examination was past; and as he had already prepared a simple and probable tale to support his pretended occupation, his hopes of ultimate success grew brighter.

After a silence of a few moments, as if adjusting his thoughts, in order to make a suitable answer to the declaration their guest had just given, another warrior arose, and placed himself in an attitude to speak. While his lips were yet in the act of parting, a low, but fearful sound, arose from the forest, and was immediately succeeded by a high, shrill yell, that was drawn out, until it equalled the longest and most plaintive howl of the wolf. The sudden and terrible interruption caused Duncan to start from his seat, unconscious of everything but the effect produced by so frightful a cry. At the same moment, the warriors glided in a body from the lodge, and the outer air was filled with loud shouts, that nearly drowned those awful sounds which the organs of Duncan occasionally announced were still ringing beneath the arches of the woods. Unable to command himself any longer, the youth broke from the place, and presently stood in the centre of a disorderly throng, that included nearly every thing having life, within the limits of the encampment. Men, women, and children; the aged, the infirm, the active, and the strong, were alike abroad; some exclaiming aloud, others clapping their hands with a joy that seemed frantic, and all expressing their savage pleasure in some unexpected event. Though astonished at first, by the uproar, Heyward was soon enabled to find its solution by the scene that followed.

There yet lingered sufficient light in the heavens, to exhibit those bright openings among the tree-tops, where different paths left the clearing to enter the depths of the wilderness. Beneath one of them, a line of warriors issued from the woods, and advanced slowly towards the dwellings. One in front bore a short pole, on which, as it afterwards appeared, were suspended several human scalps. The startling sounds that Duncan had heard were what the whites have, not inappropriately, called the "death halloo"; and each repetition of the cry was intended to announce to the tribe, the fate of an enemy.

When at the distance of a few hundred feet from the lodges, the newly arrived warriors halted. Their plaintive and terrific cry, which was intended to represent equally the wailings of the dead and the triumph of the victors, had entirely ceased. One of their number now called aloud, in words that were far from appalling, though not more intelligible for whose ears they were intended, than their expressive yells. It would be difficult to convey a suitable idea of the savage ecstasy with which the news thus imparted, was received. The whole encampment, in a moment, became a scene of the most violent bustle and commotion. The warriors drew their knives, and flourishing them on high, they arranged themselves in two lines, forming a lane, that extended from the war-party to the lodges. The squaws seized clubs, axes, or whatever weapon of offence first offered itself to their hands, and rushed eagerly to act their part in the cruel game that was at hand. Even the children would not be excluded; but boys, little able to wield the instruments, tore the tomahawks from the belts of their fathers, and stole into the ranks, apt imitators of the savage traits exhibited by their parents.

Large piles of brush lay scattered about the clearing, and a wary and aged squaw was occupied in firing as many as might serve to light the coming exhibition. As the flame arose, its power exceeded that of the parting day, and assisted to render objects at the same time more distinct and more hideous. The whole scene formed a striking picture, whose frame was composed by the dark and tall border of pines. The warriors just arrived were the most distant figures. A little in advance, stood a man, apparently selected from the rest, as the principal actor in what was to follow. The light was not strong enough to render his features distinct.

He stood erect and firm, prepared to meet his fate like a hero. The high-spirited Duncan felt a powerful impulse of admiration and pity towards him, though no opportunity could offer to exhibit his generous emotions. He watched the slightest movement, however, with eager eyes: and as he traced the fine outline of his admirably proportioned and active frame, he endeavoured to persuade himself, that if the powers of man, seconded by such noble resolution, could bear one harmless through so severe a trial, the youthful captive before him might hope for success in the hazardous race he was about to run. Insensibly the young man drew nigh to the swarthy lines of the Hurons, and scarcely breathed, so intense became his interest in the spectacle. Just then the signal yell was given, and the momentary quiet which had preceded it was broken by a burst of cries, that far exceeded any before heard. The man bounded from the place, at the cry, with the activity and swiftness of a deer. Instead of rushing through the hostile lines, as had been expected, he just entered the dangerous defile, and before time was given for a single blow, turned short, and leaping the heads of a row of children, he gained at once the exterior and safer side of the formidable array. The artifice was answered by a hundred voices raised in imprecations, and the whole of the excited multitude broke out of their order, and spread themselves about the place in wild confusion.

It will be easily understood, that amid such a concourse of vindictive enemies, no breathing time was permitted to the fugitive. There was a single moment, when it seemed as if he would have reached the forest, but the whole body of his captors threw themselves before him, and drove him back into the centre of his relentless persecutors. Turning like a headed deer, he shot with the swiftness of an arrow, through a pillar of forked flame, and passing the whole multitude harmless, he appeared on the opposite side of the clearing. Here, too, he was met and turned by a few of the older and more subtle of the Hurons.

Profiting by a momentary opening, the captive darted from among the warriors, and made a desperate, and what seemed to Duncan, a final effort to gain the wood. As if aware that no danger was to be apprehended from the young soldier, the fugitive nearly brushed his person in his flight. A tall and powerful Huron, who had husbanded his forces, pressed close upon his heels, and with an uplifted arm, menaced a fatal blow. Duncan thrust forth a foot, and the shock precipitated the eager savage headlong, many feet in advance of his intended victim. Thought itself is not quicker than was the motion with which the latter profited by the advantage; he turned, gleamed like a meteor again before the eyes of Duncan, and at the next moment, when the latter recovered his recollection, and gazed around in quest of the captive, he saw him leaning against a small painted post, which stood before the door of the principal lodge.

Apprehensive that the part he had taken in the escape might prove fatal to himself, Duncan left the place without delay. He followed the crowd, which drew nigh the lodges, gloomy and sullen, like any other multitude that had been disappointed in an execution. Curiosity, or perhaps, a better feeling, induced him to approach the stranger. He found him, standing with one arm cast about the protecting post, and breathing thick and hard, after his incredible exertions, but still disdaining to permit a single sign of suffering to escape. His person was now protected by immemorial and sacred usage, until the tribe in council had deliberated and determined on his fate.

There was no term of abuse known to the Huron vocabulary, that the disappointed women did not lavishly expend on the successful stranger. But the stranger was superior to all their efforts. His head was immovable; nor did he betray the slightest consciousness that any were present, except when his haughty eye rolled proudly towards the dusky forms of the warriors, who stalked in the background, silent and sullen observers of the scene.

The effect of his indifference began to extend itself to the other spectators; and a youngster who was just quitting the condition of a boy, to enter the state of manhood, attempted to assist the termagant, by flourishing his tomahawk before their victim, and adding his empty boasts to the taunts of the women. Then, indeed, the captive turned his face towards the light, and looked down on the stripling with a loftiness of expression, that was even superior to contempt. At the next moment, he resumed his quiet and reclining attitude against the post. But the action and the change of posture had permitted Duncan to exchange glances with the firm and piercing eyes of Uncas.

Breathless with amazement, and heavily oppressed with the critical situation of his friend, Heyward recoiled before the look, trembling lest its meaning expression might in some unknown manner, hasten the prisoner's fate. There was not, however, any instant cause for such an apprehension. Just then a warrior forced his way into the exasperated crowd. Motioning the women and children aside with a stern gesture, he took Uncas by the arm, and led him towards the door of the council lodge. Thither all the chiefs, and most of the distinguished warriors, followed, among whom the anxious Heyward found means to enter, without attracting any dangerous attention to himself.

A few minutes were consumed in disposing of those present in a manner suitable to their rank and influence in the tribe. An order very similar to that adopted in the preceding interview was observed; the aged and superior chiefs occupying the area of the spacious apartment, within the powerful light of a glaring torch, while their juniors and inferiors were arranged in the background, presenting a dark outline to the picture, of swarthy and sternly marked visages. In the very centre of the lodge, immediately under an opening that admitted the twinkling light of one or two stars, stood Uncas, calm, elevated, and collected. His high and haughty carriage was not lost on his captors, who often bent their looks on his person, with eyes, which, while they lost none of their inflexibility of purpose, plainly betrayed their admiration of the stranger's daring.

Chapter 22

Thus spoke the sage; the kings without delay
Dissolve the council, and their chief obey.
                                    Pope's Iliad.

HEYWARD had not long occupied the seat he had wisely taken, a little in the shade, when another of the elder warriors, who spoke the French language, addressed him—

"My Canada father does not forget his children!" said the chief; "I thank him. An evil spirit lives in the wife of one of my young men. Can the cunning stranger frighten him away?"

Heyward possessed some knowledge of the mummery practised among the Indians, in the cases of such supposed visitations. He saw, at a glance, that the circumstance might possibly be improved to further his own ends. It would, therefore, have been difficult, just then, to have uttered a proposal that would have given him more satisfaction. Aware of the necessity of preserving the dignity of his imaginary character, however, he repressed his feelings, and answered with suitable mystery—

"Spirits differ; some yield to the power of wisdom, while others are too strong."

"My brother is a great medicine!" said the cunning savage; "he will try?"

A gesture of assent was the answer. The Huron was content with the

96

assurance, and resuming his pipe, he awaited the proper moment to move.

When the chief had finished his pipe, he made a final and successful movement towards departing. A motion of the finger was the intimation he gave the supposed physician to follow; and passing through the clouds of smoke, Duncan was glad, on more accounts than one, to be able at last to breathe the pure air of a cool and refreshing summer evening.

Instead of pursuing his way among those lodges where Heyward had already made his unsuccessful search, his companion turned aside, and proceeded directly toward the base of an adjacent mountain, which overhung the temporary village. A thicket of brush skirted its foot, and it became necessary to proceed through a crooked and narrow path. The boys had resumed their sports in the clearing, and were enacting a mimic chase to the post among themselves. In order to render their games as like the reality as possible, one of the boldest of their number had conveyed a few brands into some piles of tree-tops, that had hitherto escaped the burning. The blaze of one of these fires lighted the way of the chief and Duncan, and gave a character of additional wildness to the rude scenery. At a little distance from a bald rock, and directly in its front, they entered a grassy opening, which they prepared to cross. Just then fresh fuel was added to the fire, and a powerful light penetrated even to that distant spot. It fell upon the white surface of the mountain, and was reflected downward upon a dark and mysterious-looking being, that arose unexpectedly in their path.

The Indian paused, as if doubtful whether to proceed, and permitted his companion to approach his side. A large black ball, which at first seemed stationary, now began to move in a manner that to the latter was inexplicable. Again the fire brightened and its glare fell more distinctly on the object. Then even Duncan knew it, by its restless and sideling attitudes, which kept the upper part of its form in constant motion, while the animal itself appeared seated, to be a bear. Though it growled loudly and fiercely, and there were instants when its glistening eyeballs might be seen, it gave no other indication of hostility. The Huron, at least, seemed assured that the intentions of this singular intruder were peaceable, for, after giving it an attentive examination, he quietly pursued his course.

Duncan, who knew that the animal was often found domesticated among the Indians, followed the example of his companion, believing that some favourite of the tribe had found its way into the thicket in search of food. They passed it unmolested. Though obliged to come nearly in contact with the monster, the Huron, who had at first so warily determined the character of his strange visitor, was now content with proceeding without wasting a moment in further examination; but Heyward was unable to prevent his eyes from looking backward in a sort of salutary watchfulness against attacks in the rear. His uneasiness was in no degree diminished, when he perceived the beast rolling along their path, and following their footsteps. He would have spoken, but the Indian at that moment shoved aside a door of bark, and entered a cavern in the bosom of the mountain.

Profiting by so easy a method of retreat, Duncan stepped after him, and was gladly closing the slight cover to the opening, when he felt it drawn from his hand by the beast, whose shaggy form immediately darkened the passage. They were now in a straight and long gallery, in a chasm of the rocks, where retreat, without encountering the animal, was impossible.

A single look was sufficient to apprize the pretended leech that the invalid was far beyond his powers of healing. She lay in a sort of paralysis, indifferent to the objects which crowded before her sight, and happily unconscious of suffering. Heyward was far from regretting that his mummeries were to be performed on one who was much too ill to take an interest in their failure or success. The slight qualm of conscience which had been excited by the intended deception was instantly appeased at the sight, and he began busily to collect his thoughts, in order to enact his part with suitable spirit, when he found he was about to be anticipated in his skill by an attempt to prove the power of music.

Gamut, who had stood prepared to pour forth his spirit in song when the visitors entered, after delaying a moment, drew a strain from his pipe, and commenced a hymn that might have worked a miracle, had faith in its efficacy been of much avail. He was allowed to proceed to the close, the Indians respecting his imaginary infirmity, and Duncan too glad of the delay to hazard the slightest interruption. As the dying cadence of his strains was falling on the ears of the latter, he started aside at hearing them repeated behind him, in a voice half human and half sepulchral. Looking around, he beheld the shaggy monster seated on end, in a shadow of the cavern, where, while his restless body swung in the uneasy manner of the animal, it repeated, in a sort of low growl, sounds, if not words, which bore some slight resemblance to the melody of the singer.

The effect of so strange an echo on David, may better be imagined than described. His eyes opened, as if he doubted their truth; and his voice became instantly mute in excess of wonder. A deep laid scheme of communicating some important intelligence to Heyward, was driven from his recollection by an emotion which very nearly resembled fear, but which he was fain to believe was admiration. Under its influence he exclaimed aloud—"She expects you, and is at hand!" and precipitately left the cavern.

Chapter 23

THERE was a strange blending of the ridiculous with that which was solemn, in this scene. The beast still continued its rolling, and apparently untiring, movements, though its ludicrous attempt to imitate the melody of David ceased the instant the latter abandoned the field. The words of Gamut were, as has been seen, in his native tongue; and to Duncan they seemed pregnant with some hidden meaning, though nothing present assisted him in discovering the object of their allusion. A speedy end was, however, put to every conjecture on the subject, by the manner of the chief, who advanced to the bedside of the invalid, and beckoned away the whole group of female attendants that had clustered there in lively curiosity to witness the skill of the stranger. He was implicitly, though reluctantly, obeyed; and when the low echo which rang along the hollow, natural gallery, from the distant closing door, had ceased, pointing towards his insensible daughter, he said—

"Now let my brother show his power."

Thus unequivocally called on to exercise the functions of his assumed character, Heyward was apprehensive that the smallest delay might prove dangerous. Endeavouring then to collect his ideas, he prepared to commence that species of incantation, and those uncouth rites, under which the Indian conjurers are accustomed to conceal their actual ignorance and impotency. It is more than probable, that, in the disordered state of his thoughts, he would soon have fallen into some suspicious, if not fatal error, had not his incipient attempts been interrupted by a fierce growl from the quadruped. Three several times did he renew his efforts to proceed, and as often was he met by the same unaccountable opposition, each interruption seeming more savage and threatening than the preceding.

"The cunning ones are jealous," said the Huron; "I go. Brother, the woman is the wife of one of my bravest young men; deal justly by her. Peace," he added, beckoning to the discontented beast to be quiet: "I go."

The chief was instantly as good as his word, and Duncan now found himself alone in that wild and desolate abode with the helpless invalid, and the fierce and dangerous brute. The latter listened to the movements of the Indian with that air of sagacity that a bear is known to possess, until another echo announced that he had also left the cavern, when it turned and came waddling up to Duncan, before whom it seated itself in its natural attitude, erect like a man. The youth looked anxiously about him for some weapon, with which he might make resistance worthy of his reputation, against the attack he now seriously expected.

It seemed, however, as if the humour of the animal had suddenly changed. Instead of continuing its discontented growls, or manifesting any further signs of anger, the whole of its shaggy body shook violently, as though it were agitated by some strange internal convulsion. The huge and unwieldy talons pawed stupidly about the grinning muzzle, and while Heyward kept his eyes riveted on its movements with jealous watchfulness, the grim head fell on one side, and in its place appeared the honest, sturdy countenance of the scout, who was indulging, from the bottom of his soul, in his own peculiar expression of merriment.

"Hist!" said the wary woodsman, interrupting Heyward's exclamation of surprise; "the varlets are about the place, and any sounds that are not natural to witchcraft, would bring them back upon us in a body!"

"Tell me the meaning of this masquerade; and why you have attempted so desperate an adventure?"

"Ah! reason and calculation are often outdone by accident," returned the scout. "But as a story should always commence at the beginning, I will tell you the whole in order. After we parted, I placed the Commandant and the Sagamore in an old beaver lodge, where they are safer from the Hurons than they would be in the garrison of Edward; for your high nor-west Indians, not having as yet got the traders much among them, continue to venerate the beaver. After which, Uncas and I pushed for the other encampment, as was agreed; have you seen the lad?"

"To my great grief!—he is captive, and condemned to die at the rising of the sun."

"I had misgivings that such would be his fate," resumed the scout, in a less confident and joyous tone. But soon regaining his naturally firm voice, he continued—"His bad fortune is the true reason of my being here, for it would never do to abandon such a boy to the Hurons! A rare time the knaves would have of it, could they tie the 'bounding elk' and the 'longue carabine,' as they call me, to the same stake! Though why they have given me such a name I never knew, there being as little likeness between the gifts of 'kill-deer' and the performance of one of your real Canada carabynes, as there is between the natur of a pipe-stone and a flint!"

"Keep to your tale," said the impatient Heyward; "we know not at what moment the Hurons may return."

"No fear of them. A conjurer must have his time, like a straggling priest in the settlements. We are as safe from interruption, as a missionary would be at the beginning of a two hours' discourse. Well, Uncas and I fell in with a return party of the varlets; the lad was much too forward for a scout; nay, for that matter, being of hot blood, he was not so much to blame; and, after all, one of the Hurons proved a coward, and in fleeing, led him into an ambushment."

"And dearly has he paid for his weakness!" exclaimed Duncan.

The scout significantly passed his hand across his own throat, and nodded, as if he said, "I comprehend your meaning." After which, he continued, in a more audible, though scarcely more intelligible language—

100

"After the loss of the boy, I turned upon the Hurons, as you may judge, myself; but that is neither here nor there. So, after I had shot the imps, I got in pretty nigh to the lodges without further commotion. Then, what should luck do in my favour, but lead me to the very spot where one of the most famous conjurers of the tribe was dressing himself, as I well knew, for some great battle with Satan—though why should I call that luck, which it now seems was an especial ordering of Providence? So, a judgematical rap over the head stiffened the lying imposture for a time, and leaving him a bit of walnut for his supper, to prevent any uproar, and stringing him up atween two saplings, I made free with his finery, and took the part of a bear on myself, in order that the operations might proceed."

"And admirably did you enact the character! the animal itself might have been shamed by the representation."

"Lord, major," returned the flattered woodsman. "I should be but a poor scholar, for one who has studied so long in the wilderness, did I not know how to set forth the movements and natur of such a beast! Had it been now a cat-o'-mount, or even a full sized painter, I would have embellished a performance for you worth regarding! But it is no such marvellous feat to exhibit the feats of so dull a beast; though, for that matter, too, a bear may be overacted! Yes, yes; it is not every imitator that knows natur may be outdone easier than she is equalled. But all our work is yet before us! where is the gentle one?"

"Heaven knows! I have examined every lodge in the village without discovering the slightest trace of her presence in the tribe."

"You heard what the singer said, as he left us—'she is at hand, and expects you.'"

"I have been compelled to believe he alluded to this unhappy woman."

"The simpleton was frightened, and blundered through his message, but he had a deeper meaning; here are walls enough to divide whole settlements. A bear ought to climb; therefore will I take a look above them. There may be honey-pots hid in these rocks, and I am a beast, you know, that has a hankering for the sweets."

The scout looked behind him, laughing at his own conceit, while he clambered up the partition, imitating, as he went, the clumsy motions of the beast he represented; but the instant the summit was gained, he made a gesture for silence, and slid down with the utmost precipitation.

"She is here," he whispered, "and by that door you will find her. I would have spoken a word of comfort to the afflicted soul, but the sight of such a monster might well upset her reason. Though, for that matter, major, you are none of the most inviting yourself in your paint."

Duncan, who had already sprung eagerly forward, drew instantly back on hearing these discouraging words.

"Am I then so very revolting?" he demanded, with an air of manifest chagrin.

"You might not startle a wolf, or turn the Royal Americans from a
101

charge; but I have seen the time when you had a better favoured look, Major," returned the scout, drily; "your streaked countenances are not ill judged of by the squaws, but young women of white blood give the preference to their own colour. See," he added, pointing to a place where the water trickled from a rock, forming a little crystal spring, before it found an issue through the adjacent crevices; "you may easily get rid of the Sagamore's daub, and when you come back, I will try my hand at a new embellishment. 'Tis as common for a conjurer to alter his paint, as for a buck in the settlements to change his finery."

The deliberate woodsman had little occasion to hunt for arguments to enforce his advice. He was yet speaking, when Duncan availed himself of the water. In a moment, every frightful or offensive mark was obliterated, and the youth appeared again in the fine and polished lineaments with which he had been gifted by nature. Thus prepared for an interview with his mistress, he took a hasty leave of his companion, and disappeared through the indicated passage.

Duncan had no other guide than a distant glimmering light, which served, however, the office of a polar to the lover. By its aid he was enabled to enter the haven of his hopes, which was merely another apartment of the cavern, that had been solely appropriated to the safe keeping of so important a prisoner as a daughter of the commandant of William Henry. It was profusely strewed with the plunder of that unlucky fortress. In the midst of this confusion, he found the maiden, pale, anxious, and terrified, but still lovely. David had prepared her for such a visit.

"Duncan!" she exclaimed, in a voice that seemed to tremble at the sounds created by itself.

"Alice!" he answered, leaping carelessly among trunks, boxes, arms, and furniture, until he stood at her side.

"I knew, Duncan, that you would never desert me," she said, looking up with a momentary glow of pleasure beaming on her otherwise dejected countenance. "But you are alone! grateful as it is to be thus remembered, I could wish to think you are not entirely alone!"

Duncan, observing that she trembled in a manner which betrayed an inability to continue standing, gently induced her to be seated, while he recounted those leading incidents which it has been our task to record. Alice listened with breathless interest; and though the young man touched lightly on the sorrows of the stricken father; taking care, however, not to wound the self-love of his auditor, the tears ran as freely down the cheeks of the daughter, as though she had never wept before. The soothing tenderness of Duncan, however, soon quieted the first burst of her emotions, and she then heard him to the close with undivided attention, if not with composure.

"And now, Alice," he added, "you will see how much is still expected of you. By the assistance of our experienced and invaluable friend, the scout, we may find our way from this savage people, but you will have to exert your utmost fortitude. Remember that you fly to the arms of your venerable parent, and how much his happiness as well as your own, depends on those exertions."

"Can I do otherwise for a father who has done so much for me?"

"And for me too!" continued the youth, gently pressing the hand he held in both his own.

The look of innocence and surprise which he received, in return, convinced Duncan of the necessity of being more explicit.

"This is neither the place nor the occasion to detain youth with selfish wishes, sweet Alice," he added; "but what heart loaded like mine would not wish to cast its burthen? They say misery is the closest of all ties: our common suffering in your behalf left but little to be explained between your father and myself."

"And dearest Cora, Duncan; surely Cora was not forgotten?"

"Not forgotten! no; regretted as woman was seldom mourned before. Your venerable father knew no difference between his children; but I—Alice, you will not be offended, when I say, that to me her worth was in a degree obscured—"

"Then you knew not the merit of my sister," said Alice, withdrawing her hand; "of you she ever speaks as of one who is her dearest friend!"

"I would gladly believe her such," returned Duncan hastily; "I could wish her to be even more; but with you, Alice, I have the permission of your father to aspire to a still nearer and dearer tie."

The maiden trembled violently, and there was an instant, during which she bent her face aside, yielding to the emotions common to her sensitive sex; but they quickly passed away, leaving her completely mistress of her deportment, if not of her affections.

"Heyward," she said, looking him full in the eye, with a touching expression of innocence and dependency, "give me the sacred presence and the holy sanction of that parent, before you urge me father."

"Though more I should not, less I could not say," the youth was about to answer, when he was interrupted by a light tap on his shoulder. Starting to his feet, he turned, and confronting the intruder, his looks fell on the dark form and malignant visage of Magua. The deep, guttural laugh of the savage, sounded at such a moment, to Duncan, like the hellish taunt of a demon. Had he pursued the sudden and fierce impulse of the instant, he would have cast himself on the Huron, and committed their fortunes to the issue of a deadly struggle. But, without arms of any description, ignorant of what succours his subtle enemy could command, and charged with the safety of one who was just then dearer than ever to his heart, he no sooner entertained, than he abandoned the desperate intention.

"What is your purpose?" said Alice, meekly folding her arms on her bosom, and struggling to conceal an agony of apprehension in behalf of Heyward, in the usual cold and distant manner with which she received the visits of her captor.

The exulting Indian had resumed his austere countenance, though he drew warily back before the menacing glance of the young man's fiery eye. He regarded both his captives for a moment with a steady look, and then stepping aside, he dropped a log of wood across a door different from that by which Duncan had entered. The latter now comprehended the manner of his surprise, and believing himself irretrievably lost, he drew Alice to his bosom, and stood prepared to meet a fate which he hardly regretted, since it was to be suffered in such company. But Magua meditated no immediate violence. His first measures were very evidently taken to secure his new captive; nor did he even bestow a second glance at the motionless forms in the centre of the cavern, until he had completely cut off every hope of retreat through the private outlet he had himself used. He was watched in all his movements by Heyward, who, however, remained firm, still folding the fragile form of Alice to his heart, at once too proud and too hopeless to ask favour of an enemy, so often foiled. When Magua had effected his object, he approached his prisoners, and said, in English—

"The pale faces trap the cunning beavers; but red-skins know how to take the Yengeese!"

"Huron, do your worst!" exclaimed the excited Heyward, forgetful that a double stake was involved in his life; "you and your vengeance are alike despised."

"Will the white man speak these words at the stake?" asked Magua; manifesting, at the same time, how little faith he had in the other's resolution, by the sneer that accompanied his words.

"Here, singly to your face," continued the undaunted Heyward, "or in the presence of your assembled nation!"

"Le Renard Subtil is a great chief!" returned the Indian; "he will go and bring his young men, to see how bravely a pale-face can laugh at the tortures."

He turned away while speaking, and was about to leave the place through the avenue by which Duncan had approached, when a low menacing growl caught his ear, and caused him to hesitate. The figure of the bear appeared in the doorway, where it sat, rolling from side to side, in its customary restlessness. Magua, like the father of the sick woman, eyed it keenly for a moment, as if to ascertain its character. He was far above the more vulgar superstitions of his tribe, and so soon as he recognised the well known attire of the conjurer, he prepared to pass it in cool contempt. But a louder and more threatening growl caused him again to pause. Then he seemed as if suddenly resolved to trifle no longer, and moved resolutely forward. The mimic animal which had advanced a little, retired slowly in his front, until it arrived again at the pass, when, rearing on its hinder legs, it beat the air with its paws, in the manner practised by its more brutal prototype.

"Fool!" exclaimed the chief, in Huron, "go play with the children and squaws; leave men to their wisdom."

He once more endeavoured to pass the supposed empiric, scorning even the parade of threatening to use the keen knife, or glittering tomahawk,

104

that was pendant from his belt. Suddenly, the beast extended its arms, or rather legs, and enclosed him in a grasp, that might have vied with the far-famed power of the "bear's hug" itself. Heyward had watched the whole procedure on the part of Hawk-eye, with breathless interest. At first he relinquished his hold of Alice; then he caught up a thong of buckskin, which had been used around some bundle, and when he beheld his enemy with his two arms pinned to his side, by the iron muscles of the scout, he rushed upon him, and effectually secured them there. Arms, legs, and feet were encircled in twenty folds of the thong, in less time than we have taken to record the circumstance. When the formidable Huron was completely pinioned, the scout released his hold, and Duncan laid his enemy on his back, utterly helpless.

Throughout the whole of this sudden and extraordinary operation, Magua, though he had struggled violently, until assured he was in the hands of one whose nerves were far better strung than his own, had not uttered the slightest exclamation. But when Hawk-eye, by way of making a summary explanation of his conduct, removed the shaggy jaws of the beast, and exposed his own rugged and earnest countenance to the gaze of the Huron, the philosophy of the latter was so far mastered, as to permit him to utter the never failing—

"Hugh!"

"Ay! you've found your tongue!" said his undisturbed conqueror; "now, in order that you shall not use it to our ruin, I must make free to stop your mouth."

As there was no time to be lost, the scout immediately set about effecting so necessary a precaution; and when he had gagged the Indian, his enemy might safely have been considered as "hors de combat."

"By what place did the imp enter?" asked the industrious scout, when his work was ended. "Not a soul has passed my way since you left me."

Duncan pointed out the door by which Magua had come, and which now presented too many obstacles to a quick retreat.

"Bring on the gentle one then," continued his friend; "we must make a push for the woods by the other outlet."

"'Tis impossible!" said Duncan; "fear has overcome her, and she is helpless. Alice! my sweet, my own Alice, arouse yourself; now is the moment to fly. 'Tis in vain, she hears, but is unable to follow. Go, noble and worthy friend; save yourself, and leave me to my fate!"

"Every trail has its end, and every calamity brings its lesson!" returned the scout. "There, wrap her in them Indian clothes. Conceal all of her little form. Nay, that foot has no fellow in the wilderness, it will betray her. All, every part. Now take her in your arms, and follow. Leave the rest to me."

Duncan, as may be gathered from the words of his companion, was eagerly obeying; and as the other finished speaking, he took the light person of Alice in his arms, and followed on the footsteps of the scout. They found the sick woman as they had left her, still alone, and passed swiftly on, by the natural gallery, to the place of entrance. As they approached the little door of bark, a murmur of voices without announced that the friends and relatives of the invalid were gathered about the place, patiently awaiting a summons to re-enter.

"If I open my lips to speak," Hawk-eye whispered, "my English, which is the genuine tongue of a whiteskin, will tell the varlets that an enemy is among them. You must give 'em your jargon, major, and say that we have shut the evil spirits in the cave, and are taking the woman to the woods, in order to find strengthening roots. Practise all your cunning, for it is a lawful undertaking."

The door opened a little, as if one without was listening to the proceedings within, and compelled the scout to cease his directions. A fierce growl instantly repelled the eavesdropper, and then the scout boldly threw open the covering of bark, and left the place enacting the character of the bear as he proceeded. Duncan kept close at his heels, and soon found himself in the centre of a cluster of twenty anxious relatives and friends.

The crowd fell back a little, and permitted the father, and one who appeared to be the husband of the woman, to approach.

"Has my brother driven away the evil spirit?" demanded the former. "What has he in his arms?"

"Thy child," returned Duncan, gravely, "the disease has gone out of her; it is shut up in the rocks. I take the woman to a distance where I will strengthen her against any further attacks. She shall be in the wigwam of the young man when the sun comes again."

Hawk-eye well knew the value of time in the present emergency. Whatever might be the extent of the self-delusion of his enemies, and however it had tended to assist his schemes, the slightest cause of suspicion, acting on the subtle nature of an Indian, would be likely to prove fatal. Taking the path, therefore, that was most likely to avoid observation, he rather skirted than entered the village.

Alice revived under the renovating influence of the open air, and as her physical rather than her mental powers had been the subject of her weakness, she stood in no need of any explanation of that which had occurred.

"Now let me make an effort to walk," she said, when they had entered the forest, blushing, though unseen, that she had not been sooner able to quit the arms of Duncan. "I am, indeed, restored."

"Nay, Alice, you are yet too weak."

The maiden struggled gently to release herself, and the reluctant Heyward was compelled to part with his precious burthen. The representative of the bear had certainly been an entire stranger to the delicious emotions of the lover, while his arms encircled his mistress, and he was, perhaps, a stranger also to the nature of that feeling of ingenuous shame, that oppressed the trembling Alice, as they made such diligent progress in their flight. But when he found himself at a suitable distance from the

106

lodges, he made a halt, and spoke on a subject of which he was thoroughly the master—

"This path will lead you to the brook," he said; "follow its northern bank until you come to a fall; mount the hill on your right, and you will see the fires of the other people. There you must go, and demand protection; if they are true Delawares, you will be safe. A distant flight with that gentle one, just now, is impossible. The Hurons would follow up our trail, and master our scalps, before we had got a dozen miles. Go, and providence be with you!"

"And you!" demanded Heyward, in surprise; "surely we part not here!"

"The Hurons hold the pride of the Delawares; the last of the high blood of the Mohicans is in their power!" returned the scout; "I go to see what can be done in his favour. Had they mastered your scalp, major, a knave should have fallen for every hair it held, as I promised; but if the young Sagamore is to be led to the stake the Indians shall see also how a man without a cross can die!"

Duncan released his hold on the arm of the scout, who turned, and steadily retraced his steps towards the lodges. After pausing a moment to gaze at his retiring form, the successful and yet sorrowful Heyward, and his mistress, took their way together towards the distant village of the Delawares.

Chapter 24

Bot. Let me play the lion too.
Midsummer-Night's Dream.

NOTWITHSTANDING the high resolution of Hawk-eye, he fully comprehended all the difficulties and dangers he was about to incur. In his return to the camp, his acute and practised intellects were intently engaged in devising means to counteract a watchfulness and suspicion on the part of his enemies, that he knew were in no degree inferior to his own.

As he approached the buildings, his steps became more deliberate, and his vigilant eye suffered no sign, whether friendly or hostile, to escape him. A neglected hut was a little in advance of the others, and appeared as though it had been deserted when half completed—most probably on account of failing in some of the more important requisites; such as of wood or water. A faint light glimmered through its cracks, however, and announced, that notwithstanding its imperfect structure, it was not now without a tenant. Thither, then, the scout proceeded, like a prudent general, who was about to feel the advanced positions of his enemy, before he hazarded his main attack.

Throwing himself into a suitable posture for the beast he represented, Hawk-eye crawled to a little opening, where he might command a view of the interior. It proved to be the abiding place of David Gamut.

First making the circuit of the hut, and ascertaining that it stood quite alone, and that the character of its inmate was likely to protect it from visitors, he ventured through its low door, into the very presence of Gamut. The position of the latter brought the fire between them; and when Hawk-eye had seated himself on end, near a minute elapsed, during which the two remained regarding each other without speaking. The suddenness and the nature of the surprise, had nearly proved too much for —we will not say the philosophy—but for the faith and resolution of David. He fumbled for his pitch-pipe, and arose with a confused intention of attempting a musical exorcism.

"Dark and mysterious monster!" he exclaimed, while with trembling hands he disposed of his auxiliary eyes, and sought his never failing resource in trouble, the gifted version of the Psalms; "I know not your nature or intents; but if aught you meditate against the person and rights of one of the humblest servants of the temple, listen to the inspired language of the youth of Israel, and repent."

The bear shook his shaggy sides in an inexplicable emotion, and then a well-known voice replied—

"Put up your tooting we'pon, and teach your throat modesty. Five words of plain and comprehensible English, are worth, just now, an hour of squalling."

"What art thou?" demanded David, utterly disqualified to pursue his original intention, and nearly gasping for breath.

"A man like yourself; and one whose blood is as little tainted by the cross of a bear as your own. Have you so soon forgotten from whom you received the foolish instrument you hold in your hand?"

"Can these things be?" returned David, breathing more freely, as the truth began to dawn upon him. "I have found many marvels during my sojourn with the heathen, but, surely, nothing to excel this!"

"Come, come," returned Hawk-eye, uncasing his honest countenance, the better to assure the wavering confidence of his companion; "you may see a skin, which, if it be not as white as one of the gentle ones, has no tinge of red on it that the winds of the heaven and the sun have not bestowed. Now let us to business."

"First tell me of the maiden, and of the youth who so bravely sought her," interrupted David.

"Ay, they are happily freed from the tomahawks of these varlets! But can you put me on the scent of Uncas?"

"The young man is in bondage, and much I fear his death is decreed. I greatly mourn that one so well disposed should die in his ignorance, and I have sought a goodly hymn——"

"Can you lead me to him?"

"The task will not be difficult," returned David, hesitating; "though I greatly fear your presence would rather increase than mitigate his unhappy fortunes."

"No more words, but lead on," returned Hawk-eye, concealing his face again, and setting the example in his own person, by instantly quitting the lodge.

As they proceeded, the scout ascertained that his companion found access to Uncas, under privilege of his imaginary infirmity. Aided by the favour he had acquired with one of the guards, who, in consequence of speaking a little English, had been selected by David as the subject of a religious conversion. How far the Huron comprehended the intentions of his new friend may well be doubted; but as exclusive attention is as flattering to a savage as to a more civilized individual, it had, assuredly, produced the effect we have mentioned. It is unnecessary to repeat the shrewd manner with which the scout extracted these particulars from the simple David, neither shall we dwell in this place on the nature of the instructions he delivered, when completely master of all the necessary facts, as the whole will be sufficiently explained to the reader in the course of the narrative.

The lodge in which Uncas was confined was in the very centre of the village, and in a situation, perhaps, more difficult than any other to approach or leave without observation. But it was not the policy of Hawkeye to affect the least concealment. Presuming on his disguise, and his ability to sustain the character he had assumed, he took the most plain and direct route to the place. The hour, however, afforded him some little of that protection, which he appeared so much to despise. The boys were already buried in sleep, and all the women, and most of the warriors, had now retired to their lodges for the night. Four or five of the latter, only, lingered about the door of the prison of Uncas, wary, but close observers of the manner of their captive.

At the sight of Gamut, accompanied by one in the well known masquerade of their most distinguished conjurer, they readily made a passage to the entrance. Still, they betrayed no intention to depart. On the other hand, they were evidently disposed to remain bound to the place by an additional interest in the mysterious mummeries that they, of course, expected from such a visit. From the total inability of the scout to address the Hurons in their own language, he was compelled to trust the conversation entirely to David. Notwithstanding the simplicity of the latter, he did ample justice to the instructions he had received, more than fulfilling the strongest hopes of his teacher.

"The Delawares are women!" he exclaimed, addressing himself to the savage, who had a slight understanding of the language in which he spoke; "the Yengeese, my foolish countrymen, have told them to take up the tomahawk, and strike their fathers in the Canadas, and they have forgotten their sex. Does my brother wish to hear 'le Cerf Agile' ask for his petticoats, and see him weep before the Hurons, at the stake?"

The exclamation "hugh," delivered in a strong tone of assent, announced the gratification the savage would receive, in witnessing such an exhibition of weakness in an enemy so long hated and so much feared.

"Then let him step aside, and the cunning man will blow upon the dog! Tell it to my brothers."

The Huron explained the meaning of David to his fellows, who, in their turn, listened to the project with that sort of satisfaction, that their untamed spirits might be expected to find, in such a refinement in cruelty. They drew back a little from the entrance, and motioned to the supposed conjurer to enter. But the bear, instead of obeying, maintained the seat it had taken, and growled.

"The cunning man is afraid that his breath will blow upon his brothers, and take away their courage too," continued David, improving the hint he received; "they must stand further off."

The Hurons, who would have deemed such a misfortune the heaviest calamity that could befall them, fell back in a body, maintaining a position where they were out of ear-shot, though at the same time, they could command a view of the entrance to the lodge. Then, as if satisfied of their safety, the scout left his position, and slowly entered the place. It was silent and gloomy, being tenanted solely by the captive, and lighted by the dying embers of a fire, which bad been used for the purposes of cookery.

Uncas occupied a distant corner, in a reclining attitude, being rigidly bound, both hands and feet, by strong and painful withes. When the frightful object first presented itself to the young Mohican, he did not deign to bestow a single glance on the animal. The scout who had left David at the door, to ascertain they were not observed, thought it prudent to preserve his disguise until assured of their privacy. Instead of speaking, therefore, he exerted himself to enact one of the antics of the animal he represented. The young Mohican, who, at first, believed his enemies had sent in a real beast to torment him, and try his nerves, detected, in those performances that to Heyward had appeared so accurate, certain blemishes, that at once betrayed the counterfeit. Had Hawk-eye been aware of the low estimation in which the more skilful Uncas held his representations, he would, probably, have prolonged the entertainment a little in pique. But the scornful expression of the young man's eye admitted of so many constructions, that the worthy scout was spared the mortification of such a discovery. As soon, therefore, as David gave the preconcerted signal, a low hissing sound was heard in the lodge, in place of the fierce growlings of the bear.

Uncas had cast his body back against the wall of the hut, and closed his eyes, as if willing to exclude such contemptible and disagreeable objects from his sight. But the moment the noise of the serpent was heard, he arose, and cast his looks on each side of him, bending his head low, and turning it inquiringly in every direction, until his keen eye rested on the shaggy monster, where it remained riveted, as though fixed by the power of a charm. Again the same sounds were repeated, evidently proceeding from the mouth of the beast. Once more the eyes of the youth roamed over the interior of the lodge, and returning to their former resting-place, he uttered in a deep, suppressed voice, the usual exclamation—

"Hugh!"

"Cut his bands," said Hawk-eye to David, who just then approached them.

The singer did as he was ordered, and Uncas found his limbs released. At the same moment, the dried skin of the animal rattled hurriedly, and presently the scout arose to his feet in his proper person. The Mohican appeared to comprehend the nature of the attempt his friends had made, intuitively; neither tongue nor feature betrayed another symptom of surprise. When Hawk-eye had cast his shaggy vestment, which was done by simple loosing certain thongs of skin, he drew a long glittering knife, and put it in the hands of Uncas.

"The red Hurons are without," he said; "let us be ready."

At the same time, he laid his finger significantly on another similar weapon; both being the fruits of his prowess among their enemies during the evening.

"We will go!" said Uncas.

"Whither?"

"To the Tortoises—they are the children of my grandfathers!"

"Ay, lad," said the scout, in English, a language he was apt to use when a little abstracted in mind; "the same blood runs in your veins, I believe; but time and distance has a little changed its colour! What shall we do with the Mingoes at the door? They count six, and this singer is as good as nothing."

"The Hurons are boasters!" said Uncas, scornfully; "their 'totem' is a moose; and they run like snails. The Delawares are children of the tortoise; and they outstrip the deer!"

"Ay, lad, there is truth in what you say; and I doubt not, on a rush, you would pass the whole nation; and in a straight race of two miles would be in, and get your breath again, afore a knave of them all was within hearing of the other village! But the gift of a white man lies more in his arms than in his legs. As for myself, I can brain a Huron as well as a better man, but when it comes to race, the knaves would prove too much for me."

Uncas who had already approached the door, in readiness to lead the way, now recoiled, and placed himself once more in the bottom of the lodge. But Hawk-eye, who was too much occupied with his own thoughts to note the movement, continued speaking more to himself than to his companion. "After all," he said, "it is unreasonable to keep one man in bondage to the gifts of another. So, Uncas, you had better take the leap, while I will put on the skin again, and trust to cunning for want of speed."

The young Mohican made no reply, but quietly folded his arms, and leaned his body against one of the upright posts that supported the wall of the hut.

"Well," said the scout, looking up at him in some surprise, "why do you tarry? there will be time enough for me, as the knaves will give chase to you at first."

"Uncas will stay," was the calm reply.

"For what?"

"To fight with his father's brother, and die with the friend of the Delawares."

"Ay, lad," returned Hawk-eye, squeezing the hand of Uncas between his own iron fingers; "'twould have been more like a Mingo than a Mohican, had you left me. But I thought I would make the offer, seeing that youth commonly loves life. Well, what can't be done by main courage, in war, must be done by circumvention. Put on the skin—I doubt not you can play the bear nearly as well as myself."

Whatever might have been the private opinion of Uncas of their respective abilities, in this particular, his grave countenance manifested no opinion of his own superiority. He silently and expeditiously encased himself in the covering of the beast, and then awaited such other movements as his more aged companion saw fit to dictate.

"Now, friend," said Hawk-eye, addressing David, "an exchange of garments will be a great convenience to you, inasmuch as you are but little accustomed to the make-shifts of the wilderness. Here, take my hunting shirt and cap, and give me your blanket and hat. You must trust me with the book and spectacles as well as the tooter, too; if we ever meet again, in better times, you shall have all back again with many thanks in the bargain."

David parted with the several articles named with a readiness that would have done great credit to his liberality, had he not certainly profited, in many particulars, by the exchange. Hawk-eye was not long in assuming his borrowed garments; and when his keen, restless eyes were hid behind the glasses, and his head was surmounted by the triangular beaver, as their statures were not dissimilar, he might readily have passed for the singer, by starlight. As soon as these dispositions were made, the scout turned to David, and gave him his parting instructions.

"Are you much given to cowardice?" he bluntly asked, by way of obtaining a suitable understanding of the whole case, before he ventured a prescription.

"My pursuits are peaceful, and my temper, I humbly trust, is greatly given to mercy and love," returned David, a little nettled at so direct an attack on his manhood; "but there are none who can say, that I have ever forgotten my faith in the Lord, even in the greatest straits."

"Your chiefest danger will be at the moment when the savages find out that they have been deceived. If you are not then knocked on the head, your being a non-compossur will protect you, and you'll then have good reason to expect to die in your bed. If you stay, it must be to sit down here in the shadow, and take the part of Uncas, until such time as the cunning of the Indians discover the cheat, when, as I have already said, your time of trial will come. So choose for yourself, to make a rush, or tarry here."

112

"Even so," said David firmly; "I will abide in the place of the Delaware; bravely and generously has he battled in my behalf, and this and more will I dare in his service."

"You have spoken as a man, and like one, who, under wiser schooling, would have been brought to better things."

So saying, the scout shook David cordially by the hand; after which act of friendship he immediately left the lodge, attended by the new representative of the beast.

The instant Hawk-eye found himself under the observation of the Hurons, he drew up his tall form in the rigid manner of David, threw out his arm in the act of keeping time, and commenced what he intended for an imitation of his psalmody. Happily for the success of this delicate adventure, he had to deal with ears but little practised in the concord of sweet sounds, or the miserable effort would infallibly have been detected. It was necessary to pass within a dangerous proximity of the dark group of savages, and the voice of the scout grew louder as they drew nigher.

Among his actual auditors, however, it merely gave him an additional claim to that respect which they never withhold from such as are believed to be the subjects of mental alienation. The little knot of Indians drew back in a body, and suffered, as they thought, the conjurer and his inspired assistant to proceed.

It required no common exercise of fortitude in Uncas and the scout, to continue the dignified and deliberate pace they had assumed; especially, as they immediately perceived that curiosity had so far mastered fear, as to induce the watchers to approach the hut in order to witness the effect of the incantation. The least injudicious or impatient movement on the part of David might betray them, and time was absolutely necessary to insure the safety of the scout. The loud noise the latter conceived it politic to continue, drew many curious gazers to the doors of the different huts as they passed; and once or twice a dark looking warrior stepped across their path, led to the act by superstition or watchfulness. They were not, however, interrupted; the darkness of the hour, and the boldness of the attempt, proving their principal friends.

The adventurers had got clear of the village, and were now swiftly approaching the shelter of the woods, when a loud and long cry arose from the lodge where Uncas had been confined. The Mohican started on his feet and shook his shaggy covering, as though the animal he counterfeited was about to make some desperate effort.

"Hold!" said the scout, grasping his friend by the shoulder, "let them yell again! 'Twas nothing but their wonderment."

He had no occasion to delay, for at the next instant a burst of cries filled the outer air, and ran along the whole extent of the village. Uncas cast his skin, and stepped forth in his own lofty and beautiful proportions. Hawk-eye tapped him lightly on the shoulder, and glided ahead.

"Now let the devils strike our scent!" said the scout, tearing two rifles, with all their attendant accoutrements, from beneath a bush, and flourishing 'kill-deer,' as he handed Uncas a weapon: "two, at least, will find it to their deaths."

Then throwing their pieces to a long-trail, like sportsmen in readiness for their game, they dashed forward, and were soon buried in the sombre darkness of the forest.

Chapter 25

> *Ant.*
> I shall remember;
> When Cæsar says, *do this,* it is performed.
> *Julius Cæsar.*

THE impatience of the savages who lingered about the prison of Uncas, as has been seen, had overcome their dread of the conjurer's breath. They stole cautiously, and with beating hearts, to a crevice through which the faint light of the fire was glimmering. For several minutes they mistook the form of David for that of their prisoner, but the very accident which Hawk-eye had foreseen, occurred. Tired of keeping the extremities of his long person so near together, the singer gradually suffered the lower limbs to extend themselves, until one of his misshapen feet actually came in contact with, and shoved aside, the embers of the fire. At first the Hurons believed the Delaware had been thus deformed by witchcraft; but when David, unconscious of being observed, turned his head, and exposed his simple, mild countenance, in place of the stern and haughty lineaments of their prisoner, it would have exceeded the credulity of even a native to have doubted any longer. They rushed together into the lodge, and laying their hands, with but little ceremony, on their captive, immediately detected the imposition. Then arose the cry first heard by the fugitives. It was succeeded by the most frantic and angry demonstration of vengeance. David, however firm in his determination to cover the retreat of his friends, was now compelled to believe that his own final hour had come. Deprived of his book and his pipe, he was fain to trust to a memory that rarely failed him on such subjects, and, breaking forth in a loud and impassioned strain, he endeavoured to smooth his passage into the other world by singing the opening verse of a funeral anthem. The Indians were seasonably reminded of his infirmity, and, rushing into the open air, they aroused the village in the manner described.

A native warrior fights as he sleeps, without the protection of any thing defensive. The sounds of the alarm were, therefore, hardly uttered, before two hundred men were afoot, and ready for the battle or the chase, as either might be required. The escape was soon known, and the whole tribe crowded in a body around the council lodge, impatiently awaiting the instruction of their chiefs. In such a sudden demand on their wisdom, the presence of the cunning Magua could scarcely fail of being needed. His name was mentioned, and all looked round in wonder that he did not appear. Messengers were then dispatched to his lodge requiring his presence.

In the mean time, some of the swiftest and most discreet of the young men were ordered to make the circuit of the clearing, under cover of the woods, in order to ascertain that their suspected neighbours, the Delawares, designed no mischief.

The clamour of many voices soon announced that a party approached, who might be expected to communicate some intelligence that would explain the mystery of the novel surprise. The crowd without gave way, and several warriors entered the place, bringing with them the hapless conjurer, who had been left so long by the scout in such a painful duresse.

Notwithstanding this man was held in very unequal estimation among the Hurons, some believing implicitly in his power, and others deeming him an impostor, he was now listened to by all with the deepest attention. When his brief story was ended, the father of the sick woman stepped forth, and in a few pithy expressions, related, in his turn, what he knew. These two narratives gave a proper direction to the subsequent inquiries, which were now made with the characteristic gravity and cunning of the savages.

Instead of rushing in a confused and disorderly throng to the cavern, ten of the wisest and firmest among the chiefs were selected to prosecute the investigation. As no time was to be lost, the instant the choice was made, the individuals appointed rose, in a body, and left the place without speaking. On reaching the entrance, the younger men in advance made way for their seniors, and the whole proceeded along the low, dark gallery, with the firmness of warriors ready to devote themselves to the public good, though, at the same time, secretly doubting the nature of the power with which they were about to contend.

The outer apartment of the cavern was silent and gloomy. The woman lay in her usual place and posture, though there were those present who had just affirmed they had seen her borne to the woods, by the supposed "medicine of the white men." Such a direct and palpable contradiction of the tale related by the father, caused all eyes to be turned upon him. Chafed by the silent imputation, and inwardly troubled by so unaccountable a circumstance, the chief advanced to the side of the bed, and stooping, cast an incredulous look at the features as if still distrusting their reality. His daughter was dead.

The unerring feeling of nature for a moment prevailed, and the old warrior hid his eyes in sorrow and disappointment. Then recovering his self-possession, he faced his companions, and pointing towards the corpse, he said, in the language of his people—

"The wife of my young man has left us! the Great Spirit is angry with his children."

The mournful intelligence was received in solemn silence. After a short pause, one of the elder Indians was about to speak, when a dark looking object was seen rolling out of an adjoining apartment into the very centre of the room where they stood. Ignorant of the nature of the beings they had to deal with, the whole party drew back a little, and gazed in admiration, until the object fronted the light, and rising frightfully on end, exhibited the distorted, but still fierce and sullen, features of Magua. The discovery was succeeded by a loud and general exclamation of amazement.

As soon, however, as the true situation of the chief was understood, several ready knives appeared, and his limbs and tongue were quickly released. The Huron arose, and shook himself like a lion quitting his lair. Not a word escaped him, though his hand played convulsively with the handle of his knife, while his lowering eyes scanned the whole party as if they sought an object suited to the first burst of his vengeance.

It was happy for Uncas and the scout, and even David, that they were all beyond the reach of his arm at such a moment, for assuredly, no refinement in cruelty would then have deferred their deaths, in opposition to the promptings of the fierce temper that nearly choked him. Meeting every where faces that he knew as friends, the savage grated his teeth together, like rasps of iron, and swallowed his passion, for want of a victim on whom to vent it. This exhibition of anger was keenly noted by all present; and, from an apprehension of exasperating a temper that was already chafed neraly to madness, several minutes were suffered to pass before another word was uttered. When, however, suitable time had elapsed, the oldest of the party spoke.

"My friend has found an enemy!" he said. "Is he nigh, that the Hurons may take revenge?"

"Let the Delaware die!" exclaimed Magua, in a voice of thunder.

Another long and expressive silence was observed, and was broken, as before, with due precaution, by the same individual.

"The Mohican is swift of foot, and leaps far," he said; "but my young men are on his trail."

"Is he gone?" demanded Magua, in tones so deep and guttural, that they seemed to proceed from his inmost chest.

"An evil spirit has been among us, and the Delaware had blinded our eyes."

"An evil spirit!" repeated the other bitterly; "tis the spirit that has taken the lives of so many Hurons. The spirit that slew my young men at the 'tumbling river'; that took their scalps at the 'healing spring,' and who has, now, bound the arms of le Renard Subtil!"

"Of whom does my friend speak?"

"Of the dog who carries the heart and cunning of a Huron under a pale skin—la Longue Carabine."

The pronunciation of so terrible a name produced the usual effect among his auditors. But when time was given for reflection, and the warriors remembered that their formidable and daring enemy had even been in the bosom of their encampment, working injury, fearful rage took the place of wonder, and all those fierce passions with which the bosom of Magua had just been struggling, were suddenly transferred to his companions. Some

116

among them gnashed their teeth in anger, others vented their feelings in yells, and some, again, beat the air as franticly, as if the object of their resentment was suffering under their blows. But this sudden outbreaking of temper, as quickly subsided in the still and sullen restraint they most affected in their moments of inaction.

Magua, who had, in his turn, found leisure for a little reflection, now changed his manner, and assumed the air of one who knew how to think and act with a dignity worthy of so grave a subject.

"Let us go to my people," he said; "they wait for us."

His companions consented, in silence, and the whole of the savage party left the cavern, and returned to the council lodge. When they were seated, all their eyes turned on Magua, who understood, from such an indication, that, by common consent, they had devolved the duty of relating what had passed on him. He arose, and told his tale without duplicity or reservation. The whole deception practised by both Duncan and Hawk-eye was, of course, laid naked; and no room was found, even for the most superstitious of the tribe, any longer to affix a doubt on the character of the occurrences. It was but too apparent, that they had been insultingly, shamefully, disgracefully deceived. When he had ended, and resumed his seat, the collected tribe—for his auditors, in substance, included all the fighting men of the party—sat regarding each other like men astonished equally at the audacity and the success of their enemies. The next consideration, however, was the means and opportunities for revenge.

Additional pursuers were sent on the trail of the fugitives; and then the chiefs applied themselves in earnest to the business of consultation. Many different expedients were proposed by the elder warriors, in succession, to all of which Magua was a silent and respectful listener. That subtle savage had recovered his artifice and self-command, and now proceeded towards his object with his customary caution and skill. It was only when each one disposed to speak had uttered his sentiments, that he prepared to advance his own opinions.

He commenced, by flattering the self-love of his auditors, a neverfailing method of commanding attention. When he had enumerated the many different occasions on which the Hurons had exhibited their courage and prowess, in the punishment of insults, he digressed in a high encomium on the virtue of wisdom. He painted the quality, as forming the great point of difference between the beaver and other brutes; between brutes and men; and finally, between the Hurons, in particular, and the rest of the human race. After he had sufficiently extolled the property of discretion, he undertook to exhibit in what manner its use was applicable to the present situation of their tribe.

In this happy state of things, it is not surprising that the management of Magua prevailed. The tribe consented to act with deliberation, and with one voice they committed the direction of the whole affair to the government of the chief, who had suggested such wise and intelligible expedients.

Magua had now obtained one great object of all his counning and enterprise. The ground he had lost in the favour of his people was completely regained, and he found himself even placed at the head of affairs. He was, in truth, their ruler; and so long as he could maintain his popularity no monarch could be more despotic, especially while the tribe continued in a hostile country. Throwing off, therefore, the appearance of consultation, he assumed the grave air of authority, necessary to support the dignity of his office.

Runners were dispatched for intelligence in different directions; spies were ordered to approach and feel the encampment of the Delawares; the warriors were dismissed to their lodges; with an intimation that their services would soon be needed; and the women and children were ordered to retire, with a warning that it was their province to be silent. When these several arrangements were made, Magua passed through the village, stopping here and there to pay a visit where he thought the presence might be flattering to the individual. He confirmed his friends in their confidence; fixed the wavering; and gratified all. Then he sought his own lodge. The wife the Huron chief had abandoned, when he was chased from among his people, was dead. Children he had none; and he now occupied a hut, without companion of any sort. It was, in fact, the dilapidated and solitary structure in which David had been discovered, and whom he had tolerated in his presence, on those few occasions when they met, with the contemptuous indifference of a haughty superiority.

Long before the day dawned, however, warrior after warrior entered the solitary hut of Magua, until they had collected to the number of twenty. Each bore his rifle, and all the other accoutrements of war; though the paint was uniformly peaceful. The entrance of these fierce looking beings was unnoticed; some seating themselves in the shadows of the place, and others standing like motionless statues, in profound silence, until the whole of the designated band was collected.

Then Magua arose, and gave the signal to proceed, marching himself in advance. They followed their leader singly, and in that well known order, which has obtained the distinguishing appellation of "Indian file." Unlike other men engaged in the spirit-stirring business of war, they stole from their camp, unostentatiously and unobserved, resembling a band of gliding spectres, more than warriors seeking the bubble reputation by deeds of desperate daring.

Instead of taking the path which led directly towards the camp of the Delawares, Magua led his party for some distance down the windings of the stream, and along the little artificial lake of the beavers. The day began to dawn as they entered the clearing, which had been formed by those sagacious and industrious animals. Though Magua, who had resumed his ancient garb, bore the outline of a fox, on the dressed skin which formed his robe, there was one chief of his party who carried the beaver as his peculiar symbol, or "totem." There would have been a species of profanity in the omission, had this man passed so powerful a community of his fancied kindred, without bestowing some evidence of his regard. Accordingly, he paused, and spoke in words as kind and friendly, as if he were addressing more intelligent beings. He called the animals his cousins, and reminded them that his protecting influence was the reason they remained unharmed, while so many avaricious traders were prompting the Indians to take their lives. He promised a continuance of his favours, and admonished them to be grateful. After which he spoke of the expedition in which he was himself engaged, and intimated, though with sufficient delicacy and circumlocution, the expediency of bestowing on their relative a portion of that wisdom for which they were so renowned.

During the utterance of this extraordinary address, the companions of the speaker were as grave and as attentive to his language, as though they were all equally impressed with its propriety. Once or twice, black objects were seen rising to the surface of the water, and the Huron expressed pleasure, conceiving that his words were not bestowed in vain. Just as he had ended his address, the head of a large beaver was thrust from the door of a lodge, whose earthen wall had been much injured, and which the party had believed, from its situation, was unihabited. Such an extraordinary sign of confidence was received by the orator as a highly favourable omen; and, though the animal retreated a little precipitately, he was lavish of his thanks and commendations.

When Magua thought sufficient time had been lost, in gratifying the family affection of the warrior, he again made the signal to proceed. As the Indians moved away in a body, and with a step that would have been inaudible to the ears of any common man, the same venerable looking beaver once more ventured his head from its cover. Had any of the Hurons turned to look behind them, they would have seen the animal watching their movements with an interest and sagacity that might easily have been mistaken for reason. Indeed, so very distinct and intelligible were the devices of the quadruped, that even the most experienced observer would have been at a loss to account for its actions, until the moment when the party entered the forest, when the whole would have been explained by seeing the entire animal issue from the lodge, uncasing, by the act, the grave and attentive features of Chingachgook from his mask of fur.

Chapter 26

Brief, I pray you; for you see 'tis a busy time with me.
Much ado about Nothing.

THE tribe, or rather half-tribe, of Delawares, which has been so often mentioned, and whose present place of encampment was so nigh the temporary village of the Hurons, could assemble about an equal number of warriors with the latter people. Like their neighbours, they had followed Montcalm into the territories of the English crown, and were making heavy and serious inroads on the hunting grounds of the Mohawks, though they had seen fit, with the mysterious reserve so common among the natives, to withhold their assistance at the moment when it was most required.

On that morning when Magua led his silent party from the settlement of the beavers into the forest in the manner described, the sun arose upon the Delaware encampment, as though it had suddenly burst upon a busy people actively employed in all the customary avocations of high noon. The women ran from lodge to lodge, some engaged in preparing their morning's meal, a few earnestly bent on seeking the comforts, necessary to their habits, but more pausing to exchange hasty and whispered sentences with their friends. The warriors were lounging in groups, musing more than they conversed; and when a few words were uttered, speaking like men who deeply weighed their opinions. The instruments of the chase were to be seen in abundance among the lodges; but none departed. Here and there a warrior might be seen examining his arms, with an attention that is rarely bestowed on the implements, when no other enemy than the beasts of the forest are expected to be encountered. And, occasionally, the eyes of a whole group were turned simultaneously towards a large and silent lodge in the centre of the village, as if it contained the subject of their common thoughts.

During the existence of this scene, a man suddenly appeared at the furthest extremity of that platform of rock which formed the level of the village. He was without arms, and his paint tended rather to soften than increase the natural sternness of his austere and marked countenance. When in full view of the Delawares he stopped, and made a gesture of amity, by throwing his arm upwards towards heaven, and then letting it fall impressively on his breast. The inhabitants of the village answered his salute by a low murmur of welcome, and encouraged him to advance by similar indications of friendship. Fortified by these assurances the dark figure left the brow of the natural rocky terrace, where it had stood a moment drawn in a strong outline against the blushing morning sky, and moved, with dignity, into the very centre of the huts. As he approached, nothing was audible but the rattling of the light silver ornaments that loaded his arm and neck, and the tinkling of the little bells that fringed his deer-skin moccasins. He made, as he advanced, many courteous signs of greeting to the men he passed, neglecting to notice the women, however, as though he deemed their favour, in the present enterprise, of no importance. When he had reached the group, in which it was evident, by the haughtiness of their common mien, that the principal chiefs were collected, the stranger paused, and then the Delawares saw that the active and erect form that stood before them, was that of the well-known Huron chief, le Renard Subtil.

His reception was grave, silent, and wary. The warriors in front stepped aside, opening the way to their most approved orator by the action; one who spoke all those languages, that were cultivated among the northern aborigines.

120

"The wise Huron is welcome," said the Delaware, in the language of the Maquas: "he is come to eat his 'suc-ca-tush' with his brothers of the lakes!"

"He is come," repeated Magua, bending his head with the dignity of an eastern prince.

The chief extended his arm, and taking the other by the wrist, they once more exchanged their friendly salutations. Then the Delaware invited his guest to enter his own lodge, and share his morning meal. The invitation was accepted, and the two warriors, attended by three or four of the old men, walked calmly away, leaving the rest of the tribe devoured by a desire to understand the reasons of so unusual a visit, and yet not betraying the least impatience by any sign or syllable.

During the short and frugal repast that followed, the conversation was extremely circumspect, and related entirely to the events of the hunt, in which Magua had so lately been engaged. It would have been impossible for the most finished breeding to wear more of the appearance of considering the visit as a thing of course, than did his hosts, notwithstanding every individual present was perfectly aware that it must be connected with some secret object, and that, probably, of the last importance to themselves. When the appetites of the whole were appeased, the squaws removed the trenchers and gourds, and the two parties began to prepare themselves for a keen and subtle trial of their wits.

"Is the face of my great Canada father turned again towards his Huron children?" demanded the orator of the Delawares.

"When was it ever otherwise?" returned Magua. "He calls my people his 'most beloved.' "

The Delaware gravely bowed his acquiescence to what he knew to be false, and continued—

"The tomahawks of your young men have been very red!"

"It is so; but they are now bright and dull—for the Yengeese are dead, and the Delawares are our neighbours!"

The other acknowledged the pacific compliment by a graceful gesture of the hand, and remained silent. Then Magua, as if recalled to such a recollection, by the allusion to the massacre, demanded—

"Does my prisoner give trouble to my brothers?"

"She is welcome."

"The path between the Hurons and the Delawares is short, and it is open; let her be sent to my squaws if she gives trouble to my brother."

"She is welcome," returned the chief of the latter nation, still more emphatically.

The baffled Magua continued silent several minutes, apparently indifferent, however, to the repulse he had received in this, his opening, effort to gain possession of Cora.

"Do my young men leave the Delawares room on the mountains for their hunts?" he at length continued.

"The Lenape are rulers of their own hills," returned the other, a little haughtily.

"It is well. Justice is the master of a red-skin! Why should they brighten their tomahawks, and sharpen their knives against each other? Are there not pale-faces for enemies!"

"Good!" exclaimed two or three of his auditors at the same time.

Magua waited a little to permit his words to soften the feelings of the Delawares, before he added—

"Have there not been strange moccasins in the woods? Have not my brothers scented the feet of white men?"

"Let my Canada father come!" returned the other evasively; "his children are ready to see him."

"When the Great Chief comes, it is to smoke with the Indians, in their wigwams. The Hurons say too he is welcome. But the Yengeese have long arms, and legs that never tire! My young men dreamed they had seen the trail of the Yengeese nigh the village of the Delawares."

"They will not find the Lenape asleep."

"It is well. The warrior whose eye is open, can see his enemy," said Magua, once more shifting his ground, when he found himself unable to penetrate the caution of his companion. "I have brought gifts to my brother. His nation would not go on the war path because they did not think it well; but their friends have remembered where they lived."

When he had thus announced his liberal intention, the crafty chief arose, and gravely spread his presents before the dazzled eyes of his hosts. They consisted principally of trinkets of little value, plundered from the slaughtered and captured females of William Henry.

The Delaware, whose name, in English, signified "Hard-heart," an appellation that the French had translated into "Le-cœurdur," forgot that obduracy of purpose, which had probably obtained him so significant a title. His countenance grew very sensibly less stern, and he now deigned to answer more directly.

"There have been strange moccasins about my camp. They have been tracked into my lodges."

"Did my brother beat out the dogs?" asked Magua, without adverting in any manner to the former equivocation of the chief.

"It would not do. The stranger is always welcome to the children of the Lenape."

"The stranger, but not the spy!"

"Would the Yengeese send their women as spies? Did not the Huron chief say he took women in the battle?"

"He told no lie. The Yengeese have sent out their scouts. They have been in my wigwams, but they found there no one to say welcome. They then fled to the Delawares—for, say they, the Delawares are our friends; their minds are turned from their Canada father!"

This insinuation was a home thrust, and one that, in a more advanced state of society, would have entitled Magua to the reputation of a skilful diplomatist. The recent defection of their tribe had, as they well knew themselves, subjected the Delawares to much reproach among their French allies, and they were now made to feel that their future actions were to be regarded with jealousy and distrust. There was no deep insight into causes and effects necessary to foresee that such a situation of things was likely to prove highly prejudicial to all their future movements. Their distant villages, their hunting grounds, and hundreds of their women and children, together with a material part of their physical force, were all actually within the limits of the French territory. Accordingly, this alarming annunciation was received, as Magua intended, with manifest disapprobation, if not with alarm.

"Let my father look in my face," said Le-cœurdur; "he will see no change. It is true, my young men did not go out on the war-path; they had dreams for not doing so. But they love and venerate the great white chief."

"Will he think so, when he hears that his greatest enemy is fed in the camp of his children? When he is told, a bloody Yengee smokes at your fire! That the pale-face, who has slain so many of his friends, goes in and out among the Delawares! Go—my great Canada Father is not a fool."

"Where is the Yengee that the Delawares fear?" returned the other; "who has slain my young men? who is the mortal enemy of my great Father?"

"La Longue Carabine."

The Delaware warriors started at the well-known name, betraying, by their amazement, they now learnt, for the first time, that one so famous among the Indian allies of France, was within their power.

"What does my brother mean?" demanded Le-cœurdur, in a tone that, by its wonder, far exceeded the usual apathy of his race.

"A Huron never lies," returned Magua coldly, leaning his head against the side of the lodge, and drawing his slight robe across his tawny breast. "Let the Delawares count their prisoners: they will find one whose skin is neither red nor pale."

A long and musing pause succeeded. Then the chief consulted, apart, with his companions, and messengers were despatched to collect certain others of the most distinguished men of the tribe.

As warrior after warrior dropped in, they were each made acquainted, in turn, with the important intelligence that Magua had just communicated. The air of surprise, and the usual low, deep guttural exclamation, were common to them all. The news spread from mouth to mouth, until the whole encampment became powerfully agitated. The women suspended their labours, to catch such syllables as unguardedly fell from the lips of the consulting warriors. The boys deserted their sports, and walked fearlessly among their fathers, looked up in curious admiration, as they heard the brief exclamations of wonder they so freely expressed, at the temerity of their hated foe. In short, every occupation was abandoned, for the time; and all other pursuits seemed discarded, in order that the tribe might freely indulge, after their own peculiar manner, in an open expression of their feelings.

When the excitement had a little abated, the old men disposed themselves seriously to a consideration of that which it became the honour and safety of their tribe to perform under circumstances of so much delicacy and embarrassment. During all these movements, and in the midst of the general commotion, Magua had not only maintained his seat, but the very attitude he had originally taken, against the side of the lodge, where he continued as immovable, and apparently as unconcerned, as if he had no interest in the result. Not a single indication of the future intentions of his hosts, however, escaped his vigilant eyes. With his consummate knowledge of the nature of the people with whom he had to deal, he anticipated every measure on which they decided; and it might almost be said, that in many instances, he knew their intentions even before they became known to themselves.

The council of the Delawares was short. When it was ended, a general bustle announced that it was to be immediately succeeded by a solemn and formal assemblage of the nation. As such meetings were rare, and only called on occasions of the last importance, the subtle Huron, who still sat apart, a wily and dark observer of the proceedings, now knew that all his projects must be brought to their final issue. He therefore left the lodge, and walked silently forth to the place, in front of the encampment, whither the warriors were already beginning to collect.

It might have been half an hour before each individual, including even the women and children, was in his place. The delay had been created by the grave preparations that were deemed necessary to so solemn and unusual a conference. But, when the sun was seen climbing above the tops of that mountain against whose bosom the Delawares had constructed their encampment, most were seated; and as its bright rays darted from behind the outline of trees that fringed the eminence, they fell upon as grave, as attentive, and as deeply interested a multitude, as was probably ever before lighted by his morning beams. Its numbers somewhat exceeded a thousand souls.

In a collection of such serious savages, there is never to be found any impatient aspirant after premature distinction, standing ready to move his auditors to some hasty, and, perhaps, injudicious discussion, in order that his own reputation may be the gainer. An act of so much precipitancy and presumption, would seal the downfall of precocious intellect for ever. It rested solely with the oldest and most experienced of the men to lay the subject of their conference before the people. Until such an one chose to make some movement, no deeds in arms, no natural gifts, nor any renown as an orator, would have justified the slightest interruption. On the present occasion, the aged warrior whose privilege it was to speak, was silent, seemingly oppressed with the magnitude of his subject. The delay had already continued long beyond the usual, deliberative pause that always precedes a conference: but no sign of impatience, or surprise, escaped even the youngest boy. Occasionally, an eye was raised from the earth, where the looks of most were riveted, and strayed towards a particular lodge, that was, however, in no manner, distinguished from those around it, except in the peculiar care that had been taken to protect it against the assaults of the weather.

At length one of those low murmurs that are so apt to disturb a multitude, was heard, and the whole nation arose to their feet by a common impulse. At that instant the door of the lodge in question opened, and three men issuing from it, slowly approached the place of consultation. They were all aged, even beyond that period to which the oldest present had reached: but one in the centre, who leaned on his companions for support, had numbered an amount of years, to which the human race is seldom permitted to attain. His frame, which had once been tall and erect, like the cedar, was now bending under the pressure of more than a century. The elastic, light step of an Indian was gone, and in its place, he was compelled to toil his tardy way over the ground, inch by inch. His dark, wrinkled countenance, was in singular and wild contrast with his long white locks, which floated on his shoulders, in such thickness, as to announce that generations had probably passed away since they had last been shorn.

The dress of this patriarch, for such, considering his vast age, in conjunction with his affinity and influence with his people, he might very properly be termed, was rich and imposing, though strictly after the simple fashions of the tribe. His robe was of the finest skins which had been deprived of their fur, in order to admit of a hieroglyphical representation of various deeds in arms, done in former ages. His bosom was loaded with medals, some in massive silver, and one or two even in gold, the gifts of various christian potentates during the long period of his life. He also wore armlets, and cinctures above the ankles, of the latter precious metal. His head, on the whole of which the hair had been permitted to grow, the pursuits of war having so long been abandoned, was encircled by a sort of silver diadem, which, in its turn, bore lesser and more glittering ornaments, that sparkled amid the glossy hues of three drooping ostrich feathers, dyed a deep black, in touching contrast to the colour of his snow-white locks. His tomahawk was nearly hid in silver, and the handle of his knife shone like a horn of solid gold.

So soon as the first hum of emotion and pleasure, which the sudden appearance of this venerated individual created, had a little subsided, the name of "Tamenund" was whispered from mouth to mouth. Magua had often heard the fame of this wise and just Delaware; a reputation that even proceeded so far as to bestow on him the rare gift of holding secret communion with the Great Spirit, and which has since transmitted his name, with some slight alteration, to the white usurpers of his ancient territory, as the imaginary tutelar saint[1] of a vast empire. The Huron chief therefore stepped eagerly out a little from the throng, to a spot whence he might catch a nearer glimpse of the features of the man whose decision was likely to produce so deep an influence on his own fortunes.

[1] St. Tammany.

The eyes of the old man were closed, as though the organs were wearied with having so long witnessed the selfish workings of human passions. The colour of his skin differed from that of most around him, being richer and darker; the latter hue having been produced by certain delicate and mazy lines of complicated and yet beautiful figures, which had been traced over most of his person, by the operation of tattooing. Notwithstanding the position of the Huron, he passed the observant and silent Magua without notice, and leaning on his two venerable supporters, proceeded to the high place of the multitude, where he seated himself in the centre of his nation, with the dignity of a monarch and the air of a father.

Nothing could surpass the reverence and affection with which this unexpected visit from one who belonged rather to another world than to this, was received by his people. After a suitable and decent pause, the principal chiefs arose, and, approaching the patriarch, they placed his hands reverently on their heads, seeming to entreat a blessing. The younger men were content with touching his robe, or even with drawing nigh his person, in order to breathe in the atmosphere of one so aged, so just, and so valiant. None but the most distinguished among the youthful warriors even presumed so far as to perform the latter ceremony; the great mass of the multitude deeming it a sufficient happiness to look upon a form so deeply venerated, and so well beloved. When these acts of affection and respect were performed, the chiefs drew back again to their several places, and a deep and breathing silence reigned in the whole encampment.

After a short delay, a few of the young men, to whom instructions had been whispered by one of the aged attendants of Tamenund, arose, left the crowd, and entered the lodge which has already been noted as the object of so much attention throughout that morning. In a few minutes they re-appeared, escorting the individuals who had caused all these solemn preparations towards the seat of judgment. The crowd opened in a lane, and when the party had re-entered, it closed in again, forming a large and dense belt of human bodies, arranged in an open circle.

Chapter 27

> The assembly seated, rising o'er the rest,
> Achilles thus the king of men address'd.
> *Pope's Homer.*

CORA stood foremost among the prisoners, entwining her arms in those of Alice, in the fondest tenderness of sisterly love. Notwithstanding the fearful and menacing array of savages on every side of her, no apprehension on her own account could prevent the nobleminded maiden from keeping her eyes fastened on the pale and anxious features of the trembling Alice. Close at their side stood Heyward, with an interest in both, that, at such a moment of intense uncertainty, scarcely knew a preponderance in favour of her whom he most loved. Hawk-eye had placed himself a little in the rear, with a deference to the superior rank of his companions that no similarity in the state of their present fortunes could induce him to forget. Uncas was not among them.

When perfect silence was again restored, and after the usual long, impressive pause, one of the two aged chiefs, who sat at the side of the patriarch, arose and demanded aloud, in very intelligible English—

"Which of my prisoners is la Longue Carabine?"

Neither Duncan nor the scout made any answer. The former, however, glanced his eyes around the dark and silent assembly, and recoiled apace, when they fell on the malignant visage of Magua. He saw, at once, that this wily savage had some secret agency in their present arraignment before the nation, and determined to throw every possible impediment in the way of the execution of his sinister plans. He had witnessed one instance of the summary punishment of the Indians, and now dreaded that his companion was to be selected for a second. In this dilemma, with little or no time for reflection, he suddenly determined to cloak his invaluable friend, at any or every hazard to himself. Before he had time, however, to speak, the question was repeated in a louder voice, and with a clearer utterance.

"Give us arms," the young man haughtily replied, "and place us in yonder woods. Our deeds shall speak for us!"

"This is the warrior whose name has filled our ears?" returned the chief, regarding Heyward with that sort of curious interest, which seems inseparable from man, when first beholding one of his fellows, to whom merit or accident, virtue or crime, has given notoriety. "What has brought the white man into the camp of the Delawares?"

"My necessities. I come for food, shelter, and friends."

"It cannot be. The woods are full of game. The head of a warrior needs no other shelter than a sky without clouds, and the Delawares are the enemies and not the friends of the Yengeese. Go—your mouth has spoken, while your heart has said nothing."

Duncan, a little at a loss in what manner to proceed, remained silent; but the scout who had listened attentively to all that passed, now advanced boldly to the front, and assumed the task of explaining.

"That I did not answer to the call for la Longue Carabine, was not owing either to shame or fear," he said: "for neither one nor the other is the gift of an honest man. But I do admit the right of the Mingoes to bestow a name on one, whose friends have been mindful of his gifts, in this particular; especially as their title is all a lie; 'kill-deer' being a genuine grooved barrel, and no carabine. I am the man, however, that got the name of Nathaniel from my kin; the compliment of Hawk-eye from the Delawares, who live on their own river; and whom the Iroquois have presumed to style the 'long rifle,' without any warranty from him who is most concerned in the matter."

The eyes of all present, which had hitherto been gravely scanning the person of Duncan, now turned, on the instant, towards the upright, iron frame of this new pretender to so distinguished an appellation. It was in no degree remarkable, that there should be found two who were willing to claim so great an honour; for impostors, though rare, were not unknown amongst the natives; but it was altogether material to the just and severe intentions of the Delawares, that there should be no mistake in the matter. Some of their old men consulted together in private, and then, as it would seem, they determined to interrogate their visitor on the subject.

"My brother has said that a snake crept into my camp," said the chief to Magua; "which is he?"

The Huron pointed to the scout, but continued silent.

"Will a wise Delaware believe the barking of a wolf?" exclaimed Duncan, still more confirmed in the evil intentions of his ancient enemy; "a dog never lies, but when was a wolf known to speak the truth?"

The eyes of Magua flashed fire; but suddenly recollecting the necessity of maintaining his presence of mind, he turned away in silent disdain, well assured that the sagacity of the Indians would not fail to extract the real merits of the point in controversy. He was not deceived; for, after another short consultation, the wary Delaware turned to him again, and expressed the determination of the chiefs, though in the most considerate language.

"My brother has been called a liar," he said; "and his friends are angry. They will show that he has spoken the truth. Give my prisoners guns, and let them prove which is the man."

Magua affected to consider the expedient, which he well knew proceeded from distrust of himself, as a compliment, and made a gesture of acquiescence, well content that his veracity should be supported by so skilful a marksman as the scout. The weapons were instantly placed in the hands of the friendly opponents, and they were bid to fire over the heads of the seated multitude, at an earthen vessel, which lay, by accident, on a stump, some fifty yards from the place where they stood.

Heyward smiled to himself, at the idea of such a competition with the scout, though he determined to persevere in the deception, until apprized of the designs of Magua. Raising his rifle, then, with the utmost care, and renewing his aim three several times, he fired. The bullet cut the wood within a few inches of the vessel, and a general exclamation of satisfaction announced that the shot was considered a singular proof of great skill in the use of the weapon. Even Hawk-eye nodded his head, as if he would say, it was better than he had expected. But instead of manifesting an intention to contend with the successful marksman, he stood leaning on his rifle for more than a minute, like a man who was completely buried in deep thought. From this reverie he was, however, speedily awakened, by one of the young Indians who had furnished the arms, and who now touched his shoulder saying in exceedingly broken English—

"Can the pale-face beat it?"

"Yes, Huron!" exclaimed the scout, raising his short rifle in his right hand, and shaking it at Magua, with as much apparent ease as though it were a reed; "yes, Huron, I could strike you now, and no power on 'arth could prevent the deed! The soaring hawk is not more certain of the dove, than I am this moment of you, did I choose to send a bullet to your heart! Why should I not? Why!—because the gifts of my colour forbid it, and I might draw down evil on tender and innocent heads! If you know such a thing as God, thank him, therefore, in your inward soul—for you have reason!"

The flushed countenance, angry eye, and swelling figure of the scout, produced a sensation of secret awe in all that heard him. The Delawares held their breath in intense expectation; but Magua himself, even while he distrusted the forbearance of his enemy, remained as immovable and calm, where he stood, wedged in by the crowd, as though he grew to the fatal spot.

"Beat it," repeated the young Delaware at the elbow of the scout.

"Beat what, fool?—What!" exclaimed Hawk-eye, still flourishing the weapon angrily above his head, though his eye no longer sought the person of Magua.

"If the white man is the warrior he pretends," said the aged chief, "let him strike nigher to the mark."

The scout laughed tauntingly, and aloud—a noise that produced the startling effect of unnatural sounds on Heyward—and then dropping the piece heavily into his extended left hand, it was discharged, apparently by the shock, driving the fragments of the vessel high into the air, and scattering them on every side of the stump. Almost at the same instant, the heavy rattling sound of the rifle was heard, as he suffered it to fall contemptuously to the earth.

The first impression of so strange a scene was deep and engrossing admiration. Then a low but increasing murmur ran through the multitude, and finally swelled into sounds, that denoted lively opposition in the sentiments of the spectators. While some openly testified their satisfaction at such unexampled dexterity, by far the larger portion of the tribe were inclined to believe the success of the shot was the result of accident. Heyward was not slow to confirm an opinion that was so favourable to his own pretensions.

"It was all a chance!" he exclaimed, "none can shoot without an aim!"

"Chance!" echoed the excited woodsman, who was now stubbornly bent on maintaining his identity, at every hazard, and on whom the secret hints of Heyward to acquiesce in the deception were entirely lost. "Does yonder lying Huron, too, think it chance? Give him another gun, and place us face to face, without cover or dodge, and let Providence, and our own eyes, decide the matter atween us! I do not make the offer to you, major; for our blood is of a colour, and we serve the same master."

"That the Huron is a liar, is very evident," returned Heyward, coolly; "you have yourself, heard him assert you to be la Longue Carabine."

It were impossible to say what violent assertion the stubborn Hawk-eye would have next made, in his headlong wish to vindicate his identity, had not the aged Delaware once more interposed.

"The hawk which comes from the clouds, can return when he will," he said; "give them the guns."

This time the scout seized the rifle with avidity; nor had Magua, though he watched the movement of the marksman with jealous eyes, any further cause of apprehension.

"Now let it be proved, in the face of this tribe of Delawares, who is the better man," cried the scout, tapping the butt of his piece with that finger which had pulled so many fatal triggers. "You see the gourd hanging against yonder tree, major; if you are a marksman fit for the borders, let me find that you can break its shell!"

Duncan noted the object, and prepared himself to renew the trial. The gourd was one of the usual little vessels used by the Indians, and was suspended from a dead branch of a small pine, by a thong of deer-skin, at the full distance of a hundred yards. So strangely compounded is the feeling of self-love, that the young soldier, while he knew the utter worthlessness of the suffrages of his savage umpires, forgot the sudden motives of the contest, in wish to excel. It has been seen, already, that his skill was far from being contemptible, and he now resolved to put forth its nicest qualities. Had his life depended on the issue, the aim of Duncan could not have been more deliberate and guarded. He fired; and three or four young Indians, who sprang forward at the report, announced with a shout, that the ball was in the tree, a very little on one side of the proper object. The warriors uttered a common ejaculation of pleasure, and then turned their eyes inquiringly on the movements of his rival.

"It may do for the Royal Americans!" said Hawk-eye, laughing once more in his own silent, heartfelt manner; "but had my gun often turned so much from the true line, many a martin, whose skin is in a lady's muff, would now be in the woods; ay, and many a bloody Mingo, who has departed to his final account, would be acting his devilries at this very day, atween the provinces. I hope the squaw who owns the gourd, has more of them in her wigwam, for this will never hold water again!"

The scout had shook his priming, and cocked his piece while speaking; and, as he ended, he threw back a foot, and slowly raised the muzzle from the earth. The motion was steady, uniform, and in one direction. When on a perfect level, it remained for a single moment without tremor or variation, as though both man and rifle were carved in stone. During that stationary instant, it poured forth its contents, in a bright glancing sheet of flame. Again the young Indians bounded forward, but their hurried search and disappointed looks announced, that no traces of the bullet were to be seen.

"Go," said the old chief to the scout, in a tone of strong disgust; "thou art a wolf in the skin of a dog. I will talk to the 'long rifle' of the Yengeese."

"Ah! had I that piece which furnished the name you use, I would obligate myself to cut the thong, and drop the gourd, instead of breaking it!" returned Hawk-eye, perfectly undisturbed by the other's manner. "Fools, if you would find a bullet of a sharp-shooter of these woods, you must look *in* the object, and not around it!"

The Indian youths instantly comprehended his meaning—for this time he spoke in the Delaware tongue—and tearing the gourd from the tree, they held it on high, with an exulting shout, displaying a hole in its bottom, which had been cut by the bullet, after passing through the usual orifice in the centre of its upper side. At this unexpected exhibition, a loud and vehement expression of pleasure burst from the mouth of every warrior present. It decided the question, and effectually established Hawk-eye in the possession of his dangerous reputation. Those curious and admiring eyes which had been turned again on Heyward were finally directed to the weatherbeaten form of the scout, who immediately became the principal object of attention to the simple and unsophisticated beings by whom he was surrounded. When the sudden and noisy commotion had a little subsided, the aged chief resumed his examination.

"Why did you wish to stop my ears?" he said, addressing Duncan; "are the Delawares fools, that they could not know the young panther from the cat?"

"They will yet find the Huron a singing bird," said Duncan, endeavouring to adopt the figurative language of the natives.

"It is good. We will know who can shut the ears of men. Brother," added the chief, turning his eyes on Magua, "the Delawares listen."

Thus singled, and directly called on, to declare his object, the Huron arose, and advancing with great deliberation and dignity, into the very centre of the circle, where he stood confronted to the prisoners, he placed himself in an attitude to speak. Before opening his mouth, however, he bent his eyes slowly along the whole living boundary of earnest faces, as if to temper his expressions to the capacities of his audience. On Hawk-eye he cast a glance of respectful enmity; on Duncan, a look of inextinguishable hatred; the shrinking figure of Alice, he scarcely deigned to notice; but when his glance met the firm, commanding, and yet lovely form of Cora, his eye lingered a moment, with an expression that it might have been difficult to define. Then, filled with his own dark intentions, he spoke in the language of the Canadas, a tongue that he well knew was comprehended by most of his auditors.

"The Spirit that made men, coloured them differently," commenced the subtle Huron. "Some are blacker than the sluggish bear. These he said should be slaves; and he ordered them to work for ever, like the beaver. You may hear them groan, when the south winds blow, louder than the lowing buffaloes, along the shores of the great salt water, where the big canoes come and go with them in droves. Some he made with faces paler than the ermine of the forests: and these he ordered to be traders; dogs to their women, and wolves to their slaves. He gave this people the nature of the pigeon; wings that never tire; young, more plentiful than the leaves on the trees, and appetites to devour the earth. He gave them tongues like the false call of the wildcat; hearts like rabbits; the cunning of the hog, (but none of the fox), and arms longer than the legs of the moose. With his tongue, he stops the ears of the Indians; his heart teaches him to pay warriors to fight his battles; his cunning tells him how to get together the goods of the earth; and his arms enclose the land, from the shores of the salt water, to the islands of the great lake. His gluttony makes him sick. God gave him enough, and yet he wants all. Such are the pale-faces."

"Some the Great Spirit made with skins brighter and redder than yonder sun," continued Magua, pointing impressively upward to the lurid luminary, which was struggling through the misty atmosphere of the horizon; "and these did he fashion to his own mind. He gave them this island as he had made it, covered with trees and filled with game. The wind made their clearings; the sun and rain ripened their fruits; and the snows came to tell them to be thankful. What needs had they of roads to journey by? They saw through the hills! When the beavers worked, they lay in the shade, and looked on. The winds cooled them in summer; in winter skins kept them warm. If they fought among themselves, it was to prove that they were men. They were brave; they were just; they were happy."

Here the speaker paused, and again looked around him, to discover if his legend had touched the sympathies of his listeners. He met every where with eyes riveted on his own, heads erect, and nostrils expanded as though each individual present felt himself able and willing, singly, to redress the wrongs of his race.

"If the Great Spirit gave different tongues to his red children," he continued in a low, still, melancholy voice, "it was that all animals might understand them. Some he placed among the snows, with their cousin the bear. Some he placed near the setting sun, on the road to the happy hunting grounds. Some on the lands around the great fresh waters; but to his greatest and most beloved, he gave the sands of the salt lake. Do my brothers know the name of this favoured people?"

"It was the Lenape!" exclaimed twenty eager voices in a breath.

"It was the Lenni Lenape," returned Magua, affecting to bend his head in reverence to their former greatness. "It was the tribes of the Lenape! The sun rose from the water that was salt and set in water that was sweet and never hid himself from their eyes. But why should I, a Huron of the woods, tell a wise people their own traditions? Why remind them of their injuries; their ancient greatness; their deeds; their glory; their happiness— their losses; their defeats; their misery? Is there not one among them who has seen it all, and who knows it to be true? I have done. My tongue is still, but my ears are open."

As the voice of the speaker suddenly ceased, every face and all eyes turned, by a common movement, towards the venerable Tamenund. From the moment that he took his seat, until the present instant, the lips of the

132

patriarch had not severed, nor had scarcely a sign of life escaped him. He had sate, bent in feebleness, and apparently unconscious of the presence he was in, during the whole of that opening scene, in which the skill of the scout had been so clearly established. At the nicely graduated sounds of Magua's voice, however, he had betrayed some evidence of consciousness, and once or twice he had even raised his head as if to listen. But when the crafty Huron spoke of his nation by name, the eyelids of the old man raised themselves, and he looked out on the multitude, with that sort of dull, unmeaning expression, which might be supposed to belong to the countenance of a spectre.

Then he made an effort to rise, and being upheld by his supporters, he gained his feet in a posture commanding by its dignity, while he tottered with weakness.

"Who calls upon the children of the Lenape?" he said, in a deep, guttural voice, that was rendered awfully audible by the breathless silence of the multitude; "who speaks of things gone? Does not the egg become a worm—the worm a fly—and perish! Why tell the Delawares of good that is past? Better thank the Manitto for that which remains."

"It is a Wyandot," said Magua, stepping nigher to the rude platform on which the other stood; "a friend of Tamenund."

"A friend!" repeated the sage, on whose brow a dark frown settled, imparting a portion of that severity, which had rendered his eye so terrible in middle age—"Are the Mingoes rulers of the earth? What brings a Huron here?"

"Justice. His prisoners are with his brothers, and he comes for his own."

Tamenund turned his head towards one of his supporters, and listened to the short explanation the man gave. Then facing the applicant, he regarded him a moment with deep attention; after which, he said in a low and reluctant voice—

"Justice is the law of the Great Manitto. My children, give the stranger food. Then, Huron, take thine own and depart."

On the delivery of this solemn judgment the patriarch seated himself, and closed his eyes again, as if better pleased with the images of his own ripened experience, than with the visible objects of the world. Against such a decree, there was no Delaware sufficiently hardy to murmur, much less oppose himself. The words were barely uttered, when four or five of the younger warriors stepping behind Heyward and the scout, passed thongs so dexterously and rapidly around their arms, as to hold them both in instant bondage. The former was too much engrossed with his precious and nearly insensible burden, to be aware of their intentions before they were executed; and the latter, who considered even the hostile tribes of the Delawares a superior race of beings, submitted without resistance. Perhaps, however, the manner of the scout would not have been so passive, had he fully comprehended the language in which the preceding dialogue had been conducted.

Magua cast a look of triumph around the whole assembly, before he proceeded to the execution of his purpose. Perceiving that the men were unable to offer any resistance, he turned his looks on her he valued most. Cora met his gaze with an eye so calm and firm, that his resolution wavered. Then recollecting his former artifice, he raised Alice from the arms of the warrior, against whom she leaned, and beckoning Heyward to follow, he motioned for the encircling crowd to open. But Cora, instead of obeying the impulse he had expected, rushed to the feet of the patriarch, and raising her voice exclaimed aloud—

"Just and venerable Delaware, on thy wisdom and power we lean for mercy! Be deaf to yonder artful and remorseless monster, who poisons thy ears with falsehoods to feed his thirst for blood. Thou, that hast lived long, and that hast seen the evil of the world, should know how to temper its calamities to the miserable."

The eyes of the old man opened heavily, and he once more looked upward at the multitude. As the full piercing tones of the suppliant swelled on his ears, they moved slowly in the direction of her person, and finally settled there, in a steady, riveted gaze. Cora, had cast herself to her knees, and with hands clenched in each other and pressed upon her bosom, she remained like a beauteous and breathing model of her sex, looking up in his faded but majestic countenance with a species of holy reverence. Gradually the expression of Tamenund's features changed, and losing their vacancy in admiration, they lighted with a portion of their intelligence, which a century before, had been wont to communicate his youthful fire to the extensive bands of the Delawares. Rising without assistance, and seemingly without an effort, he demanded, in a voice that startled its auditors by its firmness—

"What art thou?"

"A woman. One of a hated race, if thou wilt—a Yengee. But one who has never harmed thee, and who cannot harm thy people if she would; who asks for succour."

"Tell me, my children," continued the patriarch, hoarsely, motioning to those around him, though his eyes still dwelt upon the kneeling form of Cora, "where have the Delawares camped."

"In the mountains of the Iroquois; beyond the clear springs of the Horican."

"Many parching summers are come and gone," continued the sage, "since I drank of the waters of my own river. The children of Miquon are the justest white men; but they were thirsty, and they took it to themselves. Do they follow us so far?"

"We follow none; we covet nothing," answered the ardent Cora. "Captives against our wills have we been brought amongst you; and we ask but permission to depart to our own, in peace. Art thou not Tamenund—the father—the judge—I had almost said, the prophet—of this people?"

"I am Tamenund, of many days."

"'Tis now some seven years that one of thy people was at the mercy of a white chief, on the borders of this province. He claimed to be of the blood of the good and just Tamenund. 'Go,' said the white man, 'for thy parent's sake, thou art free.' Dost thou remember the name of that English warrior?"

"I remember, that when a laughing boy," returned the patriarch, with the peculiar recollection of vast age, "I stood upon the sands of the sea-shore, and saw a big canoe with wings whiter than the swan's and wider than many eagles, come from the rising sun——"

"Nay, nay; I speak not of a time so very distant; but of favour shown to thy kindred by one of mine, within the memory of thy youngest warrior."

"Was it when the Yengeese and the Dutchemanne fought for the hunting grounds of the Delawares? Then Tamenund was a chief, and first laid aside the bow for the lightning of the pale-faces——"

"Nor yet then," interrupted Cora again, "by many ages; I speak of a thing of yesterday. Surely, surely, you forget it not?"

"It was but yesterday," rejoined the aged man, with a touching pathos in his hollow voice, "that the children of the Lenape were masters of the world! The fishes of the salt lake, the birds, the beasts and the Mengwe of the woods, owned them for Sagamores."

Cora bowed her head in the anguish of disappointment, and for a bitter moment, struggled with her chagrin. Then elevating her rich features and beaming eyes, she continued, in tones scarcely less penetrating than the unearthly voice of the patriarch himself.

"Tell me, is Tamenund a father?"

The old man looked down upon her, from his elevated stand, with a benignant smile on his wasted countenance, and then casting his eyes slowly over the whole assemblage, he answered—

"Of a nation."

"For myself I ask nothing. Like thee and thine, venerable chief," she continued, pressing her hands convulsively on her heart, and suffering her head to droop, until her burning cheeks were nearly concealed in the maze of dark, glossy tresses that fell in disorder upon her shoulders, "the curse of my ancestors has fallen heavily on their child. But yonder is one who has never known the weight of Heaven's displeasure until now. She is the daughter of an old and failing man, whose days are near their close. She has many, very many, to love her, and delight in her; and she is too good, much too precious, to become the victim of that villain."

"I know that the pale-faces are a proud and hungry race. I know that they claim, not only to have the earth, but that the meanest of their colour is better than the Sachems of the red man. The dogs and crows of their tribes," continued the earnest old chieftain, without heeding the wounded spirit of his listener, whose head was nearly crushed to the earth in shame, as he proceeded, "would bark and caw, before they would take a woman to their wigwams, whose blood was not of the colour of snow. But let them not boast before the face of the Manitto too loud. They entered the land at the rising, and may yet go off at the setting sun! I have often seen the locusts strip the leaves from the trees, but the season of blossoms has always come again!"

"It is so," said Cora, dawing a long breath, as if reviving from a trance, raising her face, and shaking back her shining veil, with a kindling eye that contradicted the death-like paleness of her countenance: "but why—it is not permitted us to inquire. There is yet one of thine own people, who has not been brought before thee; before thou lettest the Huron depart in triumph, hear him speak."

Observing Tamenund to look about him doubtingly, one of his companions said—

"It is a snake—a red-skin in the pay of the Yengeese. We keep him for the torture."

"Let him come," returned the sage.

Then Tamenund once more sunk into his seat, and a silence so deep prevailed, while the young men prepared to obey his simple mandate, that the leaves which fluttered in the draught of the light morning air, were distinctly heard rustling in the surrounding forest.

Chapter 28

If you deny me, fie upon your law!
There is no force in the decrees of Venice:
I stand for judgment: answer; shall I have it?
Shakespeare.

THE silence continued unbroken by human sounds for many anxious minutes. Then the waving multitude opened, and shut again, and Uncas stood environed by the living circle. All those eyes which had been curiously studying the lineaments of the sage, as the source of their own intelligence, turned on the instant, and were now bent in secret admiration on the erect, agile, and faultless person of the captive; but neither the presence in which he found himself, nor the exclusive attention that he attracted, in any manner disturbed the self-possession of the young Mohican. He cast a deliberate and observing look on every side of him, meeting the settled expression of hostility, that lowered in the visage of the chiefs, with the same calmness as the curious gaze of the attentive children. But when, last, in his keen and haughty scrutiny, the person of Tamenund came under his glance, his eye became as fixed as though all other objects were already forgotten. Then advancing, with a slow and noiseless step, up the area, he placed himself immediately before the footstool of the sage. Here he stood unnoted, though keenly observant himself, until one of the chiefs apprized the latter of his presence.

"With what tongue does the prisoner speak to the Manitto?" demanded the patriarch, without unclosing his eyes.

"Like his fathers," Uncas replied; "with the tongue of a Delaware."

At this sudden and unexpected annunciation, a low, fierce yell ran through the multitude, that might not inaptly be compared to the growl of the lion, as his choler is first awakened—a fearful omen of the weight of his future anger. The effect was equally strong on the sage, though differently exhibited. He passed a hand before his eyes, as if to exclude the least evidence of so shameful a spectacle, while he repeated, in his low and deeply guttural tones, the words he had just heard.

"A Delaware! I have lived to see the tribes of the Lenape driven from their council fires, and scattered like broken herds of deer among the hills of the Iroquois; I have seen the hatchets of a strange people sweep woods from the valleys, that the winds of heaven had spared! The beasts that run on the mountains, and the birds that fly above the trees, have I seen living in the wigwams of men; but never before have I found a Delaware so base as to creep, like a poisonous serpent, into the camps of his nation."

"The singing-birds have opened their bills," returned Uncas, in the softest notes of his own musical voice; "and Tamenund has heard their song."

The sage started and bent his head aside, as if to catch the fleeting sounds of some passing melody.

"Does Tamenund dream!" he exclaimed. "What voice is at his ear! Have the winters gone backward! Will summer come again to the children of the Lenape!"

A solemn and respectful silence succeeded this incoherent burst from the lips of the Delaware prophet. His people readily construed his unintelligible language into one of those mysterious conferences, he was believed to hold so frequently, with a superior intelligence, and they waited the issue of the revelation in secret awe. After a long and patient pause, however, one of the aged men, perceiving that the sage had lost the recollection of the subject before them, ventured to remind him again of the presence of the prisoner.

"The false Delaware trembles lest he should hear the words of Tamennund," he said. "'Tis a hound that howls, when the Yengeese show him a trail."

"And ye," returned Uncas, looking sternly around him, "are dogs that whine when the Frenchman casts ye the offals of his deer!"

Twenty knives gleamed in the air, and as many warriors sprang to their feet, at this biting, and perhaps merited, retort; but a motion from one of the chiefs suppressed the outbreaking of their tempers, and restored the appearance of quiet. The task might possibly have been more difficult, had not a movement, made by Tamenund, indicated, that he was again about to speak.

"Delaware," resumed the sage, "little art thou worthy of thy name. My people have not seen a bright sun in many winters; and the warrior who deserts his tribe, when hid in clouds, is doubly a traitor. The law of the Manitto is just. It is so; while the rivers run and the mountains stand, while the blossoms come and go on the tress, it must be so. He is thine, my children; deal justly by him."

Not a limb was moved, nor was a breath drawn louder or longer than common, until the closing syllable of this final decree had passed the lips of Tamenund. Then a cry of vengeance burst at once, as it might be, from the united lips of the nation; a frightful augury of their fierce and ruthless intentions. In the midst of these prolonged and savage yells, a chief proclaimed, in a high voice, that the captive was condemned to endure the dreadful trial of torture by fire. The circle broke its order, and screams of delight mingled with the bustle and tumult of instant preparation. Heyward struggled madly with his captors; the anxious eye of Hawk-eye began to look around him with an expression of peculiar earnestness; and Cora again threw herself at the feet of the patriarch, once more a suppliant for mercy.

Throughout the whole of these trying moments, Uncas had alone preserved his serenity. He looked on the preparations with a steady eye, and when the tormentors came to seize him, he met them with a firm and upright attitude. One among them, if possible more fierce and savage than his fellows, seized the hunting-shirt of the young warrior, and at a single effort, tore it from his body. Then, with a yell of frantic pleasure, he leaped towards his unresisting victim, and prepared to lead him to the stake. But, at that moment, when he appeared most a stranger to the feelings of humanity, the purpose of the savage was arrested as suddenly, as if a supernatural agency had interposed in the behalf of Uncas. The eyeballs of the Delaware seemed to start from their sockets; his mouth opened, and his whole form became frozen in an attitude of amazement. Raising his hand, with a slow and regulated motion, he pointed with a finger to the bosom of the captive. His companions crowded about him, in wonder, and every eye was, like his own, fastened intently on the figure of a small tortoise, beautifully tattooed on the breast of the prisoner, in a bright blue tint.

For a single instant, Uncas enjoyed his triumph, smiling calmly on the scene. Then motioning the crowd away, with a high and haughty sweep of his arm, he advanced in front of the nation, with the air of a king, and spoke in a voice louder than the murmur of admiration that ran through the multitude.

"Men of the Lenni Lenape!" he said, "my race upholds the earth! Your feeble tribe stands on my shell! What fire, that a Delaware can light, would burn the child of my fathers?" he added, pointing proudly to the simple plazonry on his skin; "the blood that came from such a stock, would smother your flames! My race is the grandfather of nations!"

"Who art thou?" demanded Tamenund, rising, at the startling tones he heard, more than any meaning conveyed by the language of the prisoner.

"Uncas, the son of Chingachgook," answered the captive, modestly turning from the nation, and bending his head in reverence to the other's character and years; "a son of the Great Unamis."[1]

"The hour of Tamenund is nigh!" exclaimed the sage; "the day is come, at last, to the night! I thank the Manitto, that one is here to fill my

[1] Turtle.

place at the council-fire. Uncas, the child of Uncas, is found! Let the eyes of a dying eagle gaze on the rising sun."

The youth stepped lightly, but proudly, on the platform, where he became visible to the whole agitated, and wondering multitude. Tamenund held him long at the length of his arm, and read every turn in the fine and lofty lineaments of his countenance, with the untiring gaze of one who recalled the days of his own happiness by the examination.

"Is Tamenund a boy?" at length the bewildered prophet exclaimed. "Have I dreamt of so many snows—that my people were scattered like floating sands—of Yengeese, more plenty than the leaves on the trees? The arrow of Tamenund would not frighten the young fawn; his arm is wither-ed like the branch of the dying oak; the snail would be swifter in the race; yet is Uncas before him, as they went to battle, against the pale-faces! Uncas, the panther of his tribe, the eldest son of the Lenape, the wisest Sagamore of the Mohicans! Tell me, ye Delawares, has Tamenund been a sleeper for a hundred winters?"

The calm and deep silence which succeeded these words, sufficiently announced the awful reverence with which his people received the com-munication of the patriarch. None dared to answer, though all listened in breathless expectation of what might follow. Uncas, however, looking in his face, with the fondness and veneration of a favoured child, presumed on his own high and acknowledged rank, to reply.

"Four warriors of his race have lived and died," he said, "since the friend of Tamenund led his people in battle. The blood of the turtle has been in many chiefs, but all have gone back into the earth, from whence they came, except Chingachgook and his son."

"It is true—it is true," returned the sage—a flash of recollection destroying all his pleasing fancies, and restoring him, at once, to a consciousness of the true history of his nation. "Our wise men have often said that two warriors of the 'unchanged' race were in the hills of the Yengeese; why have their seats at the council-fires of the Delawares been so long empty?"

At these words, the young man raised his head, which he had still kept bowed a little in reverence, and lifting his voice, so as to be heard by the multitude, as if to explain, at once, and for ever, the policy of his family, he said, aloud—

"Once we slept where we could hear the salt lake speak in its anger. Then we were rulers and Sagamores over the land. But when a paleface was seen on every brook, we followed the deer back to the river of our nation. The Delawares were gone! Few warriors of them all stayed to drink of the stream they loved. Then said my fathers— 'here will we hunt. The waters of the river go into the salt lake. If we go towards the setting sun, we shall find streams that run into the great lakes of the sweet water, there would a Mohican die, like fishes of the sea, in the clear springs. When the Manitto is ready, and shall say, "come," we will follow the river to the sea, and take our own again.' Such Delawares, is the belief of the children of the Turtle! Our eyes are on the rising, and not towards

the setting sun! We know whence he comes, but we know not whither he goes. It is enough."

The men of the Lenape listened to his words, with all the respect that superstition could lend, finding a secret charm even in the figurative language with which the young Sagamore imparted his ideas. Uncas himself watched the effect of his brief explanation with intelligent eyes, and gradually dropped the air of authority he had assumed, as he perceived that his auditors were content. Then permitting his looks to wander over the silent throng that crowded around the elevated seat of Tamenund, he first perceived Hawk-eye, in his bonds. Stepping eagerly from his stand, he made a way for himself to the side of his friend, and cutting his thong with a quick and angry stroke of his own knife, he motioned to the crowd to divide. The grave and attentive Indians silently obeyed, and once more they stood ranged in their circle, as before his appearance among them. Uncas then took the scout by the hand, and led him to the feet of the patriarch.

"Father," he said, "look at this pale-face; a just man, and the friend of the Delawares."

"Is he a son of Miquon?"[1]

"Not so; a warrior known to the Yengeese, and feared by the Maquas."

"What name has he gained by his deeds?"

"We call him Hawk-eye," Uncas replied, using the Delaware phrase; "for his sight never fails. The Mingoes know him better by the death he gives their warriors; with them he is the 'long rifle.'"

"La Longue Carabine!" exclaimed Tamenund, opening his eyes, and regarding the scout, sternly. "My son has not done well to call him friend."

"I call him so who proves himself such," returned the young chief, with great calmness, but with a steady mien. "If Uncas is welcome among the Delawares, then is Hawk-eye with his friends."

"The pale-face has slain my young men; his name is great for the blows he has struck the Lenape."

"If a Mingo has whispered that much in the ear of the Delaware, he has only manifested that he is a singing-bird," said the scout, who now believed it was time to vindicate himself from such offensive charges, and who spoke in the tongue of the man he addressed, modifying his Indian figures, however, with his own peculiar notions. "That I have slain the Maquas, I am not the man to deny, even at their own council-fires; but that, knowingly, my hand has ever harmed a Delaware, is opposed to the reason of my gifts, which is friendly to them, and all that belongs to their nation."

A low exclamation of applause passed among the warriors, who exchanged looks with each other, like men that first began to perceive their error.

"Where is the Huron?" demanded Tamenund. "Has he stopped my ears?"

[1] William Penn.

140

Magua, whose feelings, during that scene in which Uncas had triumphed, may be much better imagined than described, now answered to the call, by stepping boldly in front of the patriarch.

"The just Tamenund," he said, "will not keep what a Huron has lent."

"Tell me, son of my brother," returned the sage, avoiding the dark countenance of le Subtil, and turning gladly to the more ingenuous features of Uncas, "has the stranger a conqueror's right over you?"

"He has none. The panther may get into snares set by the women, but he is strong, and knows how to leap through them."

"La Longue Carabine?"

"Laughs at the Mingoes. Go, Huron! ask your squaws the colour of a bear!"

"The stranger and the white maiden that came into my camp together?"

"Should journey on an open path."

"And the woman that the Huron left with my warriors?"

Uncas made no reply.

"And the woman that the Mingo has brought into my camp?" repeated Tamenund, gravely.

"She is mine!" cried Magua, shaking his hand in triumph at Uncas. "Mohican, you know that she is mine."

"My son is silent," said Tamenund, endeavouring to read the expression of the face that the youth turned from him in sorrow.

"It is so," was the low and brief reply.

A short and impressive pause succeeded, during which it was very apparent with what reluctance the multitude admitted the justice of the Mingo's claim. At length the sage, on whom alone the decision depended, said, in a firm voice—

"Huron, depart."

"As he came, just Tamenund?" demanded the wily Magua; "or with hands filled with the faith of the Delawares? The wigwam of le Renard Subtil is empty. Make him strong with his own."

The aged man mused with himself for a time, and then bending his head towards one of his venerable companions, he asked—

"Are my ears open?"

"It is true."

"Is this Mingo a chief?"

"The first in his nation."

"Girl, what wouldst thou! a great warrior takes thee to wife. Go, thy race will not end."

"Better a thousand times it should," exclaimed the horror-struck Cora, "than meet with such a degradation!"

"Huron, her mind is in the tents of her fathers. An unwilling maiden makes an unhappy wigwam."

"She speaks with the tongue of her people," returned Magua, regarding his victim with a look of bitter irony. "She is of a race of traders, and will bargain for a bright look. Let Tamenund speak the words?"

"Take you the wampum, and our love."

"Nothing hence, but what Magua brought hither."

"Then depart with thine own. The Great Manitto forbids that a Delaware should be unjust."

Magua advanced, and seized his captive strongly by the arm; the Delawares fell back, in silence; and Cora, as if conscious that remonstrance would be useless, prepared to submit to her fate without resistance.

"Hold, hold!" cried Duncan, springing forward; "Huron, have mercy! Her ransom shall make thee richer than any of thy people were ever yet known to be."

"Magua is a red-skin; he wants not the beads of the pale-faces."

"Gold, silver, powder, lead, all that a warrior needs, shall be in thy wigwam; all that becomes the greatest chief."

"Le Subtil, is very strong," cried Magua, violently shaking the hand which grasped the unresisting arm of Cora; "he has his revenge!"

"Mighty Ruler of Providence!" exclaimed Heyward, clasping his hands together in agony, "can this be suffered? To you, just Tamenund, I appeal for mercy."

"The words of the Delaware are said," returned the sage, closing his eyes, and dropping back into his seat, alike wearied with his mental and his bodily exertion. "Men speak not twice."

"That a chief should not mis-spend his time in unsaying what he has once spoken, is wise and reasonable," said Hawk-eye, motioning to Duncan to be silent; "but it is also prudent in every warrior to consider well before he strikes his tomahawk into the head of his prisoner. Huron, I love you not; nor can I say that any Mingo has ever received much favour at my hands. It is fair to conclude, that if this war does not soon end, many more of your warriors will meet me in the woods. Put it to your judgment, then, whether you would prefer taking such a prisoner as that lady into your encampment, or one like myself, who am a man that it would greatly rejoice your nation to see with naked hands."

"Will the 'long rifle' give his life for the woman?" demanded Magua, hesitatingly; for he had already made a motion towards quitting the place with his victim.

"No, no; I have not said so much as that," returned Hawk-eye, drawing back, with suitable discretion, when he noted the eagerness with which Magua listened to his proposal. "It would be an unequal exchange, to give a warrior, in the prime of his age and usefulness, for the best woman on the frontiers. I might consent to go into winter quarters, now—at least six weeks afore the leaves will turn—on condition you will release the maiden."

Magua shook his head in cold disdain, and made an impatient sign for the crowd to open.

"Well, then," added the scout, with the musing air of a man who had not half made up his mind, "I will throw 'kill-deer' into the bargain. Take the word of an experienced hunter, the piece has not its equal atween the provinces."

Magua still disdained to reply, continuing his efforts to disperse the crowd.

"Perhaps," added the scout, losing his dissembled coolness, exactly in proportion as the other manifested an indifference to the exchange, "if I should condition to teach your young men the real virtue of the we'pon, it would smooth the little differences in our judgments."

Le Renard fiercely ordered the Delawares, who still lingered in an impenetrable belt around him, in hopes he would listen to the amicable proposal, to open his path, threatening, by the glance of his eye, another appeal to the infallible justice of their "prophet."

"What is ordered, must sooner or later arrive," continued Hawk-eye, turning with a sad and humbled look to Uncas. "The varlet knows his advantage, and will keep it! God bless you, boy; you have found friends among your natural kin, and I hope they will prove as true as some of you have met, who had no Indian cross. As for me, sooner or later, I must die; it is therefore fortunate there are but few to make my death-howl! After all, it is likely the imps would have managed to master my scalp, so a day or two will make no great difference in the everlasting reckoning of time. God bless you," added the rugged woodsman, bending his head aside, with quivering muscles, and then instantly changing his direction again, with a wistful look towards the youth; "I loved both you and your father, Uncas, though our skins are not altogether of a colour, and our gifts are somewhat different. Tell the Sagamore I never lost sight of him in my greatest trouble; and as for you, think of me sometimes, when on a lucky trail; and depend on it, boy, whether there be one heaven or two, there is a path in the other world, by which honest men may come together again. You'll find the rifle in the place we hid it; take it and keep it for my sake; and harkee, lad, as your natural gifts don't deny you the use of vengeance, use it a little freely on the Mingoes; it may unburthen your grief at my loss, and ease your mind. Huron, I accept your offer; release the lady. I am your prisoner."

A suppressed, but still distinct murmur of approbation ran through the crowd at this generous proposition; even the fiercest among the Delaware warriors manifesting pleasure at the manliness of the intended sacrifice. Magua paused, and for an anxious moment, it might be said, he doubted; then casting his eyes on Cora, with an expression in which ferocity and admiration were strangely mingled, his purpose became fixed for ever.

He intimated his contempt of the offer, with a backward motion of his head, and said, in a steady and settled voice—

"Le Renard Subtil is a great chief; he has but one mind. Come," he added, laying his hand too familiarly on the shoulder of his captive, to urge her onward; "a Huron warrior is no tatler; we will go."

The maiden drew back in a lofty, womanly reserve, and her dark eye kindled, while the rich blood shot, like the passing brightness of the sun, into her very temples, at the indignity.

"I am your prisoner, and at a fitting time shall be ready to follow, even to my death. But violence is unnecessary," she coldly said; and immediately turning to Hawk-eye, added, "Generous Hunter! from my soul I thank you. Your offer is vain, neither could it be accepted; but still you may serve me, even more than in your own noble intention. Look at that dropping, humble child! Abandon her not until you leave her in the habitations of civilized men. I will not say," wringing the hard hand of the scout, "that her father will reward you—for such as you are above the rewards of men—but he will thank you, and bless you. And, believe me, the blessing of a just and aged man has virtue in the sight of Heaven. Would to God I could hear one from his lips at this awful moment!" Her voice became choked, and for an instant she was silent; then advancing a step nigher, to Duncan, who was supporting her unconscious sister, she continued, in more subdued tones, but in which her feelings, and the habits of her sex, maintained a fearful struggle. "I need not tell you to cherish the treasure you will possess. You love her, Heyward; that would conceal a thousand faults, though she had them. She is as kind, as gentle, as sweet, as good, as mortal may be. There is not a blemish in mind or person, at which the proudest of you all would sicken. She is fair—Oh! how surpassingly fair!" laying her own beautiful, but less brilliant hand, in melancholy affection, on the alabaster forehead of Alice, and parting the golden hair which clustered about her brows; "and yet her soul is as pure and spotless as her skin! I could say much—more, perhaps, than cooler reason would approve; but I will spare both you and myself——" Her voice became inaudible, and her face was bent over the form of her sister. After a long and burning kiss, she arose, and with features of the hue of death, but without even a tear in her feverish eye, she turned away, and added, to the savage, with all her former elevation of manner—"Now, Sir, if it be your pleasure, I will follow."

"Ay, ho," cried Duncan, placing Alice in the arms of an Indian girl; "go, Magua, go. These Delawares have their laws which forbid them to detain you; but I—I have no such obligation. Go, malignant monster—why do you delay?"

It would be difficult to describe the expression of features with which Magua listened to his threat to follow. There was at first a fierce and manifest display of joy, and then it was instantly subdued in a look of cunning coldness.

"The woods are open," he was content with answering; "the 'open hand,' can follow."

"Hold," cried Hawk-eye, seizing Duncan by the arm, and detaining him by violence; "you know not the craft of the imp. He would lead you to an ambushment, and your death."

"Huron," interrupted Uncas, who, submissive to the stern customs of his people, had been an attentive and grave listener to all that passed; "Huron, the justice of the Delawares comes from the Manitto. Look at the sun. He is now in the upper branches of the hemlock. Your path is short and open. When he is seen above the trees, there will be men on your trail."

"I hear a crow!" exclaimed Magua, with a taunting laugh. "Go," he added, shaking his hand at the crowd, which had slowly opened to admit his passage—"Where are the petticoats of the Delawares? Let them send their arrows and their guns to the Wyandots; they shall have venison to eat, and corn to hoe. Dogs, rabbits, thieves—I spit on you!"

His parting gibes were listened to in a dead, boding silence; and with these biting words in his mouth, the triumphant Magua passed unmolested into the forest, followed by his passive captive, and protected by the inviolable laws of Indian hospitality.

Chapter 29

Flue. Kill the poys and the luggage! 'tis expressly against the law of arms; 'tis as arrant a piece of knavery, mark you now, as can be offered in the 'orld.   *King Henry V.*

So long as their enemy and his victim continued in sight, the multitude remained motionless, as being charmed to the place by some power that was friendly to the Huron; but the instant he disappeared, it became tossed and agitated by fierce and powerful passion. Uncas maintained his elevated stand, keeping his eyes on the form of Cora, until the colours of her dress were blended with the foliage of the forest, when he descended, and moving silently through the throng, he disappeared in that lodge from which he had so recently issued. A few of the graver and more attentive warriors, who caught the gleams of anger that shot from the eyes of the young chief in passing, followed him to the place he had selected for his meditations; after which, Tamenund and Alice were removed, and the women and children were ordered to disperse. During the momentous hour that succeeded, the encampment resembled a hive of troubled bees, who only awaited the appearance and example of their leader, to take some distant and momentous flight.

A young warrior, at length, issued from the lodge of Uncas, and moving deliberately, with a sort of grave march, towards a dwarf pine that grew in the crevices of the rocky terrace, he tore the bark from its body, and then returned whence he came, without speaking. He was soon followed by another, who stripped the sapling of its branches, leaving it a naked and "blazed" trunk. A third coloured the posts with stripes of a dark red paint; all which indications of a hostile design in the leaders of the nation, were received by the men without in a gloomy and ominous silence. Finally, the Mohican himself reappeared divested of all his attire, except his girdle and leggings, and with on half of his fine features hid under a cloud of threatening black.

Uncas moved with a slow and dignified tread towards the post, which he immediately commenced encircling with a measured step not unlike an ancient dance, raising his voice, at the same time, in the wild and irregular chant of his war-song. The notes were in the extremes of human sounds, being sometimes melancholy and exquisitely plaintive, even rivalling the melody of birds—and then, by sudden and startling transitions, causing the auditors to tremble by their depth and energy. The words were few, and often repeated, proceeding gradually from a sort of invocation, or hymn, to the Deity, to an intimation of the warrior's object, and terminating, as they commenced, with an acknowledgment of his own dependence on the Great Spirit. If it were possible to translate the comprehensive and melodious language in which he spoke, the ode might read something like the following:

> Manitto! Manitto! Manitto!
> Thou art great—thou art good—thou art wise—
> Manitto! Manitto!
> Thou art just!
>
> In the heavens, in the clouds, Oh! I see
> Many spots—many dark—many red—
> In the heavens, Oh! I see
> Many clouds.
>
> In the woods, in the air, Oh! I hear
> The whoop, the long yell, and the cry—
> In the woods, Oh! I hear
> The loud whoop.
>
> Manitto! Manitto! Manitto!
> I am weak—thou art strong—I am slow—
> Manitto! Manitto!
> Give me aid.

At the end of what might be called each verse, he made a pause, by raising a note louder and longer than common, that was peculiarly suited to the sentiment just expressed. The first close was solemn, and intended to convey the idea of veneration; the second descriptive, bordering on the alarming; and the third was the well-known and terrific war-whoop, which burst from the lips of the young warrior, like a combination of all the frightful sounds of battle. The last was like the first, humble, meek, and imploring. Three times did he repeat this song, and as often did he encircle the post in his dance.

At the close of the first turn, a grave and highly esteemed chief of the Lenape followed his example, singing words of his own, however, to a music of a similar character. Warrior after warrior enlisted in the dance, until all of any renown and authority were to be numbered in its mazes. The spectacle now became wildly terrific; the fierce looking and menacing visages of the chiefs receiving additional power from the appalling strains in which they mingled their guttural tones. Just then, Uncas struck his tomahawk deep into the post, and raised his voice in a shout, which might be termed his own battle cry. The act announced that he had assumed the chief authority in the intended expedition.

146

It was a signal that awakened all the slumbering passions of the nation. A hundred youths, who had hitherto been restrained by the diffidence of their years, rushed in a frantic body on the fancied emblem of their enemy, and severed it asunder, splinter by splinter, until nothing remained of the trunk but its roots in the earth. During this moment of tumult, the most ruthless deeds of war were performed on the fragments of the tree, with as much apparent ferocity, as though they were the actual living victims of their cruelty. Some were scalped; some received the keen and trembling axe; and others suffered by thrusts from the fatal knife. In short, the manifestations of zeal and fierce delight were so great and unequivocal, that it was soon apparent the expedition was unqualifiedly declared to be a war of the nation.

The instant Uncas had struck the blow, he moved out of the circle, and cast his eyes up at the sun, which was just gaining the point, when the truce with Magua was to end. The fact was soon announced by a significant gesture, accompanied by a corresponding cry, and the whole of the excited multitude abandoned their mimic warfare, with shrill and loud yells of pleasure, to prepare for the more hazardous experiment of the reality.

The calm, but still impatient Uncas, now collected his chiefs, and divided his power. He presented Hawk-eye as a warrior, often tried, and always found deserving of confidence. When he found his friend met with a favourable reception, he bestowed on him the command of twenty men, like himself, active, skilful, and resolute. He gave the Delawares to understand the rank of Heyward among the troops of the Yengeese, and then tendered to him a trust of equal authority. But Duncan declined the charge, professing his readiness to serve as a volunteer by the side of the scout. After this disposition, the young Mohican appointed various native chiefs to fill the different situations of responsibility, and the time now pressing, he gave forth the word to march. He was cheerfully, but silently obeyed, by more than two hundred men.

Their entrance into the forest was perfectly unmolested; nor did they encounter any living objects, that could either give the alarm, or furnish the intelligence they needed, until they came upon the lairs of their own scouts. A halt was then ordered, and the chiefs were assembled in front to hold a "whispering council." At this meeting, divers plans of operation were suggested, though none of a character to meet the wishes of their ardent leader. Had Uncas followed the promptings of his own inclinations, he would have led his followers to the charge without a moment's delay, and put the conflict to the hazard of an instant issue; but such a course would have been in opposition to all the received practices and opinions of his countrymen. He was, therefore, fain to adopt a caution, that, in the present temper of his mind, he execrated, and to listen to advice at which his fiery spirit chafed, under the vivid recollection of Cora's danger, and Magua's insolence.

After an unsatisfactory conference of many minutes, a solitary individual was seen advancing from the side of the enemy, with such apparent haste, as to induce the belief he might be a messenger charged with some pacific overtures. When within a hundred yards, however, of the cover, behind which the Delaware council had assembled, the stranger hesitated, appeared uncertain what course to take, and finally halted. All eyes were now turned on Uncas, as if seeking directions how to proceed.

"Hawk-eye," said the young chief, in a low voice, "he must never speak to the Hurons again."

"His time has come," said the laconic scout, thrusting the long barrel of his rifle through the leaves, and taking his deliberate and fatal aim. But, instead of pulling the trigger, he lowered the muzzle again, and indulged himself in a fit of his pecular mirth. "I took the imp for a Mingo, as I'm a miserable sinner," he said; "but when my eye ranged along his ribs, for a place to get the bullet in—would you think it, Uncas—I saw the musicianer's blower! and so, after all, it is the man they call Gamut, whose death can profit no one, and whose life, if his tongue can do anything but sing, may be made serviceable to our own ends. If sounds have not lost their virtue, I'll soon have a discourse with the honest fellow and that in a voice he'll find more agreeable than the speech of 'kill-deer.' "

So saying, Hawk-eye laid aside his rifle, and crawling through the bushes, until within hearing of David, he attempted to repeat the musical effort, which had conducted himself with so much safety and éclat, through the Huron encampment.

The exquisite organs of Gamut could not readily be deceived, (and, to say the truth, it would have been difficult for any other than Hawk-eye to produce a similar noise,) and consequently, having once before heard the sounds, he now knew whence they proceeded. The poor fellow appeared instantly relieved from a state of great embarrassment; for, immediately pursuing the direction of the voice—a task that to him was not much less arduous, than it would have been to have gone up in face of a battery, he soon discovered the hidden songster who produced such melodious strains.

"I wonder what the Hurons will think of that!" said the scout, laughing, as he took his companion by the arm, and urged him swiftly towards the rear. "If the knaves lie within ear shot, they will say there are two non-compossurs, instead of one! But here we are safe," he added, pointing to Uncas and his associates. "Now give us the history of the Mingo inventions, in natural English, and without any ups-and-downs of voice."

David gazed about him, at the fierce and wild-looking chiefs, in mute wonder; but assured by the presence of faces that he knew, he soon rallied his faculties so far as to make an intelligent reply.

"The heathen are abroad in goodly numbers," said David; "and as I fear, with evil intent. There has been much howling and ungodly revelry, together with such sounds as it is profanity to utter, in their habitations, within the past hour, so much so, in truth, that I have fled to the Delawares in search of peace."

"Your ears might not have profited much by the exchange, had you

148

been quicker of foot," returned the scout, a little drily. "But let that be as it may; where are the Hurons?"

"They lie hid in the forest, between this spot and their village, in such force, that prudence would teach you instantly to return."

Uncas cast a proud glance along the range of trees which concealed his own band, and then mentioned the name of—

"Magua?"

"Is among them. He brought in the maiden that had sojourned with the Delawares, and leaving her in the cave, has put himself, like a raging wolf, at the head of his savages. I know not what has troubled his spirit so greatly!"

"He has left her, you say, in the cave!" interrupted Heyward; "'tis well that we know its situation. May not something be done for instant relief?"

Uncas looked earnestly at the scout, before he asked—

"What says Hawk-eye?"

"Give me my twenty rifles and I will turn to the right, along the stream, and passing by the huts of the beaver, will join the Sagamore and the Colonel. You shall then hear the whoop from that quarter; with this wind one may easily send it a mile. Then, Uncas, do you drive in their front; when they come within range of our pieces, we will give them a blow, that, I pledge the good name of an old frontiersman, shall make their line bend like an ashen bow. After which, we will carry their village, and take the woman from the cave; when the affair may be finished with the tribe, according to a white man's battle, by a blow and a victory; or in the Indian fashion, with dodge and cover. There may be no great learning, major, in this plan, but with courage and patience it can all be done."

"I like it much," cried Duncan, who saw that the release of Cora was the primary object in the mind of the scout; "I like it much. Let it then be instantly attempted."

After a short conference, the plan was matured, and rendered more intelligible to the several parties; the different signals were appointed, and the chiefs separated, each to his allotted station.

Chapter 30

"But plagues shall spread, and funeral fires increase,
Till the great king, without a ransom paid,
To her own Chrysa, and the blue-eyed maid."—
Pope.

DURING the time Uncas was making this disposition of his forces, the woods were as still, and, with the exception of those who had met in council, apparently, as much untenanted, as when they came fresh from the hands of their Almighty Creator. The eye could range, in every direction, through the long and shadowed vistas of the trees; but no where was any object to be seen, that did not properly belong to the peaceful and

149

slumbering scenery. Here and there a bird was heard fluttering among the branches of the beeches, and occasionally a squirrel dropped a nut, drawing the startled looks of the party, for a moment, to the place; but the instant the casual interruption ceased, the passing air was heard murmuring above their heads, along that verdant and undulating surface of the forest, which spread itself unbroken, unless by stream or lake over such a vast region of country. Across the tract of wilderness, which lay between the Delawares and the village of their enemies, it seemed as if the foot of man had never trodden, so breathing and deep was the silence in which it lay. But Hawk-eye, whose duty now led him foremost in the adventure, knew the character of those with whom he was about to contend, too well to trust the treacherous quiet.

When he saw his little band again collected, the scout threw "kill-deer" into the hollow of his arm, and making a silent signal that he would be followed, he led them many rods towards the rear, into the bed of a little brook, which they had crossed in advancing. Here he halted, and after waiting for the whole of his grave and attentive warriors to close about him, he spoke in Delaware, demanding—

"Do any of my young men know whither this run will lead us?"

A Delaware stretched forth a hand, with the two fingers separated; and indicating the manner in which they were joined at the root, he answered—

"Before the sun could go his own length the little water will be in the big." Then he added, pointing in the direction of the place he mentioned, "the two make enough for the beavers."

"I thought as much," returned the scout, glancing his eye upward at the opening in the tree-tops, "from the course it takes, and the bearings of the mountains. Men, we will keep within the cover of its banks till we scent the Hurons."

His companions gave the usual brief exclamation of assent; but perceiving that their leader was about to lead the way in person, one or two made signs that all was not as it should be. Hawk-eye, who comprehended their meaning glances, turned, and perceived that his party had been followed thus far by the singing-master.

"Do you know, friend," asked the scout gravely, and perhaps with a little of the pride of conscious deserving in his manner, "that is a band of rangers, chosen for the most desperate service, and put under the command of one, who, though another might say it with a better face, will not be apt to leave them idle. It may not be five, it cannot be thirty, minutes before we tread on the body of a Huron, living or dead."

"Though not admonished of your intentions in words," returned David, whose face was a little flushed, and whose ordinarily quiet and unmeaning eyes glimmered with an expression of unusual fire, "your men have reminded me of the children of Jacob going out to battle against the Shechemites, for wickedly aspiring to wedlock with a woman of a race that was favoured of the Lord. Now, I have journeyed far, and sojourned much, in good and evil, with the maiden ye seek; and, though not a man

150

of war, with my loins girded and my sword sharpened, yet would I gladly strike a blow in her behalf."

The scout hesitated, as if weighing the chances of such a strange enlistment in his mind, before he answered—

"You know not the use of any we'pon. You carry no rifle; and, believe me, what the Mingoes take, they will freely give again."

"Though not a vaunting and bloodily disposed Goliath," returned David, drawing a sling from beneath his parti-coloured and uncouth attire, "I have not forgotten the example of the Jewish boy. With this ancient instrument of war have I practised much in my youth, and peradventure the skill has not entirely departed from me."

"Ay!" said Hawk-eye, considering the deer-skin thong and apron, with a cold and discouraging eye; "the thing might do its work among arrows, or even knives; but these Mengwe have been furnished by the Frenchers with a good grooved barrel a man. However, it seems to be your gift to go unharmed amid a fire; and as you have hitherto been favoured— Major, you have left your rifle at a cock; a single shot before the time, would be just twenty scalps lost to no purpose.—Singer, you can follow; we may find use for you in the shoutings."

"I thank you, friend," returned David, supplying himself, like his royal namesake, from among the pebbles of the brook; "though not given to the desire to kill, had you sent me away, my spirit would have been troubled."

"Remember," added the scout, tapping his own head significantly on that spot where Gamut was yet sore, "we come to fight, and not to musickate. Until the general whoop is given, nothing speaks but the rifle."

David nodded, as much as to signify his acquiescence with the terms, and then Hawk-eye casting another observant glance over his followers, made the signal to proceed.

Their route lay, for the distance of a mile, along the bed of the water course. Though protected from any great danger of observation by the precipitous banks, and the thick shrubbery which skirted the stream, for the whole distance, no precaution, known to an Indian attack, was neglected. A warrior rather crawled than walked on each flank, so as to catch occasional glimpses into the forest; and every few minutes the band came to a halt, and listened for hostile sounds, with an acuteness of organs, that would be scarcely conceivable to a man in a less natural state. Their march was, however, unmolested, and they reached the point where the lesser stream was lost in the greater, without the smallest evidence that their progress had been noted. Here the scout again halted, to consult the signs of the forest.

"We are likely to have a good day for the fight," he said, in English, addressing Heyward, and glancing his eye upwards at the clouds, which began to move in broad sheets across the firmament; "a bright sun and a glittering barrel are no friends to true sight. Every thing is favourable; they have the wind, which will bring down their noises and their smoke too, no little matter in itself; whereas, with us, it will be first a shot, and then a clear view. But here is an end of our cover; the beavers have had the range of this stream for hundreds of years, and what atween their food and their dams there is, as you see, many a girdled stub, but few living trees."

Hawk-eye had, in truth, in these few words, given no bad description of the prospect that now lay in their front. The brook was irregular in its width, sometimes shooting through narrow fissures in the rocks, and at others spreading over acres of bottom land, forming little areas that might be termed ponds. Every where along its banks were the mouldering relics of dead trees, in all the stages of decay, from those that groaned on their tottering trunks, to such as had recently been robbed of those rugged coats, that so mysteriously contain their principle of life. A few long, low, and moss-covered piles, were scattered among them, like the memorials of a former and long departed generation.

All these minute particulars were now noted by the scout, with a gravity and interest, that they probably had never before attracted. He knew that the Huron encampment lay a short half mile up the brook, and, with the characteristic anxiety of one who dreaded a hidden danger, he was greatly troubled at not finding the smallest trace of the presence of his enemy. Once or twice he felt induced to give the order for a rush, and to attempt the village by surprise; but his experience quickly admonished him of the danger of so useless an experiment. Then he listened intently and with painful uncertainty, for the sounds of hostility in the quarter where Uncas was left; but nothing was audible except the sighing of the wind, that began to sweep over the bosom of the forest in gusts, which threatened a tempest. At length, yielding rather to his unusual impatience, than taking counsel for his knowledge, he determined to bring matters to an issue, by unmasking his force, and proceeding cautiously, but steadily, up the stream.

The scout had stood, while making his observations, sheltered by a brake, and his companions still lay in the bed of the ravine through which the smaller stream debouched; but on hearing his low, though intelligible signal, the whole party stole up the bank, like so many dark spectres, and silently arranged themselves around him. Pointing in the direction he wished to proceed, Hawk-eye advanced, the band breaking off in single files, and following so accurately in his footsteps, as to leave, if we accept Heyward and David, the trail of but a single man.

The party was, however, scarcely uncovered, before a volley from a dozen rifles was heard in their rear, and a Delaware leaping high into the air, like a wounded deer, fell at his whole length, perfectly dead.

"Ah; I feared some devilry like this!" exclaimed the scout in English: adding, with the quickness of thought, in his adopted tongue, "to cover, and charge!"

The band dispersed at the word, and before Heyward had well recovered from his surprise, he found himself standing alone with David. Luckily the Hurons had already fallen back, and he was safe from their fire. But this state of things was evidently to be of short continuance, for the scout set the example of pressing on their retreat, by discharging his rifle, and darting from tree to tree, as his enemy slowly yielded ground.

It would seem that the assault had been made by a very small party of the Hurons, which, however, continued to increase in numbers, as it retired on its friends, until the return fire was very nearly, if not quite, equal to that maintained by the advancing Delawares. Heyward threw himself among the combatants, and imitating the necessary caution of his companions, he supported quick discharges with his own rifle. The contest now grew warm and stationary. Few were injured, as both parties kept their bodies as much protected as possible by the trees; never, indeed, exposing any part of their persons, except in the act of taking aim. But the chances were gradually growing unfavourable to Hawk-eye and his band. The quick-sighted scout, perceived all his danger, without knowing how to remedy it. He saw it was more dangerous to retreat than to maintain his ground; while he found his enemy throwing out men on his flank, which rendered the task of keeping themselves covered so very difficult to the Delawares, as nearly to silence their fire. At this embarrassing moment, when they began to think the whole of the hostile tribe was gradually encircling them, to their destruction, they heard the yell of combatants, and the rattling of arms, echoing under the arches of the wood, at the place where Uncas was posted; a bottom which, in a manner, lay beneath the ground on which Hawk-eye and his party were contending.

The effects of this attack were instantaneous, and to the scout and his friends greatly relieving. It would seem, that while his own surprise had been anticipated, and had consequently failed, the enemy in their turn having been deceived in its object and in his numbers, had left too small a force to resist the impetuous onset of the young Mohican. This fact was doubly apparent, by the rapid manner in which the battle in the forest rolled upward towards the village, and by an instant falling off in the number of their assailants, who rushed to assist in maintaining their front, and, as it now proved to be, their principal point of defence.

Animating his followers by his voice, and his own example, Hawk-eye then gave the word to bear down upon their foes.

The charge, in that rude species of warfare, consisted merely in pushing from cover to cover, nigher to the enemy; and in this manœuvre he was instantly and successfully obeyed. The Hurons were compelled to withdraw, and the scene of the contest rapidly changed from the more open ground on which it had commenced, to a spot where the assailed found a thicket to rest upon. Here the struggle was protracted, arduous, and seemingly of doubtful issue, the Delawares, though none of them fell, beginning to bleed freely, in consequence of the disadvantage at which they were held.

In this crisis, Hawk-eye found means to get behind the same tree as that which served for a cover to Heyward, most of his own combatants being within call, a little on his right, where they maintained rapid, though fruitless, discharges, on their sheltered enemies.

"You are a young man, major," said the scout, dropping the butt of 'kill-deer' to the earth, and leaning on the barrel, a little fatigued with his previous industry; "and it may be your gift to lead armies, at some future day, ag'in these imps, the Mingoes. You may here see the philosophy of an Indian fight. It consists, mainly, in a ready hand, a quick eye, and a good cover. Now, if you had a company of the Royal Americans here, in what manner would you set them to work in this business?"

"The bayonet would make a road."

"Ay, there is white reason in what you say; but a man must ask himself in this wilderness, how many lives he can spare. No—horse," continued the scout, shaking his head, like one who mused, "horse, I am ashamed to say, must, sooner or later, decide these skrimmages. The brutes are better than men, and to horse must we come at last! Put a shodden hoof on the moccasin of a red-skin, and if his rifle be once emptied, he will never stop to load it again."

"This is a subject that might better be discussed another time," returned Heyward; "shall we charge?"

"I see no contradiction to the gifts of any man, in passing his breathing spells in useful reflections," the scout mildly replied. "As to a rush, I little relish such a measure, for a scalp or two must be thrown away in the attempt. And yet," he added, bending his head aside, to catch the sounds of the distant combat, "if we are to be of use to Uncas, these knaves in our front must be now gotten rid of!"

Then turning, with a prompt and decided air, from Duncan, he called aloud to his Indians, in their own language. His words were answered by a shout, and at a given signal, each warrior made a swift movement around his particular tree. The sight of so many dark bodies, glancing before their eyes at the same instant, drew a hasty, and, consequently, an ineffectual fire from the Hurons. Then without stopping to breathe, the Delawares leaped, in long bounds, towards the wood, like so many panthers springing upon their prey. Hawk-eye was in front brandishing his terrible rifle, and animating his followers by his example. A few of the older and more cunning Hurons, who had not been deceived by the artifice which had been practised to draw their fire, now made a close and deadly discharge of their pieces, and justified the apprehensions of the scout, by felling three of his foremost warriors. But the shock was insufficient to repel the impetus of the charge. The Delawares broke into the cover with the ferocity of their natures, and swept away every trace of resistance by the fury of the onset.

The combat endured only for an instant hand to hand, and then the assailed yielded ground rapidly, until they reached the opposite margin of the thicket, where they clung to their cover, with a sort of obstinacy that is so often witnessed in hunted brutes. At this critical moment, when the success of the struggle was again becoming doubtful, the crack of a rifle was heard behind the Hurons, and a bullet came whizzing from among some beaver lodges, which were situated in the clearing, in their

154

rear, and was followed by the fierce and appalling yell of the war-whoop.

"There speaks the Sagamore!" shouted Hawk-eye, answering the cry with his own stentorian voice; "we have them now in face and back!"

The effect on the Hurons was instantaneous. Discouraged by so unexpected an assault, from a quarter that left them no opportunity for cover, their warriors uttered a common yell of disappointment and despair, and breaking off in a body, they spread themselves across the opening, heedless of every other consideration but flight. Many fell, in making the experiment, under the bullets and the blows of the pursuing Delawares.

We shall not pause to detail the meeting between the scout and Chingachgook, or the more touching interview that Duncan held with the anxious father of his mistress. A few brief and hurried words served to explain the state of things to both parties, and then Hawk-eye, pointing out the Sagamore to his band, resigned the chief authority into the hands of the Mohican chief. Chingachgook assumed the station to which his birth and experience gave him so distinguished a claim, with the grave dignity that always gives force to the mandates of a native warrior. Following the footsteps of the scout, he led the party back through the thicket, his men scalping the fallen Hurons, and secreting the bodies of their own dead as they proceeded, until they gained a point where the former was content to make a halt.

The warriors who had breathed themselves so freely in the preceding struggle, were now posted on a bit of level ground, sprinkled with trees, in sufficient numbers to conceal them. The land fell off rather precipitously in front, and beneath their eyes stretched for several miles a narrow, dark, and wooded vale. It was through this dense and dark forest, that Uncas was still contending with the main body of the Hurons.

The Mohican and his friends advanced to the brow of the hill, and listened, with practised ears, to the sounds of the combat. A few birds hovered over the leafy bosom of the valley, as if frightened from their secluded nests, and here and there a light vapoury cloud, which seemed already blending with the atmosphere, arose above the trees, and indicated some spot where the struggle had been more fierce and stationary than usual.

"The fight is coming up the ascent," said Duncan, pointing in the direction of a new explosion of fire-arms; "we are too much in the centre of their line to be effective."

"They will incline into the hollow, where the cover is thicker," said the scout, "and that will leave us well on their flank. Go, Sagamore; you will hardly be in time to give the whoop, and lead on the young men. I will fight this skrimmage with warriors of my own colour! You know me, Mohican; not a Huron of them all shall cross the swell, into your rear, without the notice of 'kill-deer.' "

The Indian chief paused another moment to consider the signs of the contest, which was now rolling rapidly up the ascent, a certain evidence that the Delawares triumphed; nor did he actually quit the place, until admonished of the proximity of his friends, as well as enemies, by the bullets of the former, which began to patter among the dried leaves on the ground, like the bits of falling hail which precede the bursting of the tempest. Hawk-eye and his three companions withdrew a few paces to a sheltered spot, and awaited the issue with that sort of calmness that nothing but great practice could impart, in such a scene.

It was not long before the reports of the rifles began to lose the echoes of the woods, and to sound like weapons discharged in the open air. Then a warrior appeared, here and there, driven to the skirts of the forest, and rallying as he entered the clearing, as at the place where the final stand was to be made. These were soon joined by others, until a long line of swarthy figures was to be seen clinging to the cover, with the obstinacy of desperation. Heyward began to grow impatient, and turned his eyes anxiously in the direction of Chingachgook. The chief was seated on a rock, considering the spectacle with an eye as deliberate, as if he were posted there merely to view the struggle.

"The time is come for the Delaware to strike!" said Duncan.

"Not so, not so," returned the scout; "when he scents his friends, he will let them know that he is here. See, see; the knaves are getting in that clump of pines, like bees settling after their flight. By the Lord, a squaw might put a bullet in such a knot of dark skins!"

At that instant the whoop was given, and a dozen Hurons fell by a discharge from Chingachgook and his band. The shout that followed was answered by a single war-cry from the forest, and then a yell passed through the air, that sounded as though a thousand throats were united in a common effort. The Hurons staggered, deserting the centre of their line, and Uncas issued, through the opening they left, from the forest, at the head of a hundred warriors.

Waving his hands right and left, the young chief pointed out the enemy to his followers, who instantly separated in the pursuit. The war now divided, both wings of the broken Hurons seeking protection in the woods again, hotly pressed by the victorious warriors of the Lenape. A minute might have passed, but the sounds were already receding in different directions, and gradually losing their distinctness beneath the echoing arches of the woods. One little knot of Hurons, however, had disdained to seek a cover, and were retiring like lions at bay, slowly and sullenly up the acclivity, which Chingachgook and his band had just deserted to mingle, more closely in the fray. Magua was conspicuous in this party, both by his fierce and savage mien, and by the air of haughty authority he yet maintained.

In his eagerness to expedite the pursuit, Uncas had left himself nearly alone; but the moment his eye caught the figure of le Subtil, every other consideration was forgotten. Raising his cry of battle, which recalled some six or seven warriors, and reckless of the disparity in their numbers, he rushed upon his enemy. Le Renard, who watched the movement, paused to receive him with secret joy. But at the moment when he thought the rashness of his impetuous young assailant had left him at his mercy, another shout was given, and la Longue Carabine was seen rushing to the rescue, attended by all his white associates. The Huron instantly turned, and commenced a rapid retreat up the ascent.

There was no time for greetings or congratulations; for Uncas, though unconscious of the presence of his friends, continued the pursuit with the velocity of the wind. In vain Hawk-eye called to him to respect the covers; the young Mohican braved the dangerous fire of his enemies, and soon compelled them to a flight as swift as his own headlong speed. It was fortunate that the race was of short continuance, and that the white men were much favoured both in the distance and the ground, by their position, or the Delaware would soon have outstripped all his companions, and fallen a victim to his own temerity. But ere such a calamity could happen, the pursuers and pursued entered the Wyandot village, within striking distance of each other.

Excited by the presence of their dwellings, and tired of the chase, the Hurons now made a stand, and fought around their council lodge with the desperation of despair. The onset and the issue were like the passage and destruction of a whirlwind. The tomahawk of Uncas, the blows of Hawk-eye, and even the still nervous arm of Munro, were all busy for that passing moment, and the ground was quickly strewed with their enemies. Still Magua, though daring and much exposed, escaped from every effort against his life, with that sort of fabled protection, that was made to overlook the fortunes of favoured heroes in the legends of ancient poetry. Raising a yell that spoke volumes of anger and disappointment, the subtle chief, when he saw his comrades fallen, darted away from the place, attended by his two only surviving friends, leaving the Delawares engaged in stripping the dead of the bloody trophies of their victory.

But Uncas, who had vainly sought him in the melee, bounded forward in pursuit; Hawk-eye, Heyward, and David, still pressing on his footsteps. The utmost that the scout could effect, was to keep the muzzle of his rifle a little in advance of his friend, to whom, however, it answered every purpose of a charmed shield. Once Magua appeared disposed to make another and a final effort to revenge his losses; but abandoning his intentions so soon as demonstrated, he leaped into a thicket of bushes, through which he was followed by his enemies, and suddenly entered the mouth of the cave already known to the reader. Hawk-eye, who had only forborne to fire in tenderness to Uncas, raised a shout of success, and proclaimed aloud that now they were certain of their game. The pursuers dashed into the long and narrow entrance, in time to catch a glimpse of the retreating forms of the Hurons. Their passage through the natural galleries and subterraneous apartments of the cavern was preceded by the shrieks and cries of hundreds of women and children. The place, seen by its dim and uncertain light, appeared like the shades of the infernal regions, across which unhappy ghosts and savage demons were flitting in multitudes.

Still Uncas kept his eye on Magua, as if life to him possessed but a single object. Heyward and the scout still pressed on his rear, actuated, though possibly, in a less degree, by a common feeling. But their way was becoming intricate, in those dark and gloomy passages, and the glimpses of the retiring warriors less distinct and frequent; and for a moment the trace was believed to be lost, when a white robe was seen fluttering in the farther extremity of a passage that seemed to lead up the mountain.

"'Tis Cora!" exclaimed Heyward, in a voice in which horror and delight were wildly mingled.

"Cora! Cora!" echoed Uncas, bounding forward like a deer.

"'Tis the maiden!" shouted the scout. "Courage, lady; we come—we come."

The chase was renewed with a diligence rendered ten-fold encouraging by this glimpse of the captive. But the way was now rugged, broken, and, in spots, nearly impassable. Uncas, abandoned his rifle, and leaped forward with headlong precipitation. Heyward rashly imitated his example, though both were, a moment afterwards, admonished of its madness, by hearing the bellowing of a piece, that the Hurons found time to discharge down the passage in the rocks, the bullet from which even gave the young Mohican a slight wound.

"We must close!" said the scout, passing his friends by a desperate leap; "the knaves will pick us all off at this distance; and, see! they hold the maiden so as to shield themselves!"

Though his words were unheeded, or rather unheard, his example was followed by his companions, who, by incredible exertions got near enough to the fugitives to perceive that Cora was borne along between the two warriors, while Magua prescribed the direction and manner of their flight. At this moment, the forms of all four were strongly drawn against an opening in the sky, and then they disappeared. Nearly frantic with disappointment, Uncas and Heyward increased efforts that already seemed superhuman, and they issued from the cavern on the side of the mountain, in time to note the route of the pursued. The course lay up the ascent, and still continued hazardous and laborious.

Encumbered by his rifle, and, perhaps, not sustained by so deep an interest in the captive as his companions, the scout suffered the latter to precede him a little; Uncas, in his turn, taking the lead of Heyward. In this manner, rocks, precipices, and difficulties, were surmounted, in an incredibly short space, that at another time, and under other circumstances, would have been deemed almost insuperable. But the impetuous young men were rewarded by finding that, encumbered with Cora, the Hurons were rapidly losing ground in the race.

"Stay, dog of the Wyandots!" exclaimed Uncas, shaking his bright tomahawk at Magua; "a Delaware girl calls stay!"

"I will go no farther," cried Cora, stopping unexpectedly on a ledge of rocks, that overhung a deep precipice, at no great distance from the summit of the mountain.

"Kill me, if thou wilt, detestable Huron, I will go no farther!"

The supporters of the maiden raised their ready tomahawks with the impious joy that fiends are thought to take in mischief, but Magua suddenly stayed their uplifted arms. The Huron chief, after casting the weapons he had wrested from his companions over the rock, drew his knife, and turned to his captive, with a look in which conflicting passions fiercely contended.

"Woman," he said, "choose; the wigwam, or the knife of le Subtil!"

Cora regarded him not; but dropping on her knees, with a rich glow suffusing itself over her features, she raised her eyes and stretched her arms towards heaven, saying, in a meek and yet confiding voice—

"I am thine! do with me as thou seest best!"

"Woman," repeated Magua, hoarsely and endeavouring in vain to catch a glance from her serene and beaming eye, "choose!"

But Cora neither heard nor heeded his demand. The form of the Huron trembled in every fibre, and he raised his arm on high, but dropped it again, with a wild and bewildered air, like one who doubted. Once more he struggled with himself, and lifted the keen weapon again—but just then a piercing cry was heard above them, and Uncas appeared, leaping frantically, from a fearful height upon the ledge. Magua recoiled a step, and one of his assistants, profiting by the chance, sheathed his own knife in the bosom of the maiden.

The Huron sprang like a tiger on his offending and already retreating countryman, but the falling form of Uncas separated the unnatural combatants. Diverted from his object by this interruption, and maddened by the murder he had just witnessed, Magua buried his weapon in the back of the prostrate Delaware, uttering an unearthly shout, as he committed the dastardly deed. But Uncas arose from the blow, as the wounded panther turns upon his foe, and struck the murderer of Cora to his feet, by an effort, in which the last of his failing strength was expended. Then, with a stern and steady look, he turned to le Subtil, and indicated, by the expression of his eye, all that he would do, had not the power deserted him. The latter seized the nerveless arm of the unresisting Delaware, and passed his knife into his bosom three several times, before his victim, still keeping his gaze riveted on his enemy, with a look of inextinguishable scorn, fell dead at his feet.

"Mercy! mercy! Huron," cried Heyward from above, in tones nearly choked by horror; "give mercy, and thou shalt receive it!"

Whirling the bloody knife up at the imploring youth, the victorious Magua uttered a cry so fierce, so wild, and yet so joyous, that it conveyed the sounds of savage triumph to the ears of those who fought in the valley, a thousand feet below. He was answered by an appalling burst from the lips of the scout, whose tall person was just then seen moving swiftly towards him, along those dangerous crags, with steps as bold and reckless, as if he possessed the power to move in middle air. But when the hunter reached the scene of the ruthless massacre, the ledge was tenanted only by the dead—

His keen eye took a single look at the victims, and then shot its fierce glances over the difficulties of the ascent in his front. A form stood at the brow of the mountain, on the very edge of the giddy height, with uplifted arms, in an awful attitude of menace. Without stopping to consider his person, the rifle of Hawk-eye was raised, but a rock which fell on the head of one of the fugitives below, exposed the indignant and glowing countenance of the honest Gamut. Then Magua issued from a crevice, and stepping with calm indifference over the body of the last of his associates, he leaped a wide fissure and ascended the rocks at a point where the arm of David could not reach him. A single bound would carry him to the brow of the precipice, and assure his safety. Before taking the leap, however, the Huron paused, and shaking his hand at the scout, he shouted—

"The pale-faces are dogs! the Delawares women! Magua leaves them on the rocks, for the crows!"

Laughing hoarsely, he made a desperate leap and fell short of his mark; though his hands grasped a shrub on the verge of the height. The form of Hawk-eye had crouched like a beast about to take its spring, and his frame trembled so violently with eagerness, that the muzzle of the half raised rifle played like a leaf fluttering in the wind. Without exhausting himself with fruitless efforts, the cunning Magua suffered his body to drop to the length of his arms, and found a fragment for his feet to rest upon. Then summoning all his powers, he renewed the attempt, and so far succeeded, as to draw his knees on the edge of the mountain. It was now, when the body of his enemy was most collected, together, that the agitated weapon of the scout was drawn to his shoulders. The surrounding rocks, themselves, were not steadier than the piece became for the single instant that it poured out its contents. The arms of the Huron relaxed, and his body fell back a little, while his knees still kept their position. Turning a relentless look on his enemy, he shook his hand at him, in grim defiance. But his hold loosened, and his dark person was seen cutting the air with its head downwards, for a fleeting instant, until it glided past the fringe of shrubbery which clung to the mountain in its rapid flight to destruction.

Printed in Germany